THE SHOOTING STAR

SWAY OF THE STARS BOOK 1

FRANCES DALL'ALBA

Poinsettia
Publishing

Also By Frances Dall'Alba

THE SHOOTING STAR

For my grandparents, who took the gamble.

Prologue

Falerna, Southern Italy 1944

Benito huddled under his coat on the verandah as rain dripped off old Mr Fetuletti's eave, making puddles in the earth. The extra layer wasn't shielding him from the cold. Not in late July. Instead, his father's oversized, heavy woollen coat hid his shaking legs. Fear churned inside his stomach.

His twin brother, Nicolo, continued to slice the shovel into the soil furiously. Benito was supposed to be on watch. With no moonlight, the night beyond the old, disused fontana dei povere was as dark as coal. Nicolo warned they had to work fast before the sky showed its first rays of dawn. Old Mr Fetuletti was deaf, but that's not what he had to look out for. Ever since Mussolini surrendered to the Allied forces six months ago, no one knew who to trust.

On a still afternoon a week ago, they'd discovered their parents' lifeless bodies. For weeks, his papà had lain on his bed recuperating from a grenade attack. That day, they opened the front door to a ransacked home. The sight of blood-splattered sheets underneath their father seared his brain. His mother, sprawled on the floor beside the bed with a bullet wound to the chest, had left his body shaking uncontrollably. Together, he and Nicolo fled their home. They stumbled and tripped higher up into the mountains behind Falerna, tears blinding their way. Benito had gagged with every step he took, the vile taste caking his mouth.

Those who killed his parents were looking for his mother's jewels. The ones passed down to her from her wealthy Roman family. Later that night, they risked everything. Before the morning servant could discover their parent's blood-drenched bodies, Benito and Nicolo snuck back to the house to check if the jewels had been stolen. They avoided their parent's bedroom. The jewels were not hidden there.

He remembered thinking how lucky it was that a year earlier, their father had shown them where the jewels were hidden, insisting they promise never to tell anyone. When they found them hidden behind a brick in the rock wall, nothing could stop the tears coursing down his face. His young mind clearly understood this was all he would ever have to remind him of his parents.

Benito blinked, sending droplets of water down his face. Dragging his thoughts back to the dark garden, he looked up just as Nicolo dropped the shovel and flung his saturated coat off, throwing it in his direction. Crouching down again, Nicolo reached into the hole with a wooden bucket tied to a sturdy piece of wood for yet another load of dirt.

Nicolo's grunts in the quiet of the night alarmed Benito, and an involuntary shiver shook his shoulders. Without warning, tears trickled down his face. Biting his lip to control his chattering teeth, he let his face drop and whispered, "Oh, Mama e Papà, who will look after us now?"

His face whipped up when he heard Nicolo hiss, "Benito, come here quick."

Dropping Nicolo's coat, he stumbled on unsteady legs and ran towards him. "What's wrong?"

Nicolo used his shirt to wipe his face of water and sweat. "Have a look. I think we've dug enough. We've been at it for a couple of hours, and I think we're close. I used this branch to measure how far down we've gone, and it looks like it's nearly four feet."

Benito peered into the dark hole. Nicolo was always the numbers and figures one. At eleven years old, he was already smarter at maths and calculus. That came from their mama. What Benito got instead was his father's height and build. 'Strong as an ox', his father used to say.

The reminder that he would never see his father again caused the constant pain around his chest to surface again. Peering down the dark hole, his hand came up and tugged at his coat's lapel to try and ease the hurt.

The last week was spent hidden in the mountains. Fear drove them to hide the jewels until this stupid war was over. Once the jewels were safely hidden, they planned to leave Falerna and make their way to Roma, where their mother's family lived.

Nicolo pulled at his sleeve and whispered, "Come on, Benito, carry those rocks over here. We need to get this done quickly and get away before the sun rises."

Focusing back on the job at hand, he raced over to the pile of rocks they'd collected on the way and easily lugged most of them to the hole's opening. His bare feet slid on the wet ground, causing the rocks to jam his thumb. Biting his tongue to stop the yelp that wanted to escape, he dropped the pile on the ground.

"We'll put a rock below and some around the jewels, if we can, then pile more on top before we push the dirt back into the hole," Nicolo quietly directed.

Benito rubbed at his sore thumb, trying to get some feeling back into it. The raindrops were falling bigger now, splashing mud onto his sodden toes. He was already soaked through, so it didn't matter how much more it rained. With the earth softened around the fontana, it was making the job easier.

His mother's jewels were wrapped in a protective leather pouch their father had made long ago. Nicolo lowered it into the deep, narrow hole.

"Okay, pass me the rest of the rocks one at a time, Benito. I'll sit them gently on top."

Nicolo used a sling made from a couple of shirts to lower them. Benito stood ready with the shovel they borrowed from Mr Fetuletti's garden.

Levelling the ground for the last time, the first faint rays of the sun crept over the mountains. They returned the shovel to where they found it propped against the garden shed and then ran back to their mountain hideout.

Tears stung Benito's eyes all the way, and his hand came up constantly to wipe his face. When they reached the hollow in the forest, it shocked him to see Nicolo crying. *Oh no, not Nicolo, too.*

Nicolo was the sensible, emotionally strong one. While Benito was physically taller and stronger, he always looked to Nicolo for direction and support. The twins' only similarity was their dark hair. Watching Nicolo cry unhinged Benito completely, and he lost himself. Collapsing to the ground, he let the wracking sobs tear from his throat.

⌒⌘⌒

They awoke hours later after sleeping in a tangle of legs. Perched in a hollow on the side of the mountain, Benito sat up and looked out over the sparkling ocean. The rain from the previous night had dispersed completely, and only a few puffy white clouds dotted the glorious blue sky.

Glancing to his side, he watched Nicolo cracking walnuts. They took the full bag their mother kept in the cellar. Last season, he and Nicolo collected them as they fell from the trees near their home. Ever since their papà went to war, he and Nicolo had grown up fast. Each day they were forced to share the chores Papà once did. The only men left in the village were injured soldiers sent home to rest, so they became responsible for much more.

"We leave for Roma tonight, Benito?" Nicolo looked up from the pile of walnuts.

Benito nodded. "Do you think Zia Rosa will take care of us?" he asked, voice cracking and full of hope that their mother's sister would look after them. Without children of her own, she had always been kind to them.

"I hope so," Nicolo replied solemnly.

Benito turned back towards the ocean, his lips quivering. *That was before the war. Was Zia Rosa still in Roma? What about the uncles and their families?* Their father told them the Germans had forced rich families out of their homes. They ransacked their paintings and jewels and used their homes as army headquarters.

Would they find their way, and would anyone still be there?

With shaking hands, he kneaded his side while cramps pressed against his stomach with each walnut he ate.

He gritted his teeth and shoved his hat on to hide his runny nose and tears. *No more, Benito. You need to make Papà proud of you.*

"Benito?" Nicolo's hand came out and rested on his shoulder. "We'll come back for the jewels one day. I won't come back without you, I promise. We'll do it together. It's the only thing we have left from Mama e Papà." He gave Benito's shoulder a quick squeeze. "We'll take care of each other, Benito. It will keep Mama e Papà happy; I know it will."

Benito swallowed. He was glad Nicolo sounded confident because he needed him to be. He didn't want to be lost and alone because then he would have no one. He sniffled again. Grabbing Nicolo's hand, he squeezed it tight. "Of course. I promise I won't come back without you either."

Turning back to the sun as it started to sink over the ocean, the last rays of the day rested on his legs. Warmth seeped into his skin, where only a constant chill had existed for the past week.

"Soon it will be time to pack our belongings, Benito."

Benito glanced at Nicolo when his twin continued to speak.

"Papà said there was danger everywhere. He always gave us good advice. We must sleep during the day and walk only at night."

Benito bobbed his head. It would be sad to leave Falerna without Mama e Papà.

Together, they watched the sun disappear. Neither moved.

A dangerous journey would begin that night.

Chapter 1

*M*alanda, Australia

Liz winced and pushed aside her phone when the front door slammed shut. It could only be her cousin, Sally. No one else would barge in that way.

She untangled her legs from underneath her backside and rose from the couch as Sally rounded the corner into the lounge room, running, chest heaving. "I ... I came as soon as I received your message. What's wrong? Is it Great Aunt? Is she okay?" Sally darted glances around the room, wringing her hands.

Liz's jaw dropped. Her message didn't sound that urgent, did it? "Oh my God, no, no, it's not Nan." She gave Sally an apologetic grimace. "I'm so sorry; I should've explained more. It's just that I need to speak to someone before I burst. I honestly didn't expect you to come until after work." Liz pulled at her collar, shamefaced for acting like an ass and putting Sally at risk of doing something stupid on the road. "Please relax. Can I get you a drink of water?"

Sally rested her hand under her breastbone, her blue eyes widening in disbelief. When she could talk again, she huffed out, "Relax? Are you crazy? You send a message telling me to get here fast because something really urgent has happened, and you tell me to relax?"

Liz flinched as Sally's words followed her to the kitchen. She didn't need to be reminded how a split-second incident on the road could change a person's life forever.

Returning with a glass of water, she pointed to the well-worn couch. "Sorry, Sal, I won't do that again. I *do* desperately need your advice, and no one is dead. Nan is having her afternoon nap."

Sally gulped down half the water and handed the glass back. Then she dramatically flopped onto the chocolate-brown couch, one leg hanging over the side. "If nothing is wrong with your grandmother, what's so important I had to drop everything and run here? They're going to kill me at work tomorrow."

Feeling guilty as hell, Liz raked a hand through her hair and sighed. It was irresponsible of her to send an urgent message, but she'd reached breaking point and needed Sally here. Who else was there?

She sat gingerly on the opposite matching couch, not sure how to start the conversation. Delaying the inevitable for a few moments, she looked up at the wall of framed photos. Her grandmother had always been an avid photographer. The photos lining the wall chronicled her life after Liz came to live with her and her grandad as a toddler. She couldn't remember anything about her parents who'd died in a fatal crash. Today she needed reminding of how lucky she was to have the world's best grandparents. They'd raised her like she was their own, and they were her everything, despite the burdening responsibilities of the past few years.

Her gaze wandered from the photos back to Sally, who sat waiting with raised eyebrows. Standing up, she cleared her throat and began pacing.

"For goodness' sake, Liz, what's wrong? Are you going to tell me? I didn't come tearing out here for nothing, did I?"

Liz stopped and chewed on the knuckle of her thumb. Then she flung her hand out in disgust and groaned. "I don't know what to do," she wailed.

Frustrated, she pushed her palms against either side of her face, walking in tight circles. Her words came out in a sudden rush. "I started cleaning out the old mechanic shop. I was going through Uncle Ben's old papers, and I came across a letter addressed to me ... I read it and—"

"Whoa, hold on there." Sally was on her feet, grabbing hold of Liz's shoulders. "Stop! How about one word at a time?" She forced Liz to sit beside her on the couch and took hold of Liz's hand, eyeing the teeth marks. "Wow, you bit through the skin. What *is* going on?"

Liz looked at her hand in disgust before reaching for the small coffee table. She picked up Uncle Ben's letter and handed it to Sally. "This is what's going on."

Sally took the bulky envelope and held it by the corner, dangling it in front of her eyes. "Is this going to kill me when I look inside?"

Liz scowled. "Don't be so dramatic."

Sally's eyebrows arched. As though insulted, she dropped the letter onto her lap. "I wasn't the one who nearly chewed my thumb off."

"Oh, for God's sake, open the letter and read it. It's been tormenting me for a week. I was hoping I could ignore it, but my head won't let me. But just be caref—"

Sally picked up the envelope, turned back the seal and held it out at arm's length so the letter could drop safely out of harm's way.

"No. Stop!" Liz shouted, stumbling off the couch and landing on her knees.

It was too late. Along with the letter, a whole wad of one-hundred-dollar notes fluttered to the floor.

Mesmerised, Sally's eyes turned to big saucers. "Holy Jesus, Liz. Did you rob a bank?"

Liz scrambled for the loose notes, tucking them back into the envelope. The letter, she handed to Sally. "Don't be so crass."

Sally eyed her dubiously. "Are you going to explain?"

Liz sat cross-legged on the floor at Sally's feet and chewed on her thumbnail this time. "The letter explains it all."

"Nuh, nuh, nuh ... no way. You're going to start *right* from the beginning and explain how this letter and ..."

"And what?"

"The money, of course, you dill. Start talking, girl. *You* have secrets I want to know about."

Liz sighed, rubbing a hand across her forehead. Grabbing a cushion from the couch, she lay on her back on the carpet and adjusted it comfortably under her head. "Ever since I inherited the old mechanic shop, I've been seriously considering selling it. I can't get a decent tenant to stay long enough, and the building needs desperate renovation work."

Sally sat back with the letter between her fingers, her eyes firmly on Liz.

"So last week, I decided it was time to clear out all the old stuff in the storage room." Lifting her arms above her head, Liz knotted her hands and let out a long sigh. "Remember Uncle Ben's stash of lollies and chocolates on his desk?"

Sally chuckled. "Yeah, and how we used to smile so innocently at him and ask for a special treat every afternoon."

"Not before he chased us around the shop. We'd be yelling and squealing, and the only safe place was Grandad's arms."

Memories of Liz's childhood filtered through her thoughts for a moment. She'd fallen and scraped her knees so many times on the uneven boards in that old building, but the old workshop where her grandad and Uncle Ben ran their business had been a happy place.

Mentally shaking the memories away, she disconnected, needing to get to the crux of today's problem. Her gaze wandered back to Sally. "Anyway, amongst all the dust, I found some really old ledger books and things of interest I'm sure the Historical Society would love."

She rolled onto her side and rested her head on her palm. "Shoved in between the pages of an old ledger book was this bulky envelope addressed to the current owner of 23 Catherine Street, Malanda."

Sally's spine straightened. "And you're the current owner, right?"

Liz nodded. "The one and only."

"Is the letter written by Uncle Ben?"

Another nod.

"He had no other family, did he?"

Liz sat up. "I'm sure you know all this, but as far as I can remember, and I discussed this with Grandad a couple of times, Grandad met Uncle Ben soon after he arrived as an immigrant from Italy. Grandad said they were both fifteen, and his family took him under their wing. After the war, lots of immigrants from Europe found their way to Australia and Uncle Ben came over with another Italian family. They were kind to him, but it wasn't long before Grandad and Uncle Ben became inseparable, despite the fact Uncle Ben couldn't speak a word of English at first."

Sally twirled a strand of her hair around her finger and sat back. "How many years has it been since Uncle Ben died?"

Liz used her fingers to add up the years. "Um, I was still in high school, so that makes it about ten years ago."

Sally sat up straight, flung her arms out wide and fell back onto the couch. "Jeez, ten whole years the money's been sitting there."

Liz nodded, understanding where Sally's thoughts were going. Grandad's cancer prognosis had gobbled up all his and Nan's savings. Liz was still paying back medical bills a year after his death. Now with her grandmother's health deteriorating and dementia getting more noticeable by the day, she was warned looking after her nan would be too much for her. The cost of a nursing home loomed on her horizon.

"You know what?" Sally sat up again.

"What?"

"I think Uncle Ben always intended for you to find it. He knew your grandfather would never go through all the stuff in the back room."

Liz had thought the same thing.

"So, what's in the letter?"

Liz ran her hand through her hair. "When you read it, you'll find Uncle Ben had an interesting history. I never knew anything about his family. I remember being told he was a war orphan. Read it and tell me what you think."

Sally unfolded the pages and laid them on her lap. Liz had initially struggled to read the spidery writing. It had taken a couple of goes before the cursive appeared as an undulating lullaby on the page, each letter a creative art form in its own right. Sally drew the pages closer and squinted, reading the letter for the first time.

Liz waited, not realising she held her breath. Sally's expressions changed as her eyes drifted down the page. When Sally reached the end of the letter, the two pages fluttered to the floor. In a trance, Sally's mouth fell and her eyes opened wide. "Sweet mother of God. Just do it, Liz."

Liz scratched her cheek, confused. "Do what?"

"Oh, for goodness' sake." Sally jumped up, and this time, *she* paced. "Go over there and find the jewels, of course. What do you think all the money is for?"

Liz rose and walked to the window. Leaning against it, she said, "Um ... duh, girl. Have you calculated how many years since they have been buried? I have. Seventy-five, just in case you haven't worked it out yet."

"So?"

"What makes you think the other twin hasn't already been and dug them out? Think about it." She tapped her head with her knuckles and turned around to face Sally. "They were separated. They never found each other. If you notice, Uncle Ben must've changed his surname when he came to Australia. His twin probably thought he was dead, so of course he went back for the jewels."

"What if ..." Sally retrieved the pages and scanned them again. "What if, what's the other twins' name? Um—Nicolo, that's it; what if he was killed?"

"What if?"

Sally sent the pages flying. "It means the jewels are still buried, that's what," she explained impatiently.

"Impossible. A lot can happen in seventy-five years. There's probably a building standing over it by now."

"Liz, listen to yourself. This is why you've been stressed for a week, isn't it? You know you've already talked yourself out of going. Now you're feeling guilty because you're going to spend all this money on sensible stuff? Girl," she growled, "just do it. Live a bit, dream a bit and for God's sake, take a holiday."

Back beside the couch, Liz slid to the floor and sunk her head in her hands. Through her fingers, her voice came out muffled. "You don't understand. Five thousand dollars is a lot of money. I'm only just getting some control over Grandad's medical bills. What about the renovations I could now afford on the old shop?"

Sally sat beside her. She jostled close enough so their shoulders touched. "I do understand. You've dealt with things at the ripe old age of twenty-six that most people don't have to until they're fifty." Sally tugged at Liz's hand. Squeezing it between her own, she continued, "You deserve some time away. So what if the jewels are gone. I still think you should do it for Uncle Ben. I'll get Mum to help and we'll look after Aunty for you."

Liz baulked. "I can't waste this money on something so far out. Then what do I do? Start digging near the fontana? I'm more likely to be thrown in jail." Her shoulders drooped, reflecting everything going on. She'd toyed with the fanciful idea of going to Italy for about three seconds, despite knowing exactly what Sally's reaction would be. "By the way, a fontana dei povere is a water fountain provided for the poor to access clean drinking water."

Sally shook beside her, laughing. "Let me guess. You've been on the internet doing research? Use your head, girl. Tell them some story—like—ah ..." She clapped her hands. "I know, tell them you're planting a new garden for the community or something in honour of your uncle. Use your imagination."

Liz's face dropped. Sally's life ambition was to constantly remind Liz she needed to live. Even Nan would agree with Sally. In her better health days, barely a few years ago, when her grandfather was at his worst and it would get Liz down, it was a constant, 'where's that sassy girl I raised?' or 'where's that cheeky, spirited girl with spunk? I want her back.' Liz had laughed plenty over the old-fashioned word and was always touched by how her grandmother championed the idea that Liz needed to live her own life and not be hampered by aging grandparents. But to abandon her now?

As they rested against the couch, Liz peered down at Sally's ankle. The rope ankle bracelet peeking out from under her work pants could easily have had a label attached to it saying 'beautiful and not a care in the world'. Sally was beautiful both inside and out, with her honey blonde hair and her sporty and fit body, and a generous soul to go with it. Liz loved her cousin better than if she'd been a sister. They were raised in the same town, were the same age, and had done some crazy stuff over the years, but ultimately it was Liz's responsibility to take care of her grandparents, more so now it was just Nan. She wouldn't have it any other way.

Sally's voice took on a dreamy tone. "Hey, Liz, think of all those gorgeous Mediterranean boys over there. I'd go in a flash."

Liz momentarily dwelled on the possibility there was room for any man in her life but cleared all such thoughts when she heard the intercom buzzer go off in the kitchen. She sighed and rose. "Grandma must be awake and needing a hand to sit up." She reached out to help Sally up. When the strong garlic and French onion smell wafted into the lounge, she said, "I better check on dinner too."

Liz didn't miss the sad lilt to Sally's smile. She knew Sally felt sorry for her and all she'd been through since Grandad's cancer diagnosis.

Sally reached for a hug and said, "I better get going. Give Aunty a hug from me, and we'll talk about this tomorrow. In the meantime, think seriously about doing this. The chance may never come again and isn't it exciting? It's like a real-life treasure hunt. Remember how we used to love that game?"

"A long time ago, maybe." Liz gave Sally a crooked smile as she waved goodbye and made for the front door. Liz also didn't miss how Sally shook her head on the way out, probably despairing of ever convincing her to do something so way out. And she'd be right. It was a crazy idea, not worth thinking about again.

This didn't stop her hand from coming up to rest on her chest, though. Uncertainty gnawed at her a lot lately. It hovered in the background, silently growing in size. The best years of her life were slipping away. If she didn't start acting her age, she would be old before her time.

Then she remembered the buzzer had sounded a couple of minutes ago and this jolted her back to the present. She sped down the hallway towards her grandmother's bedroom. This was her real life. Expenses to pay, an almost finished occupational therapist degree—if only she had time to go back and complete it—and an aging grandmother who deserved the best.

Chapter 2

*T*oronto, Canada

Connor reached for the silverware tongs and placed extra ice cubes in his scotch. He'd have it straight tonight. God knows he needed it.

"He asked to speak to both of us tonight." Connor's pulse ticked on either side of his forehead as he spoke to his father. Ice tinkled against the Swarovski crystal glass as he swirled the liquid. He tried to concentrate on the simple chiming sound to ignore the thumping inside his head.

He brought the glass up to his lips and bit on the edge. Tipping his head back, the amber liquid burned its way down his throat.

"Isn't he dead yet?" His father loosened his tie as he sank back onto the soft leather couch. With one leg resting on his knee, he showed no traces of sorrow.

Connor swallowed another mouthful. Sighing into his glass, his shoulders dropped. His life was a sham. His mother fidgeted on the other side of the room with a fake smile. Gritting his teeth, he met his father's eyes. "The doctor doesn't think he'll live more than a few days."

His father's smug smile always left a horrible taste in his mouth.

"I haven't given a shit about him for a long time. The sooner he's gone, the sooner I can take control of the empire." His father's laugh sounded depraved. "I can't believe the bastard has hung on for this long."

For Connor, it was hard to pinpoint when he began to despise his father.

Was it when he read the social pages of the Toronto newspapers and found many photos over the years of his father with a constant stream of different women? His friends treated it as a joke, but it had torn the safe and secure part of his life into shreds.

Was it when he realised his father was lazy with no desire to work alongside his own father? Instead, Connor thrived beside his grandfather, forging a solid bond.

Was it when he learnt his father was eroding the family fortune with his excessive gambling habits? It only fortified Connor's efforts to work harder.

Or was it when he learnt too late his father was an alcoholic, incapable of completing a full day of work?

Staring past him, his eyes rested on the polished timber staircase leading three stories up. A house lavished with every comfort available. The lights from the chandelier flickered across his vision. It was easy for three people to live separate lives in a house this large.

When his sister Lucia left two years ago, she vowed never to return. *God, how I miss her.* She never tolerated their mother's misery. Couldn't look her in the eye when she understood how their father treated her. "Why the hell does she stay?" Lucia used to ask.

"The sooner the old bastard dies, the sooner I can be free of him. Tell him that from me."

Connor's heart thumped against his chest at his father's words. Why so much hate? He loved his grandfather with such intensity that it shook him to his very core whenever his father spoke this way.

Two months ago, he insisted his grandfather move into Lucia's room. Connor knew his days were numbered and wanted to be as close as possible to him until the end. An old man rumbling alone in a mansion as large as theirs made no sense.

Ignoring his father, he turned towards his mother. He understood the look she gave him. He had grown up learning to understand it at an early age. His mother's hand shook when she brought the wineglass up to her lips. He suspected it hadn't left her hand all day. As she sipped, Connor looked into her sad, addled eyes. It was her usual nonverbal response whenever their father graced their presence: Don't start anything. Keep the peace. Pretend we're a happy family.

Lucia was the smart one. London suited her. He was simply tired.

His chest tightened as he continued to stare at his mother. Her personal assistant had straightened her creamy hair and set it neatly against her neck. The expensive matching sky-blue blouse and skirt complemented the high-heeled shoes enclosing her stockinged feet. Why does she bother? The bastard doesn't even look at her. His mother was beautiful. He vaguely remembered her vigour and cheerfulness. Her laughter had once been contagious. How many years since he last heard it? Connor could barely remember. Whatever she had left was leeching out, leaving an empty shell devoid of happiness and relying on alcohol and antidepressants to get her through the day.

Placing his glass down, he walked over to his mother and reached down to hug her. When he stepped back, moisture had built up around her soft brown eyes. Not wanting to upset her further, he hastily kissed her forehead and turned towards the elegant, sweeping staircase. It was time to check on his grandfather.

⁘

Connor's bare feet sunk into the plush carpet as he loosened his tie and top button. Then he moved the chair closer to his grandfather's bed and sat.

The hired nurse entered the room from the connecting door, her handbag hanging from her shoulder. "He's had a peaceful day but hasn't eaten much, preferring to sleep a lot."

Connor nodded. "Thanks."

The nurse stood with her hands clasped in front of her neat uniform. "Your mum spent an hour with him earlier today. It seemed to perk him up."

Chewing on his bottom lip, he continued to nod. "Thanks again for everything. I better let you go home. I'll see you tomorrow morning?"

The nurse went to walk past him but stopped. Her hand reached out and lightly squeezed his shoulder. In a hushed tone, she said, "He won't make it past the weekend. Spend as much time as you can with him."

Connor's heart tripped again. No preparation would prepare him for his grandfather's death. The doctor had given him the same verdict.

The nurse smiled sadly, and genuine warmth surrounded her. "Your grandfather's very lucky he's not in a great deal of pain. Be grateful for that."

He tried not to fall apart. With his teeth clamped down on his tongue, not even the acrid taste of blood could stop the stray tear trickling down his cheek. He nodded and turned towards the bed.

The nurse left the room, the door clicking softly behind her. He reached for his grandfather's arthritic hand and held it gently between his. Taking a deep breath, he wiped his face on his sleeve and massaged the old man's fingers. "Hey, Grandad, I'm home."

Instead of the larger-than-life booming voice his grandfather always had, Connor concentrated hard to make out the words that croaked from his throat. "Connor is … is your father here, too?"

He hated having to lie, but he would never convey the hate his father felt towards this man. "He was busy tonight, Grandad."

His grandfather shook his head. "Connor, don't blame him. I was not a good father."

"No," Connor vehemently denied, "you did nothing wrong."

"Shh, my boy, listen to me. I know I don't have much longer to live." His voice seemed to find strength from an inner source, and Connor didn't have to strain so much to make out his words.

"I was always too busy for him." He coughed, and Connor reached for the glass and straw by his bed. After a couple of sips, he continued, "By the time I realised I needed to spend more time with him, he was no longer interested."

Connor had difficulty breathing, the ache in the back of his throat worsening. His grandfather must've sensed his anguish because, with surprising strength, he squeezed his hand. Connor's face fell onto their clasped hands, and the tears flowed freely, spilling onto the sheets.

When Connor's tears dried up, he sat back and reached for the box of tissues. His grandfather's misted green eyes matched his own, but it was his smile that brought momentary joy to Connor's ravaged heart.

"You remind me of Benito. Built like an ox but always so emotional."

Benito?

"Sit closer. Before I die, I have a story to tell you. I've only ever told your grandmother. I need you to do something for me after I'm gone."

His heart wrenched. "Please don't talk about after you're gone. While you're alive, I want only good memories."

"Then give me a smile so I can bring it away with me. You've been my greatest joy from the day you were born. It's not your fault you resemble Benito."

"Who's Benito?"

His grandfather's eyes closed for a moment, but not before tears trickled past his eyelids. "Benito was my twin brother. I tried so hard to find him. I never stopped looking." His frail hand came up to rest on his chest. "We were separated by an isolated group of German soldiers. He would've been so lost without me." With surprising strength, his hand thumped his chest. "All these years, I could feel it in my heart that he was still alive somewhere." His eyes flicked open. "Benito didn't die; otherwise, I would have felt it here"—his hand struck his chest again but not so hard this time—"but I never found him. He must've changed his surname. We talked about it once."

Connor's frown deepened. "How come I never knew about a twin brother?"

His grandfather relaxed against his pillow. His arms lay by his side; his fingers curled towards his palms. For a few moments, he didn't speak, and Connor sensed his grandfather's mind had left the room.

"Some mornings, I'd wake and think it was all a dream. That I never really had a twin brother."

He blinked a couple of times and turned his face towards Connor. "About five years ago, I wrote everything down and left it with my will. It's addressed to you. I was going to share the story with your father tonight, but now I'll leave it up to you who you tell."

Connor rested his elbows on the side of the bed. His grandfather was flagging and would probably fall asleep soon. "What happened to your parents?"

His hand came up and rested on Connor's cheek. "It was towards the end of the war. My father was recovering from a grenade attack. They were murdered looking for my mother's famous jewels."

Jewels? Famous?

His grandfather's hand dropped away from his cheek, exhaustion setting in. His breathing sounded heavier. "They never found them. Father hid them well and showed us where they were. We snuck back and took them, burying them a week later."

His raspy breath echoed in the room.

"Shh, Grandad, don't tire yourself. I'll read the letter one day."

His grandfather's lips moved rapidly, but Connor heard no sound. His Adam's apple bobbed up and down. Alarm bells rang when his grandfather started to choke. In a swift action, Connor raised him off the bed to help steady his breathing.

"Shh, Grandad, don't get upset."

When minutes passed and his grandfather's breathing was under control, Connor gently lowered him back onto his pillow.

His grandfather's eyes were closed, and he looked asleep. Then his voice, clear and full of strength, startled Connor as he moved to sit back on the chair. "Connor, I need you to promise me something. I want you to dig up the jewels. I know they're still there. Benito promised we'd do it together."

Fumbling, he found Connor's hand and, with the strength of an arm wrestler, squeezed it. "Promise me, Connor. Go back to Falerna and find the jewels. If you ever find Benito and his family, tell him I never stopped looking for him. I missed him so much."

"I promise, Grandad." Connor tucked the promise securely away knowing he would never break it.

His hand slipped out of Connor's hold, and within seconds, his breathing turned regular as he drifted to sleep.

Connor lovingly tucked his grandfather's arms under the sheet and covered his chest. He reached over and placed a kiss on his pale, sunken cheek, which was once so healthy and full. The memories flittered past. The camping trips, fishing, hiking, snow skiing and even the times his grandfather came skateboarding. His friends loved his easy banter and great jokes.

Connor recalled the years they'd worked side by side. The confidence his grandfather instilled in him, the business acumen he'd passed on, and the finance empire Connor successfully managed with him, shouldering the burden more so in the later years.

His vision swam. With heavy limbs he registered how weary he was. The pressures of work and his grandfather's final days were taking their toll. He rested his face on his grandfather's shoulder and closed his eyes. As sleep overtook his exhausted body, his grandfather's heart beat one last time.

Chapter 3

S ix Months Later

Liz fingered the lucky charm of a shooting star attached to her backpack as she followed the other passengers streaming towards the exit. Sally had clipped it on a mere thirty-eight hours ago when they parted at the airport.

Tightening the straps over her shoulders, she continued to smooth her fingers over its chrome surface. Not for the first time since leaving home did she ask herself what the hell she was doing. She shook her head, fatigue clouding her usually organised and meticulous brain. For every kilometre the plane flew her away from the sleepy, little town of Malanda, the worse her anxiety shot up. She was already regretting her impulsiveness. Not to mention the enormous waste of money this wild goose chase was, despite Sally's reassurances.

She made her way out of customs and jostled past crowds of passengers, swinging her backpack to her front so it wouldn't hit anyone. Her chest tightened, recalling the goodbye to her grandmother. She knew it was only three weeks, but it hurt. The signs of dementia were getting worse. Liz swallowed back the lump in her throat. Too soon she was going to lose the one person who had nurtured her all her life.

But Sally was relentless. *Throw caution to the wind, drop everything and just do it.* She never let up. Liz found every reason not to surrender. Her mind kept warning her it couldn't be true. Put the money to better use.

The bills would keep coming, and renovations were long overdue on the old mechanic shop.

Until two weeks ago when Sally's last argument finally penetrated her stubbornness. It was the push Liz needed to get her backside on the plane. If she found the damn jewels, it would ensure the best medical care for her grandmother. She'd surrendered without any further argument until the plane took off and, all alone, her doubts resurfaced.

Raising her downcast eyes, she found herself surrounded by families and loved ones reuniting. She took a deep breath and released it slowly, keeping her nerves at bay. It was time to push aside all the reasons she shouldn't have been so impulsive. She was here now, and despite all her misgivings, every trick in the book couldn't stop the smile stretching across her face. *I'm actually here. Rome's Fiumicino International Airport.* She rolled her tongue around the word Fiumicino, trying to get the right sound and feel for it before she gave up and laughed at herself. Only last week her neighbour told her anything could be spoken to sound Italian as long as you rolled your 'r', and where possible, ended every word with an 'a'.

Smiling, she tucked a loose strand of hair falling out of its ponytail behind her ear. What a mess she must look. She'd run a comb through it during her stopover in Singapore, but there was no time to worry about grooming now. She needed to find her connecting train to Falerna.

Knowing she would need her translator app soon, she reached into the pocket of her creased track pants for her phone. She straightened her cheap cotton t-shirt and sighed at her scuffed trekking boots. Not wanting to waste any money on a new wardrobe for this short stint, she planned to return home with most of the spending money she'd brought with her.

She switched on her phone, and a message popped up a few moments later, reminding her what she needed to do before boarding the train. Travel advice on the small village of Falerna, chiselled into the side of a mountain, recommended she carry euro. It looked a world away from the busy tourist strip of Falerna Marina on the seashore, with all its modern facilities.

A money exchange booth sat just inside the arrivals hall, and she dodged weary travellers to reach it. Her stomach grumbled as the strong aroma of garlic and bolognaise sauce caught her right in her middle. It had been hours since her last decent meal, and the smells assailing her nose were making food a top priority. She would exchange some money first and then head back for food. Problem solved.

Shouts of 'taxi!' and 'taxi signorina!' rang out, and remembering the stern warnings on internet sites advising care about taxis, she ignored them. Not all were honest and safe.

She felt for the leather money pouch hanging around her neck, hidden underneath her clothes, and lifted the cord over her neck. Along with a credit card, she'd also brought some US notes. It was those notes she would exchange for euros.

Unzipping the pouch, Liz reached for a small bundle of notes just as her arm was forced back with a painful yank. She spun around, dazed, but snapped to when the pouch was gone. *Oh my God, I've been robbed.*

"Help!" she yelled. "Help, my money's been stolen!"

Sprinting as fast as her backpack allowed, she followed the thief, running only metres ahead. As she continued to shout, a man began to run alongside her. With his long strides, he overtook her clumsy gait and gained on the thief.

The stranger shouted something in Italian, and the crowds parted, allowing him easy passage, just like the sea that had parted in a biblical story she'd once read. The babble of noise as the people in the crowd began to shout and point at the man grew. In the next instant, two young, strong men scrambled from the throng and tackled the thief. He fell onto his stomach, hitting the tiled floor. At the same time, the stranger reached them and toppled onto the pile, adding an extra pair of arms around the thief.

Liz might've pulled herself up short if her backpack hadn't been so heavy, but unable to stop in time, she saw no option but to plough headlong into the stranger. With her chest heaving, she fell towards him as his hand wrenched her pouch and belongings from the robber, smacking her on the cheek with its force.

Liz groaned, the strength of the hit sending her sprawling backwards onto her back. Stars sparkled behind her closed eyelids. She struggled to breathe. Gasping for air, her hand came up and rested on her chest. The surrounding noise dimmed. Her hand jerked up to her cheek when the pain from the strike eclipsed all other thoughts.

"Are you okay?" Someone tried to cradle her head in their hands. "Answer me if you can," a man pleaded. "I didn't mean to hit you."

Liz's eyes snapped open at the panicked voice. The dark-haired man running alongside her was now holding her head. She tried to make sense of her surroundings. Trying to nod, a wave of dizziness made her stomach churn. She collapsed against his arms.

"Would you like me to call a doctor?"

Swallowing back nausea, Liz concentrated on the stranger. He spoke with an American accent, but she could've sworn he'd shouted in Italian.

Pain flickered behind her eyes as she rolled onto her knees. His hand came out to help her stand, but not before her eyes latched onto his polished black leather shoes. She leant heavily on his hand, hoisting herself up, allowing her eyes to follow the perfect cut of his designer-cut pants. His silver cufflinks shot off sparkling flashes as his sturdy, muscled hand clasped tighter around hers. Getting her legs to work of their own accord, she slowly drew her face up but stopped abruptly near his neatly knotted, and what looked to be an expensive silk tie.

Liz swallowed, heat rushing up the back of her neck and suffusing her cheeks. She drew level with his face and collided with sea-green eyes, wide with concern. Finally, she released the breath she'd been holding and forced her shoulders to relax. "Um, th—thank you. I think I'm fine." She pressed her palm over her cheek, where his hand had connected.

His hand clutched hers tighter as though afraid she would topple over. "I'm so sorry," he said, reaching for her face and halting. "I didn't know you were right behind me and ..." His hand dropped away, but he kept searching her face. "I think all of your things are here. Would you like to check?"

The pouch, my money, my ... of course ... Liz reached for the pouch and checked the contents. She sorted through them, mentally ticking her list: passport, credit card, cash ... Her hand froze, and she swivelled her head from side to side. "Where is he? Where did he go? He took my letter. Oh my God, he has Uncle Ben's letter."

She shoved the contents roughly into the pouch and secured the strap around her neck. "I have to find him. Did the police take him away somewhere?" She took a few steps to the left, stopped and swung back towards the stranger. She bumped into someone going the opposite direction and snapped, "For goodness' sake, can you tell me where they took the thief?"

The man who'd hit her stood with his feet firmly planted, his arms crossed and eyebrows arched in surprise. Travellers ducked around to avoid walking into him. "You're an Aussie girl, I assume? I thought you lot were a friendly bunch."

Aghast, Liz's face dropped. He was right. She could hear her grandmother's voice reprimanding her. *Bugger!*

With her bottom lip caught between her teeth, she looked up, forced a smile and extended her hand. Sighing and hoping she looked apologetic, she said, "And you're an American, a very helpful one." Shrugging, she continued, "Please excuse my rudeness. This was so unexpected. I'm not normally like this."

The stranger took hold of her hand and squeezed it. Heat lingered in her palm as it nestled comfortably against his larger one. His eyes surveyed her, wincing when they reached her cheek, then did a cursory glance at her shirt and creased pants. Uncomfortable with the scrutiny of her clothes, she jerked her hand away. "Um ... the letter the thief stole is the reason why I'm here. It was only a copy, but it had some personal information on it."

The man's hand fell by his side, and he rocked back on his heels. "Actually, I'm Canadian, and in all the confusion he took off so fast we didn't have time to restrain him. I was more concerned about the hit you took, and I thought I'd snatched everything back from him."

Liz winced, rubbing the back of her neck. "Er ... thank you."

His eyes crinkled at the edges, his dark hair brushing his forehead. "What for? For hitting you?"

Taking a deep breath, she tilted her face. "I'm sorry about the American thing. At least give me a chance to thank you properly for saving my stuff."

The man's hand came out again. "It's Connor, and I only wish I'd saved the letter too."

Liz's hand sunk into his warmth again. Why were her legs suddenly a teeny bit shaky? It must be the after-effect of the head knock. "You saved enough, thank you. I'll get my cousin to email me another copy of the letter."

"Well, I'm glad that's settled. I feel better now about the thief getting away with only the letter."

Liz dismissed the slight niggle about what was in the letter. Hopefully, the thief couldn't read English and would toss it away. Time to move on.

With her hand free again, she brought it up to rest on her cheek, which suddenly tingled from the hit. "Thank you again for everything. I won't hold you up anymore. I—I'll be right from here."

He took a step closer, and Liz's breath caught in her throat when his hand touched her cheek. Staring at it, he exclaimed, "Damn! I can't believe I hit you so hard." He gently pushed aside her hand and fingered the tender spot. "I think you're going to end up with a bruise unless you can get some ice on it soon."

Liz inwardly groaned. Where was Sally when she needed her? Tall, dark and gorgeous was standing right in front of her, and she was coming across like a helpless idiot.

Liz tried to take a step back, but he continued to hold her face. Through the lump in her throat, she managed to say, "At least I'll be a bruised Aussie with a passport *and* money. Honestly, the bruise is no big deal. It won't kill me, so don't worry about it."

A dimple flashed on Connor's cheek as he gave her a broad smile, and that was all it took for Liz's heart to miss a beat. How did one male get all the good-looking genes in the world?

Chuckling, he said, "Okay. So ... ah ... I'll just leave now? Are you sure you'll be all right? I'm really sorry about the hit."

She nodded and bent to pick up her backpack. Her lucky charm tinkled against a metal buckle, but before she could correlate shaking legs with a solid chest, Connor put one hand on her shoulder and gave it a quick squeeze. She was close enough to inhale all the spicy scents of expensive aftershave. This was a never to be repeated freak moment in her life. A story to laugh over with Sally and a strong coffee.

Pulling away, he said, "I hope the rest of your holiday goes well. It was a pleasure to help you."

Alarmed, she remembered the money she still had to exchange and a train to catch very soon. Swinging her backpack over her shoulder, she blurted, "I need to go, or I'll miss my train. I ... um ... thank you again, and I hope *your* holiday is fantastic. I owe you one."

She turned to leave when his hand brushed her arm. She half twisted back.

"You didn't tell me your name?"

Huh? "My name? Oh, it's Liz," she offered before turning away and briskly searching for the foreign exchange booth.

While she appreciated all he'd done to help, what were the chances she'd ever run into him again?

Zilch.

Chapter 4

Liz flung herself into the train carriage as the door slid shut behind her. She tripped on her own foot and landed on her knees, a stinging pain jarring her body. "Ouch!" For the second time that day, she concentrated on her breathing, willing the pain to dissipate. That was too close a call. She didn't want to calculate how much more it would have cost to stay an extra night in Rome if she'd missed the train.

"Are you okay?"

Her face snapped up to see the smiling face of a young, dark-haired woman. Still struggling for breath after running what felt like a three-kilometre-long platform, she asked, "You speak English?"

"Nah," the woman replied, her smile turning mischievous, "I speak Australian, and so do you, by the sounds of it. Need a hand up?"

Liz's jaw dropped as she rubbed her knee. Surely her day was improving if she'd already run into another Aussie. Grabbing onto a chrome handhold, she shook her head and picked herself up, tightening her grip as the train swayed. She slid her backpack off and dropped it to the floor, sitting opposite the woman. The small cabin had seats facing each other, which folded out into a bed when you were travelling overnight.

The vibrations as the carriage lurched along the train tracks rubbed her backpack against her sore knee. She pushed it away with her foot and removed her water bottle from a side pouch.

"Roberta's the name. What part of Oz are you from?"

Pressing her water bottle closed after a sip, Liz smiled at the woman. "I'm Liz and give me a second. I just need to catch my breath."

The woman's laughter rang around the small cabin. "Yep, I think you had about one second to spare when you threw yourself in."

Liz chuckled. What a sight she must have looked. Now that the real fear of missing her train had passed, she relaxed, easing the tension from her shoulders. She pulled her hair tie off with every intention of tidying up her ponytail. "I live in Malanda, a small town in North Queensland. What about yourself?"

"Melbourne. You know the place? Has more Italians than Italy itself."

Sitting back, Liz smiled. With a huge sigh of relief, she turned to her left to glance at the passing landscape of old buildings, tacked on together one after the other, as the train departed Rome. She conjured up another smile for the elderly lady sitting near the window. She was the only other passenger in their cabin. Then looked on enviously as she took out a thermos and what looked like a container of food from the cooler bag on her lap.

Dragging her eyes away, she remembered the garlic and bolognaise smells that had prompted her to make food a priority about an hour ago. With all the drama, she never made it back, and her stomach grumbled in protest.

Liz turned back to Roberta when she asked, "Is Lamezia Terme where you're headed?"

"Yes, but then I have to make my way to a small village called Falerna."

"Are you serious? Nobody has ever heard of Falerna when I tell them I'm going to visit my aunt."

"You're joking?" Liz exclaimed. "You're travelling to the same place?"

Roberta pointed her thumb at her chest. "Would a face like mine joke to you?"

The dark curls and the even-darker brown eyes twinkled back, and Roberta's light-hearted laughter pealed around the tiny cabin. Its contagious gaiety had Liz grinning from ear to ear. "What a small world."

"Heck, yeah. But tell me, why is an Australian who doesn't look one speck Italian going to Falerna of all places?"

Liz shrugged. She never expected to have to explain her travel plans. "I ... I'm fulfilling the last wish for an adopted uncle born there." She remembered Sally's idea and blurted, "I'm going to plant a tree in his memory. Then I might do some research and find out if there's any family of his living in the village."

Roberta arched a brow. "Hmm, interesting. Maybe I can help. I speak the lingo, and it might help kill the boredom. Then you and I could have ourselves a good time down at the marina. Where are you staying?"

Scrounging around in her backpack, Liz pulled out an envelope. "I didn't have much choice, but I found this."

Roberta sat back and folded her arms. Nodding, she said, "Let me guess, Zia Maria's Casa, by any chance?"

She turned the envelope up the right way. "Yeah, that's the place."

"Thought so. There's nowhere else unless you stay on the beach at Falerna Marina."

"Have you been to Falerna before?" Liz asked.

"This is my third time. My aunt's filthy rich, and her only sibling is my father. She never married and has no kids. She paid for my first holiday at twenty-one, and my brother and I have taken turns each year since. It's three weeks of being totally spoilt if you can find enough stuff to do and someone to do it with. She bankrolls it, and we spend it." Roberta's infectious laughter rang out again, filling all the spaces of the cabin.

It was hard not to grin, flippant as Roberta was. There was never anyone throwing money her way when she needed it. The usual balloon of fear that jiggled inside her chest reminded her of the many sleepless nights she'd had over the years worrying over how some bills were going to be paid. "That's very generous of her."

"Yeah, I know. She's not a bad old bird. A bit set in her ways, though."

For some people, money was just that. Some people had it, others not quite so much. A sigh escaped, but Liz made a snap decision to stop worrying over how much of it she was wasting on this trip. If Sally was sitting beside her, she'd be a constant harp in her ear. *Live life. Enjoy being young. You'll be old before your time.*

Roberta and the elderly lady started a conversation in Italian. Liz sat mesmerised by Roberta's animated face when she spoke. The way her eyes lit up and her curls bounced around her face projected a naturally happy person. A quick calculation of her age made her about twenty-five. Maybe sharing some holiday time with Roberta wasn't such a bad idea. It would be like having Sally around.

Roberta turned to Liz. "She wants to know if you want a sandwich. She has plenty to spare."

As if on cue, her stomach grumbled, the sound filtering around the confined air conditioned cabin.

"Sounds like a yes to me," Roberta said with a chuckle.

Heat rushed along Liz's neck. "I could use some food. I had some drama earlier and ran out of time to eat."

"Well, turn to her and say *si signora*, and when she hands it to you, say *grazie*."

She did as told and sank her teeth into a thick slab of homemade bread. Roberta accepted a sandwich, too, and informed Liz the filling was salami and goat's cheese.

It was heaven.

As they ate, Roberta continued with a string of questions. "So, how long are you spending in Falerna?"

"Three weeks," Liz answered in between chewing and swallowing.

"Are you spending all that time in Falerna?"

She nodded before swallowing the last of the sandwich.

"By the way, my aunt's place is next door to where you're staying. And to fill your days, you can spend one locked away in the local church because that, my darling, is the only place a town like Falerna keeps the records that might contain details of your uncle. Only the bigger places have a town hall for record keeping. Then," she continued, "you and I can do some sightseeing, bum a lift to the marina coastal strip and check out some of the tourist joints."

Roberta took a gulp of water from her bottle, then kept talking. "How about coming with me to Pompeii for a couple of days? It's on the way and shouldn't interfere with your plans."

Liz watched Roberta in fascination, remembering films her grandfather used to show on his old projector. She used to love the noise the reel made as it spun out at the end of the film. In an absurd way, its sound reminded her of Roberta's babble.

"So, what do you think?"

Her mouth opened and closed, but no sound came out.

"Well?"

When common sense washed over her, her shoulders dropped. "Roberta, it all sounds like fun, but I don't have spare cash. My uncle left me some money for this trip, but I should've spent it on more important things back home. So, my answer has to be no."

Roberta continued talking as though Liz hadn't spoken. "Great, my aunt has already deposited a stack of money in my account, and there will be more when I arrive. I'll do the paying; you follow my lead. As for Pompeii, I'll handle the accommodation and organise for your train ticket to include a few more days. Agreed?"

"What?"

"Come on, Liz. I could use a friend. It gets lonely travelling by myself, and it's hard to say no to my aunt when she offers to pay us to visit her. She's not bad, and it's not her fault she has no one else to spend her money on. Just don't blame me when you find out Falerna is a backwater place compared to Melbourne and whatever place you're from."

Liz chewed on her bottom lip. It was better not to tell her how small Malanda was. Now to decide whether this girl was a crazy psycho or plain genuine? Would it hurt to do a spot of sightseeing at someone else's expense? Not something she'd done before or was comfortable with, but what the heck. Time to follow through on all of Sally's nagging. If Sally was here, she'd have her hand up in the air, agreeing to the arrangement without a second thought.

"If the money side of things worries you, how about we make a pact?"

A pact? Liz frowned.

"Yeah. You're going to need a translator, you know, someone who can speak the lingo."

"Yes ..." She nodded slowly. "That could be handy."

"Well, I'm it. You drag me around for one day so you can get your research done, then your part of the deal is to keep me company for the rest of the time. Look at it as paying your own way."

A chuckle burst past Liz's lips. A translator sounded like a great idea. She'd deal with the rest as it happened. Somehow, the jewels had to be dug up, too, if she could find them. "Okay, you're on."

Chapter 5

"So, why are you travelling to southern Italy?" Lucia tilted her head before lifting her cappuccino with both hands for another sip.

"If you're good to me, I'll tell you one day," Connor told her with a wry grin.

"Oh, poop Connor. You know I hate secrets. If it's some southern Italian princess you've discovered, shouldn't I know about it?"

Connor laughed. A sound he hadn't heard for a long time. Certainly not since his grandfather had passed away. Lucia could always drag him out of the darkness he sometimes found himself in. Spending a few days with her in London was what his overwrought head needed. "No, it's not." For now, he was keeping the contents of his grandfather's letter to himself.

"Phew. For a minute there, I was worried. It's not your usual hunting ground."

Lucia had their mother's colouring, pale complexion and hair, but her eyes matched his. Their sea-green vividness sparkled in her pretty face.

"I'm not sure what my usual hunting ground is anymore."

"Spend more than three days with me and I'll lead you in the right direction." Lucia's laughter tinkled around them, causing other café patrons to look up from their coffees and croissants. Lucia always brightened up a room, and he didn't doubt she could match him with a hundred pretty girls, all perfectly groomed and coming from the right family.

Connor took a moment to inhale the rich smell of his coffee as it wafted up. He'd just eaten a slice of sweet apple crumble, and the taste sat well. After landing in Rome, he'd made a swift change of plans and come to London for a few days to see Lucia. He was leaving that afternoon and making his way back to Rome and then onto southern Italy to fulfil his grandfather's promise.

"Who did you leave in charge? And please don't tell me it was Dad because you'll return to wrack and ruin."

Connor grimaced at Lucia's spot-on assessment. "Phil Baxter. Remember him? Lost his wife in a car accident?"

"I do. He was one of the decent ones."

"Yeah, worked his way up. We nearly lost him when his wife died, but he's since become a grandfather, and I think it's given him reason to get up each day."

A week ago, he'd dismissed Phil's misgivings about being able to look after the company on his own. Connor was leaving him in charge for a month. He was their staunchest supporter, and there was no one else Connor trusted.

Lucia sighed, which was unusual for her. "Connor, when do you know if you've met the one."

Connor flicked his gaze up, witnessing a misty-eyed Lucia for the first time ever. "I'm not sure I can answer that."

"I get what happened to Phil. There's someone I've met and —."

Quirking an eyebrow, Connor respected the momentous occasion this was in Lucia's life. After watching their father embarrass the family for years, she vowed never to get married or settle down. This declaration was huge. "How come I haven't met him yet?"

Her face dropped, and she fiddled with her spoon. "He doesn't know how I feel. He thinks I'm some spoilt, rich girl without a brain in my head."

This time Connor's laughter roared out loud and clear. Enough for others to look his way and for Lucia to drop her frustrated look. She finally laughed along, too, before scrunching up a clean serviette and throwing it at him. Connor frowned. That was all he needed, paparazzi and a camera shot showing a flying piece of serviette.

He stopped the serviette midair before it dropped to the ground.

"It's not funny." She pouted.

Connor smiled again. "Little sis, it's hilarious. For the first time in your life, you haven't got men grovelling at your feet, mesmerised by your beauty and money. This time you're going to have to work for this man's attention."

Lucia pulled her shoulders back, indignation written all over her face. "Well, you're no better. When are you going to finally snap up some rich, gorgeous girl and give me some nieces and nephews? You're not getting any younger."

"Puh … twenty-nine isn't old, and anyway, I'm not sure what I'm looking for anymore." He concentrated on stirring the remains of his coffee and ignored the beeping of his phone.

For a few weeks, he wanted to forget the burden of what awaited him back home. As if he had time to pursue a relationship. The last girlfriend barely lasted a month when she learnt he was chained to an office desk and not her.

In the six months since his grandfather's death, Connor found the gaping hole in his life still too large to cross. A legal minefield where each day he'd drag his boots up out of the squelching mud to take a step forward, only to have his father haul them back behind the starting line. Always with the promise made to his grandfather reverberating in the back of his head.

He'd read and reread the pages of the letter his grandfather left him, surprised he'd never spoken about his twin brother. How did he expect him to find his twin when all the money in the world couldn't find him in nearly eighty years?

Connor had toyed with the idea of using private investigators to retrieve the jewels, but something held him back. He'd made a promise and he wouldn't go back on his word. Finally, one morning he woke up knowing he would do it himself. It was what his grandfather wanted.

"How's Mum?"

Connor glanced up again and grimaced. "Not getting any better, and she won't leave him."

"Won't or can't?"

Knots of anxiety twisted in his stomach as he shrugged. He wasn't so sure anymore. Each morning he woke up wanting to escape the clutches of his overbearing, lazy father, whose infidelities embarrassed him. He despised him for the hurt he imparted on his mother and how much he'd hurt their family. He had the strongest urge to protect his mother and encourage her to leave and enjoy a decent life of her own. Her dependency on booze and pills worried him endlessly, but he couldn't force her to do anything.

Connor sat back and ran a hand over his stubbled chin. "She's not her usual self." Lucia dabbed at her eyes with a tissue. "Hey, what's up?"

"I'm sorry, Con. I didn't mean to leave you with all the headaches. I just couldn't take it anymore. It was dragging me down."

Connor grabbed hold of her hand and squeezed it. "I'm managing. To be honest, I'd love nothing more than to sell everything, go somewhere new and start from scratch. Grandad arrived in Canada penniless. If he could do it, so can I."

"Except you wouldn't be penniless." Lucia gave him a twisted smile. "And where would you go?"

Connor stretched his legs and leant back. It was hard to forget the echo of his grandfather's voice over the years: money won't necessarily bring you happiness. Remember that, my grandson.

The sigh that left his chest sounded weary. "Doesn't matter what I want to do. What about all our loyal staff? Trust me, I'd love nothing more than to disappear and do my own thing, but I won't. As to where I'd go —"

His thoughts filtered back to the attractive woman with the caramel brown hair he helped at the airport. Australia was far enough away, wasn't it? Liquidate his assets and get the hell out of Toronto. Except he would never leave his mother with that monster, and she'd never be brave enough to leave.

"Africa, Asia or Australia. They all start with the first letter of the alphabet. The start of something new. What do you think, Sis?"

Now the tears flowed freely down her face.

"What the heck? I was trying to be funny." Connor shoved his chair back and rose. "Come here and give me a hug. I'm going to need it, and so do you, by the looks of it."

He wound his arms around his sister and squeezed hard, letting her release the tears. This was not the Lucia he knew. She was headstrong, independent and a staunch supporter. A knot tightened in his chest. Their father had a lot to answer for. He'd screwed up their once tight-knit family. Once upon a time, their mother laughed a lot. She used to be funny, told knock knock jokes and made them smile often.

Then and there, Connor vowed to see his mother happy again. He also wanted more than anything to see the old Lucia smiling every day. As for his life, well, he'd worry about that some other time. His list consisted of: finding his grandfather's twin or family, unearthing the jewels, and then getting on with life. Fingers crossed, it would all fall into place.

With one last squeeze, he stepped back and looked at his sister's blotchy face. "I have to leave, Sis, if I'm going to make it to the airport in time."

She nodded, wiping her face with a tissue she found in her pocket. "It's so good to see you, Connor. I didn't realise how much I missed my annoying older brother."

"Hey, enough of that," he rebuffed with a smile.

He dragged her closer for one final hug while making a promise to himself to salvage what was good of their family and protect it with everything he had.

First things first—the promise to his grandfather.

Chapter 6

Liz scrunched her face as she took another sip of bitter, strong coffee from the tiny ceramic cup. "Jeez, Roberta, how do you drink this stuff? Look, it's not even a liquid." She placed her spoon upright, and it refused to fall sideways.

Roberta's sparkling laughter floated away from under the faded, red and white striped awning with the sultry breeze. They sat at Falerna's only outdoor café, and the other patrons turned in their direction. Roberta's laughter replaced complacent and bored expressions with smiles. She had that effect on people. In the four days since they'd met on the train, it had become a medicinal and therapeutic balm for Liz. So used to having to deal with stressful situations, being around Roberta allowed her to feel young and impulsive for the first time in a long time.

Liz pulled her shirt away from her sweaty back, and it flapped in the breeze. July was the start of Europe's tourist season, but Falerna wasn't the sort of place teeming with tourists. She slid the distasteful cup of coffee to the other side of the table and switched her laptop on.

The day before, at the marina, she'd sourced free internet. To her relief, Sally had emailed her another copy of the letter and some notes. "Okay, this is the information I have about his family." She scrolled to the top of the page, then handed pen and paper to Roberta. "Ready?"

With reluctance, Roberta took hold of the stationery, but her eyes stayed glued to something behind Liz. "Come on, Roberta. You promised you'd help me for one whole day."

The pen dropped from Roberta's hand and clattered on the tabletop. "Yeah, but you didn't warn me that the world's most gorgeous man would be in this dead-end place."

Groaning, Liz reached for the pen. Taking it back, she started to write the details down. "Every man we've passed is the world's most gorgeous man. I refuse to take another look until some research is done."

"But he keeps looking at us. Or is he looking at you, Liz?"

Liz continued to scribble notes, her other hand massaging her temple. "I'm dead certain he's not looking at me."

"You've been wrong before."

Liz looked up. "What? As in wrong when that middle-aged, balding man was supposedly looking at me in Pompeii?"

"Exactly. Don't you get it? You look different from the norm here. You naturally attract attention."

"Attention I don't want, so can we get back to work?"

Roberta snatched the pen back. "Okay, I'm focused again. Let's get to work. What do we know about your uncle?"

Uttering a soft sigh, Liz was inwardly relieved Roberta was willing to help. After a single night at Zia Maria's accommodation, Roberta insisted she move into her auntie's home and save money. At Liz's protests, since Roberta's aunt, Fiorina refused to take a single cent, Zia Maria assured Liz she already had another two bookings and was nearly at capacity. This helped ease the guilt of cancelling the booking.

The inability to speak Italian was something else she had not considered before leaving Australia. Roberta's ease at speaking it had already proved helpful over the past few days. Slumping in her chair, she read from the notes on the screen. "Okay, he changed his surname when he moved to Australia to Menorico. His real name was Benito Enrico." Liz spelt out his surname. "His twin was called Nicolo, and their parents were Frederico and Giovanna. His mother came from a wealthy, central Italian family known as the Frevannini Dynasty. They were murdered in Falerna in 1944." Liz looked up from the letter, her short fingernails clicking against the table. "Am I going too fast?"

Roberta hunched further as her brow creased in concentration. "No, no, I'm nearly there. What year was the murder?"

"1944."

Roberta finished writing and sat back. "Well, that's a good start. Names and dates are always helpful." She reached for her bag and pulled out her mobile phone. "I'll call my aunt and check whether she could get us a time to meet the priest." She grimaced. "Be warned; apparently, he's nearly ninety years old." Roberta pushed her sunglasses to the top of her head and lifted her cup to drink more coffee. "As long as he's not deaf *and* sleazy, I should be able to handle him."

Liz jerked her shoulders back. "Roberta," she admonished.

Roberta tilted her face and feigned innocence. "What? I can handle this, okay?"

Liz shook her head. "You ring Fiorina. I'm going to buy some water to wash the espresso down."

As she shut down her laptop, Liz wondered at her reluctance to mention the buried jewels. How did she bring them up? Pushing her chair back, she pressed against the plastic cushion with her hands, nudging her sweaty legs off. "Want anything?" she asked, grabbing her money pouch from her backpack.

"Nah," Roberta replied and turned her attention back to her phone.

Liz walked to the front entrance of the café, glancing at her profile in the shadowed glass walls. Her short legs hung out of frayed denim shorts while her loose cotton shirt fitted against her small torso. She sighed, noting her hair was in its usual messy ponytail. As her rubber thongs flopped on the concrete floor in the outdoor dining area, she glanced at the decorated cornice along the building's façade and wondered how old it was. Everything in this place was ancient.

Weaving around the tables, Liz reached the heavy front door and pushed on it. Her vision blurred when three children came tearing inside from behind her, shoving her towards the opposite door panel, yelling, "*Mi scusi. Mi scusi.*"

Her hand reached out to steady herself. She only *just* managed to grab hold of the doorframe with her fingertips when her money pouch dropped to the ground. Her vision turned fuzzy again when a fourth child raced through the door and tripped on Liz's legs. Unable to hold onto the door any longer, she fell to the floor with the child landing on her stomach and sucking the wind out of her.

The child started crying, "Mama, Mama," then scrambled up and ran towards the back kitchen area where the other children must have disappeared.

Liz shuffled to her feet and attempted to stand, pressing the sore spot on her tummy, when a familiar accented male voice said, "I recognise this pouch."

She looked up. A strangled sound escaped her lips, her hand flying to her chest. With her breath caught in her throat, her ability to breathe worsened when his hand reached out to help her up.

The same warmth from a few days earlier enclosed her hand, and her legs trembled as she rose and stared at him. Gently tugging at her hand, she freed it. With relief, her lungs began to function again.

"I thought you looked familiar from where I sat, but I didn't think it was possible to run into you again, let alone save your money pouch *twice*."

When she remained speechless, he handed it back. "Liz, isn't it?"

Jeez, girl, answer him. In a halting voice, she stuttered, "Th … thank you. Yes, it is, and I can't believe it's happened either." She took hold of her pouch and clutched it tight between her fingers. "And you're Connor from Canada?"

That dimpled smile … Her hand subconsciously came up to stroke her throat. His shining-green eyes brushed over her face, and her hand stilled when their gazes caught. When her little finger began to twitch, an invisible cord pull-started her back to life and she coughed lightly.

Taking a deep breath, she braced her shoulders and allowed a tentative smile to build when a massive racket erupted from the kitchen area. Patrons inside the café turned to look when a short, chubby woman came tearing towards the front door where Liz and Connor stood. Wisps of dark hair were stuck to her sweaty, round face. Her hands moved at a hundred miles in time with her speech, making it impossible for anyone to keep up.

Liz didn't understand a word but could tell her tirade was an apology of sorts. The woman nervously wrung her hands around her Napoletana-stained apron and visibly relaxed when Connor replied in Italian. She repeatedly bowed her head and said grazie a few times.

When the woman returned to the kitchen, Connor asked, "Do you speak Italian?"

Shaking her head, Liz rubbed her temple. "No, but I did understand her thank you at the end."

"She wanted to check we were okay and to apologise for her children's rough behaviour. I assured her we were and that I would take care of you."

A heat crept up her neck. She averted her eyes. Licking her dry lips, her eyes fell to his shoes. They were the same designer pair he wore in Rome. How did he wear closed-in shoes on such a hot day?

"How long are you in Falerna?"

With her bottom lip still caught between her teeth, she lifted her face to meet his eyes. Once again, she was struck by their intensity. "Ah ... I have two and a half weeks left. I'm here to do some research on an adopted uncle who was born in Falerna. Today is my first attempt at it."

Her teeth clamped together when his hand touched the pale yellow bruise on her cheek. "It's not as bad as I thought it would be."

When his hand fell to his side, she straightened her shirt and smoothed down her shorts. "I knew it wouldn't be a big deal. Um ... I really should go. I've got someone outside waiting who has agreed to be my translator."

Liz disentangled the strap of her money pouch and placed it around her neck. With a shy shrug, she said, "I never expected to see you again. Are you visiting family in Falerna?"

Grinning, Connor leant against the door with his legs crossed at the ankles and his arms folded against his chest. "I'm searching for the lost family of my late grandfather. I only arrived in Falerna this morning, and I came inside to ask the owners if they could suggest where I might start looking."

Liz quirked a brow. *He's kidding, of course.*

"You don't believe me?" Connor asked, his lips twitching.

"It's the best pick-up line I've heard in a long time." Where Liz found some long-ago hidden sass, she'd never know.

Connor burst out laughing and straightened, towering over her. "I promise you it's the truth. He left Italy for Canada after the war ended. He was born in Falerna."

Liz tried to ignore the tingling along her skin. She looked anywhere except his face, filling her lungs with the same fragrant aftershave she remembered from the airport. When she did eventually connect with his gaze, her breath was sucked out of her chest, forcing her lungs to work extra hard just to say something.

And make it clever, girl, she reminded herself. If her long-ago hidden sassiness was going to re-emerge now, when Mr Gorgeous was saving her pouch for a second time, she had to make it worth her while.

"Even if I did believe you, I bet Roberta won't."

"Huh?" Connor frowned.

Liz inwardly cringed. Was that the best she could muster? She fumbled when her hand caught in her shirt. Finally freed, she pointed outside to show who she was talking about. "Roberta, a fellow Aussie, is visiting her aunt in Falerna. I met her on the train from Rome. Her advice was to start at the local church, and her aunt is organising an appointment for us today. We're about to head in that direction now. I was just buying a bottle of water to wash down the horrible taste of the coffee that everyone drinks here."

Connor chuckled. "It's certainly an acquired taste. Here, let me get the water for you."

When he made to walk towards the counter, Liz grabbed his arm. "It's not necessary. You've done enough favours for me. I'll get it, thanks."

Smiling and causing Liz's pulse on her neck to thud, he said, "Allow me today." He rested his hand on her arm to halt her progress any further. "I haven't forgotten you still 'owe me one', but it can wait for another day."

Her heart did a funny jig. *He remembers me saying that?* At the counter, he leant against it and blazed another dazzling smile in her direction, causing her stomach to tumble. *Calm down, girl.* Inwardly groaning, she fervently wished Sally was by her side. She always knew how to handle these situations.

Within a matter of minutes, they were both shooed out the front door with a bottle of water each and no money exchanged. The harried mother with the four children refused to take anything for their troubles.

Chapter 7

C onnor blinked in the sun, following Liz to the outdoor tables. Cool droplets from the water bottle tickled his palm as his fingers tightened around its neck. He switched the bottle to his other hand and dried his palm against his pants. When his eyes adjusted to the outdoor light, he rested them on Liz's silhouette. With an appreciative smile, he acknowledged her curves as his gaze wound its way down her slim, tanned legs, peeking out of casual denim shorts. When his gaze dropped further, he appreciated the dark purple nail polish on her toenails and her shapely feet in flip-flops as she made her way around the café tables.

She stopped suddenly, causing him to bump into her back. He looked up, grimacing. "Sorry."

When she glanced back, chuckling, her hazelnut eyes latched onto his for a moment. A tingle fluttered over his chest. This woman intrigued him.

While Liz chatted with Roberta, he was drawn to the loose wisps of hair clinging to her neck. For some absurd reason, he itched to touch their softness. Until common sense set off alarm bells and he pulled out a chair and sat.

"*He's* the Canadian who helped you at the airport?"

Connor faced the dark-haired Roberta sitting across from him. When Liz pulled up a chair beside him, his hand accidentally touched her hip in the confined space. He tried to ignore the stirring in his body and forced himself to concentrate on the woman ogling him from across the small round table.

Roberta sat back and placed her hands on her hips. "My God, Liz. You didn't tell me he was good looking." Her chair scraped loudly on the concrete pavers as she pushed it back and stood, walking to his side of the table. "*He* was the one sitting over there"—she pointed to the table where Connor had sat earlier—"and you were *too* busy to turn around and look at him."

Beautiful but blunt. Liz groaned as though embarrassed by the woman's words.

"I'm Roberta, by the way."

"It's a pleasure to meet you, Roberta. Liz tells me you're helping her with the language here."

Roberta undressed him with her eyes. They casually roved his body from top to bottom. It only took a matter of seconds, but within that time, she managed to move even closer and could've easily fallen onto his lap.

"Hmm." She bent closer and shoved her nose near Connor's chest, inhaling. "You, Connor, smell of money. We girls could have some fun with you." She straightened and rolled her eyes in Liz's direction. "She claims to have come all this way to research her adopted uncle. I'm not going to let her spend all her time in stuffy churches and town halls."

Connor leant back and chuckled. *Forward, but harmless. Not my type.* He was used to women attracted to his money. He didn't like it, and a section of his brain always hoped that one day he would find someone who liked him for who he was, not what he owned.

And pigs will fly.

Beside him, Liz fidgeted, so he mustered a friendly smile and approached Roberta with caution. "I would appreciate your help, too. I'm here to learn about the history of my grandfather's family. He died six months ago, and all I really know is that he was born in Falerna."

Roberta's expression instantly changed from flirtatious to serious. She cocked her head to one side and narrowed her eyes. Thrusting her shoulders back, she eyed him warily. "Um, let me get this right. *You* turn up in Rome at the same time Liz does. You're a complete stranger who just *happens* to be at the right place at the right time, and *you* help Liz fight off a thief."

Connor nodded.

She clutched the back of the chair belonging to another table. Rocking it back and forth, she continued, "*Then*, you find yourself in Falerna of all the backwater places, needing to do family research? Coincidently, Liz is here doing the same thing."

Roberta pushed the chair under the table with a loud scrape and turned to Liz. "I smell a rat. He may be drop-dead gorgeous, but this is too sus for me."

Liz picked up her backpack she'd left leaning against the table leg. "I 'owe him one' for the favour in Rome." She glanced at Connor with a wry smile, and something moved in his chest when their gazes met. "I've invited him to come with us to the church. Surely, we're safe from strangers there, don't you think, Roberta? Did you manage to make a time with the priest?"

"Yeah," Roberta replied, cagily, "any time we're ready. The priest is there for the rest of the day."

Liz reached for her laptop and shoved it into her backpack. "Well, what are we waiting for? Do you know the way?"

Roberta sent a probing look his way. "Connor, can you speak any Italian?"

He rose, shoved the water bottle inside his soft, leather travel bag and leant back against the empty table behind him. "It's passable. It's the old dialect my grandfather was taught."

Roberta threw her hands in the air. "Okay, okay, enough on the grandfather bit. I'm still not sure I believe your story, but since you can speak the lingo, how about you help Liz with her research? I promised her one full day; I'm not sure I can stomach more than that."

A jolt flogged its way through his body. The idea excited him, and he wiped his palms down his pants. This wasn't his usual way with women. Normally it involved high society, expensive champagne and lots of diamonds. Hesitantly, he replied, "I'm happy to help Liz."

"How long are you in town?" Roberta threw over her shoulder as they moved away from the café.

"A few weeks."

She about-turned, doubt written all over her face. "You're not by any chance the thief from the airport or his accomplice?"

Connor placed his hands on her shoulders and spun her back towards the church. "Roberta, you have the most amazing imagination. I am definitely *not* the thief. Now, get us to this church. We have less than *three* weeks, remember?"

Growling, Roberta turned to Liz and wagged her finger. "Liz, be wary of rich, foreign men. He may be good-looking, but this isn't fate." She chewed on her bottom lip and cast a glance his way as they continued to walk away. "I'm worried. You're too naïve and trusting for the likes of him."

"I can hear you, Roberta," Connor threw at her, dodging vehicles on the narrow bitumen road between the centuries-old buildings.

As Connor's gaze lingered over the rock and cement buildings all tagged onto each other, he refused to believe Liz was naïve. He'd sensed a spirit coming from her earlier in the café. More brazen and cheeky, not naïve. Nothing like what he was used to, but since he was questioning a lot of things about his life, why not question this? Three short weeks didn't present much time to achieve anything, let alone some sort of relationship. A short fling was more like his style before they realised what his life entailed. But if he was digging up jewels, he'd have to work hard and fast to achieve anything.

As he followed the two women down a narrow street, his gaze followed long cracks that worked their way along old concrete walls. They reached the second stories, which were topped with faded, terracotta tiled roofs. The only splash of colour was the washed-out blue or green shuttered doors and windows, laced with scrolled balconies or narrow cement staircases leading directly off the street.

A smile stretched across his face. Walking in the shadow of the buildings, he looked up at the few puffy white clouds dotting the blue sky.

For some reason, Roberta's words didn't concern him. *A thief?* He almost laughed out loud but bit his tongue to pull himself together. He was determined to prove them wrong. *He* couldn't believe he had encountered Liz twice in a foreign country. For some inexplicable reason, he wanted to spend time with her. Get to know her. Connor was a big believer in gut instinct, and his was throwing out good vibes.

Liz slowed her step to allow Connor to catch up. With one hand perched on her hip, she cast him a wary look. "I've got nothing worth stealing."

What? His jaw slackened. When did he become the bad guy?

"What about your innocence?" Roberta flung at her from a few paces away.

Connor ignored the unexpected swell thrashing about his insides when their gazes caught for an instant. Liz didn't need Roberta's protection; she looked perfectly capable of standing on her own two feet. But he appreciated Roberta's concern.

"Are you really here to research your grandfather's past?" Liz asked.

Connor straightened. "Yes."

"Okay, let's do this then," she said with a grin and swung away in the direction Roberta was headed.

Chapter 8

From the street, the church looked no different from the buildings beside it, not even a cross fixed to the front. Connor's eyes widened when he passed through the heavy, wooden door Roberta held open. The simple exterior of the building was very deceptive when the cavernous interior became visible.

The door clanged shut behind them, the cast-iron rings rattling against its aged wood. He stood looking towards the breathtakingly beautiful marble altar and its intricately sculptured relief images and inhaled the familiar smell of a Catholic Church. Burning oils, incense and wax candles. It would've smelt this way a hundred years ago. A combination of scents slowly absorbed by the furniture, pews and statues, day after day.

The dust motes lent a musky, aged feel. The sun streamed through the spectacular stained-glass windows, with images depicting the Stations of the Cross. Connor dipped his fingers into the holy water before making the sign of the cross with them. This small action released a flood of memories. He and Lucia would often attend mass with their grandparents when they were much younger. By the end of the mass, they would be crouched on the pew kneeler, giggling and whispering inane things, occasionally inviting a frown from their grandfather. A smile tugged at the corners of his mouth. Even after all these years, the good memories were still there and strong.

He followed Roberta and Liz between the pews as they made their way to the altar. They whispered in hushed tones, respectful of the holy place.

Roberta indicated with a nod that they should wait near the front pew. She crossed the threshold and walked directly to a door on the right-hand side of the altar. Her knock on the door reverberated around the vast interior and disturbed a bird flying around the ceiling. It quickly disappeared through an open window. When there was no response, she raised her hand to knock again as the door opened to reveal a short, hunched priest. Dressed in neat black pants with a white button-up shirt, he shuffled slowly out of the room. He stopped a few paces from the door before inviting them to join him with a wave of his hand.

Touching her shoulder, Connor let Liz walk into the room before him, and his hand tremored from the warmth of her soft skin. She acknowledged his courteous gesture with a gentle smile, and his heart struck his ribs when her eyes brushed over his.

The small, cramped room was filled with books and binders neatly stacked on shelves on all sides. Connor let Roberta do all the talking, but he was relieved to understand the priest, who also spoke the old dialect.

The priest, in his slow gait, lightly fingered the ledgers on one wall, finally stopping at one. He nudged his glasses back up his nose and pulled out the binder. He placed it on the shelf in front of where he stood and took another moment to catch his breath. Connor shot out of his chair and reached out to carry the binder back for the priest, who waved him away with a frown, telling him to sit down.

Roberta laughed and, in English, said, "I think he just put you in your place, mate. Don't mess with the old man."

Smiling, Connor returned to his chair. Liz and Roberta followed suit. The old priest mumbled under his breath, but enough for Connor to understand the priest was letting them know he could still fulfil his tasks, despite his age.

Connor looked at the binding. The date printed in gold thread was 1931–1950. He brought his attention back to the priest when he asked Roberta for the year Liz's uncle was born.

Roberta thrust her hand out towards Liz. "Can I have the piece of paper with the details?"

Liz dug around in her backpack and pulled it out.

Roberta took it and spread it on the small table where they sat. "Did we work out exactly what year your uncle was born?"

Liz squished her eyebrows together. "Well, in his letter, he says he was nearly eleven years old in 1944 when his parents were murdered, so that would make it 1933."

Turning to the priest, Roberta explained the year he was born and his full name, Benito Enrico.

The instant after Roberta uttered Benito's name, the priest gasped and slumped to the ground, his head dangerously close to the shelf behind him. At that same moment, Connor yelped and scraped his chair back, nearly causing it to topple.

"Holy shit, we didn't do a thing to him." Roberta frowned.

"Quick, help me get him into a sitting position." Liz was already down on her knees, holding one shoulder.

"Is he dead?"

"Shush, Roberta, his chest is moving. Let's give him a moment to recover."

"What if it's a heart attack or stroke?"

Connor remained frozen, somehow managing to remain in his chair.

The priest slowly regained consciousness and began taking deep breaths. After a few minutes, he seemed to recover his composure and waved at the girls to sit down.

Liz crouched beside him. "Let's get him up into a chair. I'm not leaving him on the floor."

Still, Connor couldn't move, and the confined space wasn't to blame.

Once they had the priest sitting in a chair, he coughed to clear his throat and began to talk. For once, Roberta looked transfixed, too busy listening, too enthralled to translate.

Connor understood every word.

He had recognised the surname immediately. Liz's adopted uncle was *his* grandfather's missing twin.

When Roberta began to translate, he tried to concentrate.

"He says it was a shock to hear the name of your uncle after all these years. He clearly remembers him and his twin Nicolo. He believed they were dead. Nobody ever saw either of them after their parents' bodies were found murdered."

In a gesture of sympathy, Roberta reached across and gently squeezed the old priest's hand. "He wants to know what happened to Benito."

Connor listened as Liz explained and Roberta translated. The twins were separated, and her adopted uncle tried unsuccessfully for years to find his twin. He found his way to Australia a few years after the war ended, where he lived the rest of his life. He passed away ten years ago.

Fidgeting on his chair, it creaked in the quiet room. Roberta turned and frowned. Too concerned with the sudden attack on the priest's health, neither had noticed Connor's reaction to the news.

Connor's breathing sounded loud in the small room, so he clenched his hands by his side to control it. His ears perked up when Roberta asked Liz, "He wants to know if you're related to Benito."

"Benito never married or had children of his own. My grandfather's family cared for him when he first arrived in Australia."

The jewels! Liz must know about them. The scraping timber chair and the heavy thud of his body when it landed on the floor were deafening in the small room. He winced at the sharp pain that ripped across his back, but at least no one heard it over the echoing noise.

Roberta stood over his splayed body with her hands on her hips. "Bloody hell, Connor, are you okay?"

Connor straightened the kink in his back and managed to nod. "Sorry," he swallowed the thick wad of emotion caught in his throat, "must be the jetlag making me feel light-headed in this small room."

"Okay, well, give us another minute," she said, righting the chair. "We'll move on to your grandfather next."

He turned towards Liz when she said, "Maybe he's claustrophobic? This room *is* small, and the dust is probably a hundred years old."

Latching onto her soft eyes full of concern, he found he could breathe again. He hoisted himself up, disguising the shudder rattling his body, and recalled the letter the thief stole. It must've contained the same details his grandfather had left him. No wonder Liz was agitated. That sort of information in the wrong hands was a problem.

Seated again, Connor didn't let a single muscle quiver. He ignored the perspiration trickling down his temple. Being in a small, stuffy room wasn't helping.

"Are you okay, Connor?"

"Thanks, Liz, yes I am. I'm not sure what just happened, but I'm okay." He prised his fingers away from his pants and steadied his breathing.

If he told them the truth, Roberta would have no trouble convincing Liz he was the thief's accomplice, only in Falerna to find the jewels—the bad guy Roberta already suspected he was. He'd give the priest the surname his grandfather took on when he moved to Canada and make a slight change to his grandfather's first name. Niculin instead of Nicolo. With no record of it, that will be the end of it. An unrecorded birth was probably not uncommon at the time. Then he would learn as much as possible before telling Liz the truth.

But where to start?

Chapter 9

While Liz tied her shoelaces, the Mediterranean balmy breeze swept across her skin. Sitting on the bottom step leading from the house to the narrow street, hemmed in by concrete walls on either side, she lifted her face, closed her eyes and inhaled the smell of freshly baked bread. Waiting for Connor to arrive from next door and Roberta to wake, she couldn't help the nervous flutter dancing around her chest. And over a man! Hadn't she learnt the hard way? Her last boyfriend had been a real loser who didn't like sharing her with a grandmother. He was flicked faster than old, rotting fruit.

Roberta hadn't lied when she said Fiorina's home was right next door to 'Zia Maria's Casa'. Connor was one of the new guests Zia Maria had spoken of, and that morning, he was treating them to breakfast. So Liz took a deep breath, determined to enjoy the treat. Her usual budget didn't allow for such extravagances.

Since she was ready early, she would soak up the sounds and smells of the gradual bustle of a village waking up in a foreign country. Something else she'd never experienced.

"Good morning."

Her eyes snapped open, and she stood. Stumbling a little, she used the wall to steady herself. *Real graceful, girl.* "Good morning," she replied, inwardly cursing her clumsiness.

Connor's eyes twinkled with laughter, his arm coming out to steady her. "Did you and Roberta get on the vino last night?"

"What?" She defiantly lifted her chin and angled her face. When Connor leant away, eyes wide, she chuckled and relaxed. "I've gotta say, in less than a week, I've decided I don't like their espresso coffee or their vino."

Connor rested his shoulder against the wall. "Is that so?"

She looked into his dancing eyes and felt trapped. She needed to look away fast to portray a look of casual indifference. "But I do love their pizza, lasagne and gelato," she burst out, then wanted to kick herself. Why couldn't she have a normal conversation with a good-looking man?

"In that order?"

"Yeah." She smiled, dragging her eyes away to the view of the ocean in the distance. She needed a moment's break to get her thoughts into order. The view was unobstructed, and the morning peaceful, but she was anything but. As Falerna was perched on the side of a mountain, she could look out over the faded orange roofs as they descended the mountain face.

"Would you care to share dinner with me tonight? I'll make sure they serve it in the order you prefer."

She turned back. In the vain hope that Roberta would magically appear, she looked up towards the front door at the top of the stairs. It didn't happen, so Liz took a lung full of air and forced her gaze back in Connor's direction. *What would Sally do? Say yes, of course.*

"Is this a good idea?" She inwardly groaned at her dumb response and dropped her face. Yep, that ought to do it. *Come on, girl, show us some of the sassiness Nan used to rave about.*

"Liz?"

Her eyes drew level with his, and she lost a little more of herself.

"I like that you're wary. It tells me you're smart and sensible, but I'm not the thief's accomplice that Roberta would have you believe, I promise."

The seconds ticked by, the silence thickening between them as she contemplated accepting the invitation. She nodded slowly before clearing her throat. "Okay, I'll come, but I owe you a favour, so how about I pay?"

With a serious face, he quirked a brow. "I was only joking when I reminded you of that."

"But I owe you something for helping me that day. Can you imagine what a nightmare it would've been if I'd lost my passport and money?"

Sporting a half smile, he joked, "I can. I'm glad I was there to help. But you know what? A thank you is enough, and you've already done that ... unless you want to come up with some ideas of what I should do in Falerna. There doesn't seem to be a whole lot to keep a tourist busy."

Liz chuckled. "You've been around Roberta too long." She eased up, relaxing against the concrete wall, allowing the warmth to seep into her skin. "Her aunt, Fiorina says the Falerna sunsets are spectacular. There's a park you can drive to at the back of town, and provided the sky is clear, it's like a big ball of fire dropping into the ocean."

I just suggested watching a sunset? Aghast, she kicked her shoe against the wall, her pulse picking up speed.

"You know what, Liz—?"

She held her breath, expecting Connor to walk away any second. She mentally repeated her stupidity to herself. Um ... gorgeous male, lots of money, plenty of spare time. *And I suggest a sunset?*

"—In Toronto, I rarely leave the office in time to see the sunset. I would love to see a Falerna sunset."

Choking on her words, her eyes widened. "Look, it was a stupid idea. It's just that I have a thing about sunsets. I probably shouldn't tell you it's almost an obsession if you count the number of photos I have. How about I ask Roberta and Fiorina for some other suggestions?"

Chuckling, he replied, "You've no idea how certain I am. I'll order a picnic dinner from Zia Maria because the sun sets late in summer. I was only reading the leaflet this morning."

Liz pushed herself away from the wall and shook her head. "No way, this is supposed to be the favour I owe you. I'll organise it."

Connor gestured impatiently by raising his hand. "Liz, *please*. I heard Roberta say yesterday you were travelling on a shoestring budget. Let me cover the costs while I'm here, not just the dinner. I don't need you stressing over money because of me." He cocked his face and raised his eyebrows, daring her to argue. "I'm enjoying your company. If I hadn't bumped into you and Roberta, I'd be doing this research on my own."

"You'd cover *all* the costs for another two weeks?"

"Look, we'll do as much research as we can on your uncle and my grandfather, do some touristy things and before you know it, it'll be time to return home. No strings attached."

This left her breathless; warning bells clanged in her head. *Spend two weeks together with no strings attached? Sally would be jumping up and down by now, with a high five all round. But could she do it? Give in to all her fears and apprehensions and enjoy the time for what it was.*

"Now," Connor moved in front of her, "how about breakfast before I fade away?"

Liz glanced up the stairs. "Roberta loves her late nights, but I swear, by the time she gets up, half the day is over."

"You sound like a morning person?" His soft gaze settled over her when she turned back.

"I have to be. I take care of my grandmother and she wakes up early."

She couldn't look away if her life depended on it and her heart pounded against her chest like her grandfather's jackhammer. Like an animal trapped in high beams, she couldn't budge. She got that Connor oozed wealth and fortune. The way he dressed, his manner and his casual indifference to how he spent money. But on the few occasions she'd glimpsed an unguarded side, she detected a vulnerability and hurt. For this, she was a sucker, with a natural caring instinct to wrap him in her arms and ease the hurt.

It would bring her down. End badly. It always did.

The front door slamming did the trick, and Liz flicked her gaze up the stairs again.

"Yeah, I'm finally ready for breakfast." Grumbling, Roberta put on her dark sunglasses and made her way down the stairs. "I swear this is the last time I'm getting up at such an indecent hour to put food into my body. Don't ask me again."

Connor burst out laughing. "So that's one strong espresso for you?"

Liz joined in with the laughter as Roberta flounced past them both, staying a couple of metres in front.

Connor reached for Liz's hand and squeezed it quickly, knocking the breath out of her lungs.

"Are you coming with us to Lamezia Terme?" Connor called to Roberta.

"No thanks," Roberta threw back over her shoulder. "I need more sleep. I've fulfilled my share of the pact."

Liz's body burned with awareness when Connor brushed up beside her. *Be careful,* she warned. *A lot can happen in two weeks.*

Connor expertly manoeuvred the open-top hire car between the crazy Italian drivers he'd only read about, managing to find a half legal car space in Lamezia Terme. Leaving Falerna nearly forty minutes ago, the descent down the mountain had involved local drivers careering wildly around the tight bends, accompanied by a blast of their horns, warning they were on the other side of the bend.

The breeze had buffeted his shirt, and the warm sun had kissed his cheeks. There had been little chance to talk while they drove. Liz's white knuckles, as her hands gripped the sides of her seat, hadn't gone unnoticed.

Before switching off the ignition, he pressed the button to close over the roof and looked across at her. "Italian drivers take a little getting used to."

She prised her fingers away from the edge of the seat and had them firmly knotted on her lap. Seriously, she said in a clipped tone, "I saw imminent death on every curve of that damn mountain, and I have never heard such excessive use of a car horn in all my driving life."

Connor chuckled. "It's not over yet. Let's see if we can find the town hall without being hit by a car." He opened his door and had one leg out when he turned back. "Want to do something with me?"

Liz twisted back with a frown. "I thought I was."

His grin stretched across his face at her confused expression. "Starting from now, let's count how many horn toots we get by the end of the day."

She climbed out of the car but not before he saw the eye roll. With her door closed, she leant against it and looked across from where she stood on the other side. "You're joking of course?"

It was a stupid and childish game to play, but Connor was having trouble keeping the smile off his face. He came around to her side, locked the vehicle and gently butted her shoulder. At the soft contact, warmth flooded his body. This was a ridiculous reaction, of course. For a man of his age and experience, this was supposed to be just another short conquest. A fling to fill in the time, if he excused the amount of headspace she was already taking up.

When her questioning eyes turned in his direction, his knees wobbled for a split second. *Jeez, old boy.* It'd been a long time since any woman had elicited that reaction.

His lips parted to speak, but no sound came out until an embarrassing cough worked its way past his throat. "Um ... did you end up finding the address of the town hall where the historical records are kept?" Maybe he should spend the next two weeks with Roberta. She looked the type for a bit of casual stuff and there wouldn't be any weak knees in the equation.

Her eyebrows rose. He reached into his pocket for his phone, confused why his body was betraying him. "If you've got it, I'll put it in the GPS so we can find it quicker."

Liz scrounged inside her bag, the tinkle of a metal charm distracting his thoughts. She pulled out a notebook, flicked a couple of pages and stopped at one. "Fiorina helped me find it last night."

When she passed it to him, a loud toot startled them. A car was trying to park on the footpath where they stood. Gesturing wildly, the driver indicated his intentions, and Connor didn't waste any time grabbing Liz's arm and steering them both to safety.

Ten metres away and feeling light-headed, he looked at Liz to check she was okay. As soon as their gazes locked, they both burst out laughing. It was the contagious type that took more than a few seconds to recover from. The longer she laughed, the harder he did. She was bent double with her hand on her stomach and only had to look up once to set them off again. A tissue was thrust under his nose. He gladly accepted it and reined in his laughter while Liz dabbed at her eyes.

"I guess that's toot number one."

"Is that a yes to the counting game?"

Liz leant against his shoulder, digging out a second tissue from her pocket. "I suppose."

Not sure why, Connor wrapped his arm around her and pulled her closer to his side. He had never been this protective of a woman, excluding his sister and mother. This close, he could inhale the citrus scents she used to wash her hair; he'd never been with any other woman that used a citrus-scented shampoo—and he liked it.

Chapter 10

L iz inserted the earplugs and played the English translation while she meandered around the town hall. Each room showcased photographs and paintings depicting stories of the people who'd made history in this part of the world.

Connor was a little further ahead, and she had to work hard to keep her pulse from racing erratically. *Okay, so the guy is cute, friendly and rich.* She knew better than to get too carried away. Plus, she didn't have time to get involved with anyone. With less than two weeks left, all her attention was needed to find the hidden jewels.

She tightened the straps of her backpack and ground her teeth. The sound of the recording hummed in the background as she worried about how to go about looking for the fontana dei Povere. It didn't feel right to talk about it to Connor. So, who? Roberta?

Unable to come up with a solution, her eyes brushed over the photos along the wall, trying to catch up with the recording. She reached a large, black-and-white photograph and halted. A chill froze her on the spot. The recording became an intrusion on her headspace, so she yanked the earplugs out and stared at the photograph, her mouth hanging open.

Intrigued by the local history, Connor pushed in his earplugs and gave Liz some space, starting his tour in a different section. He glanced over a couple of times to watch her. She ran her hand through her hair once. Another time she was reading a notice board. At one stage she fiddled with her phone and adjusted her earplugs. Everything about her he liked. Even the inexpensive clothing she wore moulded her body in all the right places, leaving him breathless somehow. The allure she exuded came from somewhere else; her striking eyes the colour of melted chocolate, her slim, trim legs and her sassiness he'd already witnessed. Added to the mix was the way her accent turned him on with every word she spoke.

This thing with Liz was new and exciting and so far off his usual radar that he had no control over how his body reacted whenever she was near. No different from a drug user needing the next fix.

Her wariness was new and as endearing as her attractive looks. It was hard to keep from touching her, but somehow, he held back, unsure of her reaction. *Hell,* women normally threw themselves at him and he was left to tactfully prise them off. *No such luck with this one,* and for once, he wanted it to happen.

Connor sighed, tapped the app on his phone and caught up with the recording.

When he neared Liz, her stance was rigid and her face pale with shock. He bolted to her side, pulling out his earplugs. "Are you okay?"

When he didn't get a response, he looked up at the photograph. In the same instant, his back stiffened and he stifled a gasp.

Liz moved closer to the photograph. "My God, Uncle Ben was the spitting image of his father."

Connor's racing heart took over his ability to move. He stared at the photograph and couldn't get over the likeness of the man to *his* grandfather. He put his earplugs back in and fumbled with his phone. Tapping back into the app, he fast-forwarded it to the section on Falerna's history.

He listened carefully and spoke the translated version softly for Liz's benefit. "This photograph is of Frederico and Giovanna Enrico. Giovanna was a distant cousin to the Frevannini Dynasty of Central Italy. They were an influential couple in Falerna and played an important role before the outbreak of war. They had twin sons named Benito and Nicolo. Frederico and Giovanna were brutally murdered in 1944. It was presumed their deaths were related to Giovanna's valuable jewels, which have never been seen since. Their murderers were never found, and their twin boys were not seen after that day. It is believed they were murdered, too, but no evidence of their bodies was ever found. Their home, which was one of the larger homes of Falerna at that time, was eventually taken over by the municipality of Falerna. Later sold, it is largely unchanged from those days and can be found at ..."

Connor stifled a gasp, pulling out the earplugs. "You're not going to believe this."

Liz seemed to come out of her trance. "Believe what?"

Connor's heart began a rapid thumping. "Fiorina owns the house your uncle used to live in."

Liz latched onto his arm. "What? Are you serious?" She shook it as though trying to prise the truth out of him.

Automatically, his free hand came to rest on hers to still the shaking. "Well, the address matches the house next door to Zia Maria's Casa."

She swayed against his body. Not sure if she was about to collapse, he wrapped his arm around her waist.

"This is so weird, Connor."

He looked at her confused frown, liking how she said his name.

"Of all the people to meet on a train in one of the world's busiest cities, I meet Roberta." Her frown deepened. "And that's not the weird bit."

When her eyes cleared of their glazed look, she twisted, realising he held her close to his chest. Taking a step back forced Connor to drop his arm, missing the warmth of her body.

"This is so bizarre," she continued. "How do two unrelated people get thrown together and then learn of a connection between them? What was the chance Fiorina lived in Uncle Ben's former home? A million to one? A trillion to one?" She shook her head, unable to grasp it, while Connor chewed on his lip.

Liz, you've got no idea how much weirder this is going to get.

She turned back to the photo and studied it again. Connor felt more like the fraud Roberta had accused him of. He knew the longer he withheld the truth, the worse it would look when it eventually came out. *So why not tell her now?*

Connor studied her back, his eyes fixed on the shiny charm on her backpack that tinkled each time she moved. *Because we're both after the jewels.* Money aside, the lure of the treasure was too real—and exciting. *Why hasn't she said anything?* His chest tightened with the truth. *She doesn't know who you are. Tell her!*

Connor took a step back and suddenly realised how alone he was. Over here, he didn't have the protection of his grandfather's name and wealth. Here he was just another face. A steely determination sprouted inside his body. The branches stretched and the leaves unfurled, reaching past his chest and extending to his arms and legs. He wanted to win her trust first. *Yes.* His fingers curled by his side. He wanted her to feel something for him. He was sick of the usual menu when it came to women. Liz was different, and it was time to change where he ate. He'd give up the jewels to have her look at him, even once, with more than worry and caution in her eyes. *No, I won't tell her the truth yet.*

"Have you found anything on your grandfather?"

Connor's face whipped up. She had turned around, and some instinct told Connor she'd been looking at him for a few moments before she spoke. "No ... um ... not yet. I was going to do a search on their computer database." He pointed in the computer's direction. "I spotted it over there when we walked in."

Liz glanced towards the computer, one hand rubbing her other arm as though cold.

"Okay. I'll have more of a look around. Do you mind if we head back to Falerna soon? I'm keen to have a chat with Fiorina."

"Sure. It'll only take me a few minutes."

Before he had a chance to walk away, her hand rested on his arm. "Thanks, Connor."

His legs almost gave way, and it was only because of how she'd said his name.

"I really do appreciate your help. Finding this photograph means a lot to me."

I can help you find the jewels, too. Trust me. He latched onto her eyes, reluctant to look away. When she finally turned back to the photo, he dragged his feet to the computer terminal.

⁂

Roberta languished on her aunt's lounge, her eyes barely open. "You're going where? Out to dinner tonight?"

Liz laughed at Roberta's cynical expression. She had just told Roberta about the exciting find in Lamezia Terme, but the news failed to raise the same level of excitement. This was a little disheartening because she was fast realising how handy Roberta's local knowledge was.

"Um ... you know ... boy meets girl, boy takes girl out for dinner sort of thing. Is something wrong with that?"

Roberta's leg hung limply over the timber armrest as though she barely had the energy to swing it, having only dragged herself out of bed again after suffering through breakfast with them earlier. "Oh, you know me, the jealous type. He's gorgeous, wears the nicest clothes, smells like he has lots of money, but ... what the hell is someone that rich doing here? People like him usually pay someone to do whatever it is he's here to do."

Liz sighed. She would be home in Australia before she knew it, and Connor had been right. They could help each other with their research and have some fun together. "He promised his grandfather he would visit Falerna."

Roberta half sat up, but her elbow gave way and she flopped back down again. "Has he found anything? Isn't it sus his grandfather's surname is not coming up anywhere? Not even on the database in Lamezia Terme?"

Pulling at her ponytail, Liz stood and looked down at Roberta. "Look, something will come up. He was probably some poor peasant and his birth never recorded. It's just that ... there's something more important I need to talk to you about."

Roberta twisted her body and sat up. "I told you, I *will* ask my aunt how many years she has owned this house and if she knows any of its history."

Liz started to pace. "No, no—yes, find out what you can. But ... there's something else, and I'm not sure how to go about it." She stopped and sank to the floor, wrapping her arms around her knees.

"What?" Roberta sat up, fully awake. "You suspect something about Connor, don't you? Is he really the thief?"

Laughing nervously, she said, "No, forget Connor; this has nothing to do with him. I'm ... I'm really here in Falerna to find the jewels my uncle and his twin brother buried before they were separated and captured."

"Jewels?"

Liz could've sworn Roberta's eyes glinted with dollar signs. Her face dropped, and the scowl returned. "Jewels?"

Sucking in a quick breath, she said, "Yes. The jewels Uncle Ben believes his parents were murdered for."

Roberta continued to glare, her fingers tapping on the armrest, the only sound in the room. "You're really going to do it, aren't you?"

Confused, Liz raised her hands, palm up. "What am I going to do?"

Roberta's expression turned meaner and crankier, forcing Liz to cringe and wonder what she had said wrong.

Watching Roberta bare her teeth, Liz experienced a shaft of fear cross her chest. She dropped her arms and sat with her breath jammed in her throat, unsure if she'd live to feel the next one.

"You have every intention of destroying my holiday, don't you? I planned orgy after orgy with every gorgeous Italian man I could lay my hands on, so that by the end of the three weeks, I'd die happily with a smile on my face. Instead, I've been stuck in churches and cafés discussing people long dead and murdered, lost and separated. And now you want me to dirty my nails and dig up some jewels? Christ, how much worse will it get? Why doesn't lover boy help you? He sure as hell can't keep his hands and eyes off you, and *don't* tell me you haven't noticed."

Liz spontaneously laughed at Roberta's tirade. As hard as it was to imagine, she honestly believed the angel Uncle Ben promised in his letter, that would guide and look after her if she travelled to Falerna, had come in the form of Roberta.

She stood up and tried to maintain a straight face. "That's my problem. I don't want Connor to know about the jewels, and don't ask me to explain because I can't. It doesn't feel right to discuss it with him."

Roberta sank back into the lounge with her arms out wide and groaned. "Okay, let loose on all the information you have and make it worth my while being awake."

Liz grinned from ear to ear. "I'll get my laptop and you can read Uncle Ben's letter and the notes he made about where to find them."

Roberta shouted to her retrieving back, "Is this the same letter the thief stole at the airport?"

"Yes," Liz replied, pleased she was finally doing something about finding the jewels and Roberta's comment about Connor not being able to keep his hands and eyes off her.

Chapter 11

The first spoonful of chocolate and hazelnut gelato slid down her throat. Liz took a second helping, closed her eyes and savoured the sweet taste, letting it sit on her tongue for a fraction longer before swallowing.

"Nice?"

Her eyes opened to sea-green pearls and a smile that had her heart racing double time. "It's divine. Thank you so much for giving me the chance to taste such delicious food."

Connor nodded, taking a spoonful of his dessert. The subdued lighting cast shadows on his jaw when it moved. The damp ocean breeze ruffled the collar of his white button-up shirt. She looked past him, mesmerised by the waves lapping at the shore only metres away from the restaurant's verandah.

"Thank *you* for sharing it with me. I've enjoyed listening to your stories. You should be proud of how you've cared for your grandparents."

She blinked and turned her attention back to her plate, continuing to eat the delicious gelato. "It hasn't always been easy. Grandad's medical bills burnt up their savings."

"What about your grandmother?"

Liz's shoulders dropped. She placed her spoon down, the gelato momentarily forgotten. "The doctors have told me when her dementia worsens, I will need to admit her to an aged-care facility, where they can provide twenty-four-hour care."

She bit her bottom lip when moisture began building up behind her eyelids. Was Nan okay? Was she missing her?

He reached across to squeeze her hand. "My grandfather was the centre of my life. When he died, I wasn't sure I could go on as usual. Losing your grandmother will hurt you in places you never knew existed."

Liz looked up with tears brimming. "But you have your parents."

Connor's nod was solemn. "Except my grandfather was more the parent to me. It's hard to explain." Connor hastily withdrew his hand and continued eating. Had he said more than he planned to?

After his last mouthful, he looked up and cocked his head. His view was of the inside dining area behind her back, and it wasn't long before the strains of a piano accordion filtered through the dining room. "Can you hear the music, Liz?"

She nodded and twisted in her chair as the music increased in volume. The musician and a group of dancers were making their way to the centre of the restaurant.

"As a kid, I often accompanied my grandparents to their Italian Club. This music is so familiar to me. They call the dance the Tarantella, and I remember dancing it with my sister, Lucia. It was lots of fun." When she turned back, he was tapping his chin with his fingers and had a faraway look in his eyes. "But that was a long time ago. I don't even know if I'll remember how it's done."

Liz grinned, the music uplifting as the dancers twirled closer to where they sat. "Well, I can't say I've ever danced it. Looks fast paced with a lot of spinning."

She studied Connor's smiling face and eyes that twinkled with joy.

"It's considered unlucky to dance the Tarantella alone." Raising an eyebrow, he asked, "Want to know how it originated?"

Liz nodded, enjoying their conversation as the dancers moved amongst the tables and diners.

"My grandfather once told me it originated from the bite of a tarantula spider. If someone was bitten, the townspeople would play this music while the victim used frenetic dancing to sweat the venom out."

Her eyes widened. "Really?"

Connor didn't get a chance to reply. A pair of dancers swirled and spun near their table, beckoning them both to rise and dance.

The music erupted when the musician appeared behind the dancers. Reluctant to stand, Liz stuttered, "But ... but ... I can't ... I don't know how to—"

Sweat dripped from the temple of the male dancer. His hand begged not to be refused as his feet moved in time with the music. Up and already standing, Connor moved towards her and shouted, "You'll have a ball. Go on, have a go."

The female dancer whirled him away, leaving her no option but to accept the outstretched hand and be dragged to the middle of the restaurant.

Within fifteen minutes, she discarded her heels. Sweat soaked her thin, white blouse, and her wispy emerald skirt stuck to her skin. She was spun, twirled and whirled as the tempo of the music quickly turned frantic and faster, eventually falling into Connor's arms.

Limp against each other, their bodies slick with moisture, Connor's breath brushed along her skin when he mouthed near her ear, "Would you like to take a walk on the beach?"

Fearless after that wild spinning and needing fresh air and cool water on her feet, she nodded and said, "Why not?"

Humming the music loud enough for Connor to hear, she spun in wild circles as Connor caught hold of her hand and laughed beside her.

On the beach, tiny granules of sand rolled under her bare feet. She continued to twirl on the end of his hand. They stopped about fifty metres from the restaurant in a fit of giggles.

"Look what happens when you have a mouthful too many of gelato. A guy can't take you anywhere."

Smiling, Liz stretched her arms out wide while the ocean breeze ruffled her hair. Taking deep breaths, she beckoned its cooling powers to brush over her heated skin.

Connor stood close behind, not quite touching, but close enough for the heat radiating from his body to touch hers. She could easily lean back and fall into his embrace. Closing her eyes, she enjoyed the blood rushing through her veins and her racing pulse.

"We'll use my jacket for sitting on," Connor suggested, hands on her hips, guiding her from behind.

Liz's eyes snapped open when she sank to the sand, her breath raspy when Connor sat close enough for their hips to touch. "But we'll ruin it."

Connor ignored her comment and lay down on the sand with his hands behind his head. "Come and join me."

Falerna Marina was well lit, with lamp posts casting golden hues and strings of oversized fairy lights, but shadows loomed from the restaurants and cafés. She looked down at Connor, who lay staring at the stars.

His hand reached over and gently tugged on hers. "I promise you're safe with me. I'll show you some of our northern constellations."

She sighed and flopped down beside him. While things were getting a little out of control, instinctively, she knew she could trust him. Which was crazy. She didn't know much about the guy except he loved his grandfather and worked in the family finance business. But it was a beautiful night and the stars twinkled brightly above.

Connor's deep rumble of a chuckle broke the comfortable silence.

"What's so funny?"

Connor rolled to his side, his head resting on his hand. "You make it sound like such a chore to lie beside me. I'm not used to that."

An unexpected tidal wave of emotions pushed against her heart when their gazes caught, and his smile slipped. A mixture of excitement and longing. "I'm not the type to throw myself at someone I barely know."

"You have no idea how refreshing that is."

Liz grimaced in the semidarkness. Why didn't she throw herself at him? Hundreds of others apparently did. This was the person she'd become. Boring, predictable, safe. Sally was shouting in her ear right now. *Get out there and live. Take a chance.*

"Are you frightened of me?" His voice was barely a whisper.

She struggled to tear her eyes away, his gaze boring deep into her soul. "No, I'm just not certain what you want in return for all your generosity. You know I can't afford to repay you, but I'm worried you expect something from me. I'll be gone in less than two weeks, and I'm not sure I can give you enough."

He reached across and trailed his fingers down her cheek, halting near her neck. All thoughts of breathing stopped. Her heart thundered in her ears, in time with the waves collapsing along the shore.

"Liz, believe me when I say *you're* doing me the favour. I had no idea what I would find in Falerna, and in all honesty, I might have been gone by now. I couldn't believe my luck when I stumbled across someone else researching their family's past." He used his thumb to brush a piece of wispy hair caught in her lash. "As for the money side of things, well … I brought extra to spend. It's no fun dining alone, and I enjoy your company." His hand moved down to rest on her shoulder, and she tensed. "And I'm not in the habit of forcing anyone to do anything they don't want to do."

Liz swallowed, a light in her peripheral vision flickering on and off. "What is it you're not used to?"

He frowned for a moment before realising it was an earlier statement he'd made. Liz made out his grin in the shadows now that the flickering light had blacked out. "Let's just say you're different from what I'm used to, and that accent of yours is crazy special."

She smiled with amusement. She'd never considered her accent anything special.

"Now, we're going to spend a few minutes doing some star gazing, then we're going to return to the restaurant for your shoes, and then"—he reached for her hand and laid it against his chest—"I'm going to drive you home."

All the pent-up air in her lungs whooshed out with relief. Which was crazy. His plan didn't sound exciting at all. Not according to the laws of Sally. But she only had herself to blame. *Come on, girl, loosen up!*

With her hand firmly enclosed in his, he added, "I thought tomorrow morning we could visit the cemetery in Falerna and find Frederico and Giovanna's graves. I'll leave you in peace for the afternoon. I want to make another trip to Lamezia Terme. I have a couple of ideas I want to check out on their data computer. I'll let you know if I find anything when we watch the sunset."

Relief swamped her again. Her emotions were seesawing so badly. She wanted to be around Connor, and she didn't. The jewels. She still had to find them and Roberta promised to help her locate some of the fontana dei poveres the next day. It was a sure bet she would not be awake and feeling alive until well into the afternoon.

But something else lodged itself in her chest. When Connor rolled back to stargaze, she licked her lips, still tasting the gelato mingled with the saltiness of her sweat. She clenched her free hand by her side to stop it from reaching over and tracing a finger down his face. *Is this the perfect time and place to live a bit?*

Liz tried to concentrate on what Connor was showing her in the sky. Her thoughts, though, rocketed back to previous boyfriends and how lacklustre they'd been. Beside this man, her skin hadn't stopped tingling, and her pulse raced erratically. A Mediterranean fling? Something to look back on with fond memories? She could already hear Sally cheering in the background.

She hadn't realised she sighed loudly until Connor's voice broke into her thoughts. "Am I boring you?"

She turned to find him facing her, probably for longer than a few moments, and giggled. She was grateful the darkness hid the blush suffusing her face. "Sorry, something else crossed my mind. But as I still owe you one, how about I make a promise to point out our Southern Cross to you one day?"

What the heck? Had she suggested taking this past the next two weeks? She reached up and covered her face. Her groan sounded like a plea to her ears, begging Connor to forgive her.

Connor chuckled. "You keep stacking them up and I'll come and collect one day, but I better get you back home before you say anything else you'll regret." He rose from the sand and reached for her hand, easily helping her.

His grin was infectious, and she couldn't help her own as it stretched across her face. He bent down to retrieve his jacket and wound his arm around her waist. They walked side by side towards the restaurant. The air smelt of garlic and onion mingled with wine and chinotto and, for some reason, she knew she'd always associate those smells with this night.

She lay her head against his shoulder while his strength pulled her across the grainy sand, each granule massaging the soles of her feet. *This would be the perfect time to reach up and kiss his cheek.* But of course, she didn't. She had buried jewels to find and her days were fast running out. *I really don't have time for this.*

Too bad her heart wouldn't listen.

Chapter 12

"**S**ixteen mother flamin' fountains, taps, ponds, waterholes, or whatever else the hell you want to call them."

Liz came face to face with Roberta, who rose midmorning after getting out of bed on the wrong side. "Sit." She steered Roberta back until her legs buckled at the couch. "I'm getting you a coffee immediately. Now, what do you mean by sixteen?"

Roberta's tangle of black curls fell across her eyes. Flicking them impatiently away, she growled. "My aunt insisted I attend a family function last night while lover boy dined *you* in fine style."

Confused, Liz continued to eye Roberta's intimidating frown. "What's that got to do with the fountains?"

"Nothing, actually." Roberta relaxed, laying back on the couch and closing her eyes. "Part way through dinner, I escaped with the most gorgeous man in the entire village." She let out a satisfied sigh, and her head fell back. "Oo laa laa."

Liz left her to her happy humming and escaped to the kitchen to check on the coffee machine, usually switched on by Fiorina each morning before she went out. Without preamble, she prepared the small cup of disgusting espresso Roberta drank.

Back in the living room, Liz sat across from her and placed the miniature coffee cup on the small table between them. Resting her elbows on her thighs, she contemplated Roberta's dreamy expression. She waited until she'd taken a couple of sips before blundering, "Okay, what are you talking about?"

Liz was fast learning that Roberta was at her most obnoxious early in the morning, but if she was prepared to put herself out and help her find the jewels, Liz didn't mind making her the occasional espresso.

Roberta's smile stretched the entire width of her face. "Well ... I promised this gorgeous Italian thing sex if he showed me every fountain, tap, pond, waterhole ..."

Jumping up, Liz shook her head. "Okay, okay, I get the picture."

Roberta gulped the hot coffee and then placed the tiny cup on the table. "No, I don't think you do. I remember the diagram from your uncle's letter, and the fountain you're looking for could be any ten of the sixteen I spotted last night."

Liz shuffled her feet and shoved her hands in the pockets of her shorts. "Damn."

"Damn, alright. Marco wants to see me every night, and God help you if my nails are caked with dirt."

Liz's shoulders relaxed, a gurgle of laughter threatening its way past her throat. She gave the smile stretching across her face free rein.

Roberta's spine straightened. "What? What calculated thought is running through your head now, girl?"

"*You*, Roberta, from plain, little Melbourne, are having the time of your life. You crave excitement, and the chase for hidden treasure fits your requirements perfectly. Fate brought us together, but time is fast running out. This Marco better be worth it if I release you into his arms each night."

Roberta ran a hand through her tangled hair and slumped back on the couch. "I won't be ready to do anything for a good couple of hours."

"Good. Connor will be here soon. We're off to the local cemetery to look for Frederico and Giovanna's graves."

Roberta groaned, covering her face with her hands. Her muffled voice told Liz her idea of a fun morning was nothing like Roberta would ever want to experience.

Leaving the room to grab her backpack, Liz turned back. "By the way, Roberta, thanks a lot. I couldn't do this without you."

Roberta rose and swayed on her feet, stretching her arms. "You're just lucky the sex was superb."

Turning to leave, Liz chuckled and shook her head. *I can't imagine being that casual with a man. I can't even reach up and give one a peck on the cheek.*

⁂

Connor parked the car under a shady tree and turned the ignition off. "I'm going to organise a local tradesman to freshen up their graves."

Liz turned in her seat, a frown etched on her brow. "But why? They're not even your family."

Wincing, Connor knew he was digging himself in deeper. "I feel they deserve it. It's something I'd like to do." They'd found the graves with some help but in a dilapidated condition. Their deterioration touched a raw spot, but it wasn't until he'd made the mad dash back to Lamezia Terme that afternoon that the idea to freshen them up had come to him.

He pushed open his door and stepped out, putting a halt to the conversation. "Come on, time to watch this sunset."

Other families were enjoying the late afternoon stillness, but Connor didn't think their sunset would be cloud free. With sweat pooling under his shirt and heavy, dark clouds directly above, it was more likely a good storm was brewing.

"I'm not sure we picked the best day for this," Liz said, reading his thoughts. She flapped her shirt against her back, drawing his attention to her perfectly scalped body.

Connor looked away and opened the boot. "Here, catch." He threw a picnic blanket her way and reached in for a couple of cushions. "Can you catch these, too?"

Tucking the blanket between her legs, Liz stretched her arms and smiled. "Easy."

He threw them one at a time, pleased she wasn't the sort of girl to worry about breaking a nail. Then he grabbed the cooler with their dinner before locking the car.

Liz stopped at a flat, shady spot and spread out the rug. "Do you have a change of clothes in your car? Shorts and a tee?"

Connor placed the cooler near the tree and straightened his back. "Is this something Australian I need to know about?"

She burst out laughing and beckoned for him to sit down. No sooner was he seated when she moved closer and undid his laces. Pulling off his shoes, she said, "Socks have to come off, too. Come on, Connor, I'm sweating just looking at you. The weather is so humid this afternoon."

She began to giggle, struggling to pull off his size eleven sock. Helpless, her contagious laughter had him falling back. He grabbed a cushion and left her to her ministrations. No sooner were his socks off than she was rolling the pants of his legs to above his knees.

"Now sit up."

She pulled at his arms until he was sitting and shifted his feet until they rested on the grass.

"Okay, now squish your toes so you can feel the grass between them."

His pale Canadian skin was no match for her golden hue and, in all honesty, he couldn't remember the last time he'd given in and let down his walls. He liked her hands on his feet. Her gentle, yet firm massage was not something he'd experienced before. He also loved her cheeky grin, and God help him, he wanted nothing more than to run his hands all over her suntanned body. With her legs bare to the top of her thighs and her shirt very loose on her body, there was a lot of it to see.

He cleared his throat and eyed her attempts to let as much sun as possible touch his skin. "I didn't plan very well for this stay, did I? Even though I'd allowed myself a few weeks, in all honesty, I thought I'd be gone after a couple of days."

With her mission complete, she lay on her stomach resembling a small child, her feet raised in the air swinging from side to side. "So, what happened this summer? Did it bypass Canada?"

The grass tickled his soles. *Cheeky Tyrant.* "Time got away from me. One minute it was freezing cold, the next ... I don't know ... I'm here, that's what happened."

How did he explain the endless hours spent at a desk?

His gaze brushed over her face. Her hands cupped her chin as she looked out over the ocean. "Vitamin D's good for you. You need to get out into the sun more."

Except I'm too busy fixing my father's reckless business dealings.

He flopped back onto the rug, shoving a cushion under his head. "I do find time to exercise, just so you know. I swim fairly regularly. Inside a heated, purpose-made, temperature-controlled building where the outside elements cannot touch me and where I follow this damn black line for hours."

She swivelled around and reached for the second cushion. With her arms around it, she hugged it against her chest like a security blanket and lay facing him. "No vitamin D there."

Her eyes latched onto his, and he forgot how to breathe. She was so close. He could reach across and touch her. Touch his fingers along her cheek. God help him, lean in closer and kiss her. In a rush, he released the breath he was holding, and for a fraction of time, the outside world intruded: children playing close by, the bark of a dog and the laughter of adults. The dry smell of undergrowth reached his nostrils, and its headiness made his thoughts fuzzy. He was drowning. In the shade of the tree where they lay, her eyes were dark pools of water, and he was fighting to come up for air.

His mind was closed to everything else, but at the edge of reason, he heard excited shouts. When they penetrated his skull, he could translate the frantic shouts spoken in Italian.

Waterspouts?

Gasping for air, he sat up and spotted three waterspouts hovering over the ocean kilometres away.

"Oh, look, are they tornadoes?" Liz had sat up, too, and was pointing towards the spectacle. She stood to get a better look. "Are we in danger, do you think?"

He had no idea but got to his feet, standing, shoulders touching. "I'll ask him." He pointed to a middle-aged man and his family sitting underneath another tree, looking at the spouts too.

Connor returned to the rug, relief rushing through his body. "He says the only danger we're in is getting caught in the storm likely to fall on us any minute. He suggests we leave if we don't want to get soaked or wait it out in the car. He assured me that waterspouts rarely touch land. They usually fizzle out in the ocean."

"They're spectacular. Look how fast they're moving."

A couple of large drops of rain landed on his nose. Looking up, he made the hasty decision to pack the gear back in the car. "Okay, Liz, everything in the car."

Fat raindrops landed on her bare arms and sun-kissed cheeks as she swiftly picked up the cushions and folded the rug.

Within minutes of packing everything back into the car, fog clouded up the windows as rain pelted down. The noise was deafening, so talking was impossible. Connor reclined his chair back and indicated Liz should do the same thing. When she'd settled, he reached across and caught her hand, gently stroking it with his thumb. *I still have to tell her what I organised today.*

The storm eventually eased and, in its place, left a mostly clear sky to watch the sun drop its red, hot orb into the ocean. Connor opened his door, and the cool breeze rushed in. The smell of newly wet grass swamped his senses, and he greedily inhaled its freshness. Something else he rarely experienced. Liz continued to lie on the passenger's seat with her eyes closed and a shadow of a smile on her lips. The urge to press his lips on hers was all he could think of; instead, he said, "Are you hungry?"

"I'm starving and thirsty." She struggled to open her eyes against the glare, so squeezed his hand.

Connor chuckled and released her hand to run it through his hair. "Then it's time to continue this picnic and watch a decent sunset. All those who agree say 'aye'."

Her smile blossomed across her face as she answered with an 'aye'.

Connor stepped out of the car, pleased Liz was a woman with a healthy appetite, unlike past girlfriends who picked at their food, relying heavily on supplements. He took another lung full of air, and its goodness filtered through his body. It'd been so long since he'd smelt damp earth and mushy leaves mixed with salty sea breezes. The muscles tightened around his chest, reminding him of the camping trips his grandfather had taken him on as a kid. That's what was missing in his life. He had to let go of the stresses of work and family disappointments and reconnect with nature again. *Why has it taken a down-to-earth woman who lives on the other side of the world for me to see this?*

They spread the rug again as the sun started its descent. Connor chewed on crusty, homemade bread filled with cheese, freshly sliced tomato and thinly cut salami, and couldn't remember eating anything so simple yet wholesome in a long time. He decided to forego the wine and drink water, which was Liz's preference.

"This is delicious, Connor. I could die for this bread. It's so fresh and so soft. Yum." She wrapped her hands around the thick layers of bread and moaned in pleasure with each bite.

He laughed as the expressions of pleasure crossed her face, which rewarded him with a cheesy grin—he was a goner.

The magnificent rays of orange and red unfurled across the sky and reflected on the water, calm after the storm. Sobering up, he wondered if his plans would upset her. *I have to tell her soon.*

After they packed away the leftovers, he slid to sit beside her and butted his shoulder with hers. Her eyes stayed glued to the descending sun, and she took the occasional photo with her phone. Its drop was too spectacular to destroy with idle talk. They sat like statues for minutes as the sun slowly lost its bottom half. When a fraction of the top half was all that remained, Connor coughed to clear his throat. "Um ... would Roberta miss you for a couple of days?"

She turned to face him, brows knitted. "What do you mean?"

He swallowed, mouth suddenly dry. *What will she think of my proposal?* "Are you able to pack an overnight bag?"

Frowning deeper, she bit her bottom lip. "I suppose."

"Well ... while in Lamezia Terme, I booked a couple of flights to Rome ... for us." *And I did a search on the fountains in Falerna.*

She swung around, and her knees collided with his. "What do you mean?"

Swiftly, he moved to squat in front of her, itching to take her hands, but when she leant away thought better of it. "I found a palace of sorts preserved as a museum. It was once owned by the Frevannini Dynasty. I thought you might like to see it. We'd spend a night in Rome, and the next day we could do some sightseeing. There's a lot to see and do."

Her mouth hung open, and in the fading light, he witnessed a speck of wariness cross her face.

"I can't afford to do this, Connor," she said as darkness crowded them.

He sat back on his bottom and crossed his legs, unsure if she meant she couldn't afford to do this financially or didn't want to risk an emotional entanglement. He opted for the money option. "It's my choice how I spend my money," he murmured, "and it would be a shame not to see some of Rome while over here."

"But—"

Throwing all caution to the wind, he gently brushed her lips with his. A whimper escaped her mouth, but he might easily have missed it because his heart beat ferociously.

When he pulled back, her hands were clenched tight against her chest, eyes darting in every direction, avoiding his. He dropped his arms by his side to hide the shaking.

"I would really enjoy your company for two days. Please say yes." *Why am I begging?*

Liz's eyes finally rested on his, and she relaxed her hands. In barely a whisper, she said, "Yes," followed by a slight nod.

For the first time, Connor admitted that around Liz, he was a lost cause.

Chapter 13

Liz scribbled the note before she changed her mind.

Gone to Rome. Back late tomorrow night. Connor found the palace owned by Uncle Ben's family. Enjoy Marco while I'm gone. I will desperately need your help to investigate the fountains when I return. Love Liz.

She hastily placed the note under the saltshaker on the kitchen table. Still hesitant about going to Rome with Connor, her fingers came to rest on her lips. She recalled the intense pleasure after Connor had brushed his lips against hers. The way desire had heated her body, the sunset the perfect backdrop. But all too soon, Connor took her home when darkness swiftly descended. Was this the message she was giving him? Look, but don't touch?

It wasn't how she pictured the night ending, but what did she expect? Her sassiness had done a runner and taken her with it. It was time to shake things up. There was no doubt who Roberta was spending the night with. Was it time for Liz to release her shackles a little? So what if she experienced a little heartache when she returned home?

All night, her thoughts had circled and swirled; the debate meaning sleep was not forthcoming. She needed to better attempt to find the fountain where the jewels were hidden. How serious would Roberta think she was after reading the note? If she didn't find them this trip, the chances of returning to Falerna were non-existent. She needed to make a decent effort now!

Her heart, though, continued to argue with her head. It didn't let up all night, and it had been only one quick graze of his lips. She straightened her shoulders and grimaced. With Roberta's help, there was still time to locate the jewels. No doubt Roberta was probably relieved she'd given her a couple of days off to spend with Marco. She deserved some fun.

Connor was the complete package, but ... *money isn't everything, girl.*

She sighed and picked up her backpack. Money sure went a long way to making life easier, and Sally's words resonated in her head. *You're on holiday, and don't forget it. Have some fun!*

Roberta wasn't wasting a single minute while Liz dithered over a couple of days. *Face it, girl, the man is gorgeous and with spare cash to spend.* She'd be nuts to pull out of the generous offer now. Yet it went against every principle her grandparents had instilled in her about how a young lady should act. But for once, she was going to throw caution to the wind. If it ended badly, Sally would be there to help her pick up the pieces. It wouldn't be the first time either one had helped the other.

Time to push the niggle of guilt to the back of her mind. That would be Sally's advice, and today she was going to take it, going in boots and all, and the first brave thing she would do was return the kiss of last night. Fast, and set the tempo for a great two days. Then she would return refreshed and ready to tackle the serious business of locating the jewels.

With her plan in place, she made her way to the front door, latched it shut quietly and stepped down the narrow concrete stairs leading onto the street.

Connor was waiting, leaning against the concrete wall of Zia Maria's Casa. As his fingers tapped and swiped his phone screen, she spent a moment taking in the all-consuming tall, dark, gorgeous man. Every woman's dream. Her mouth dried, and her heart galloped around her chest. She was on the job, and there was no backing out. Willing her feet to keep moving, she closed the last few metres and stood before him.

"Why so serious?" Connor straightened, sliding his phone into his pocket, a frown beginning to form.

"Uh, I—" She reached up and pressed her lips to his. "Good morning."

A burst of laughter escaped Connor, but in two seconds flat, it was gone and replaced with a serious look. He clasped his arms around her waist and eyes the colour of the Adriatic Sea locked with hers. A rush of breath left her mouth, and words jammed in her throat when his lips descended towards hers. All coherent thoughts fled her mind.

Connor easily lifted her a step back against the white-painted concrete wall, his mouth never leaving hers. She leant heavily against it, unsure her shaking legs would hold her up.

Connor's tongue darted into the softness of her mouth, the pleasure shaking her body to its core. At the same time, he reached around her waist and pulled her up against his chest. His expensive spicy aftershave seeped into her skin, and she tasted peppermint as his mouth pressed against hers.

Her hands crept up to cradle his head, her fingers knotting themselves in his short, dark hair as the kiss went on and on. Until the pressure in her lungs expanded to bursting point, forcing them apart.

With her chest heaving in time with Connor's, he rested his forehead against hers, his warm breath rushing past her cheek. "I'm so glad you made the first move because I've been thinking of doing just that all night." When he stepped back, their gazes locked. "I wasn't sure whether it was something you wanted."

An embarrassing garbled reply caught in her throat and she chuckled instead, willing her legs to stop shaking.

Connor must've taken pity on her because he swooped in for another quick hug before kissing the top of her head. "We need to go, or we'll miss our flight."

All plans to tell Connor she shouldn't go to Rome disappeared in an instant. She loved that kiss and God help her, she wanted more.

"Ready?"

She wiped her palms on her shorts before looking into his direct gaze. A delicious distraction already. She nodded, debating whether or when she should tell him about the hidden jewels.

Connor took hold of her backpack and wrapped his arm around her waist. As he steered her towards the hire car, she vowed to tell him when they returned to Falerna. Another couple of days shouldn't matter.

⁕

Connor stood behind Liz with his arms looped comfortably around her waist. That first kiss had definitely started something.

"Not a bad photo." They inspected the life-size enlargement of an old black-and-white photo showing Giovanna's parents and siblings. "Look, only two daughters and six sons."

He nuzzled the back of her neck and pressed his lips behind her ear, causing her to shiver. He hadn't let go of her since *that* kiss blasted all his senses to smithereens. She turned and, oblivious to the other tourists in the palace, let him kiss her deeply.

When she pulled away, he couldn't believe how much he craved her touch.

With a gorgeous smile, she turned back to the photo and settled comfortably against his chest. "The other sister was Rosa." With her finger pointed towards the photo, she read out the siblings' names.

He couldn't believe his luck. The palace was everything he'd hoped it would be. They found it on the outskirts of Rome, surrounded by lush, green lawns, a rarity in such an ancient city where space was unheard of. These people were his ancestors, and he knew the time was fast approaching when he'd have to tell Liz the truth. As she continued to study the photo, he rested his hands on her hips and gazed down the length of the long hall, feasting on frescos and carvings tastefully dotted along the walls. Not all rooms were opened to the public, but they'd seen enough to know his ancestors were once wealthy, with a history extending well into past centuries.

Dark burgundy brocades hid tall, narrow windows. Those tied at their centres revealed spectacular stained-glass windows depicting Roman life centuries ago. One caught his interest. A naked woman with a curvaceous body held a large urn with water pouring out. The sudden arousal pushing at his pants surprised him, and he took a step back to not alarm Liz. The last thing he wanted to do was frighten her away.

To feign his real reasons for letting go, he moved to a noticeboard a few metres away. Carefully reading the Italian words, a rush of excitement swirled around his chest.

"Hey, Liz, come here, quick."

Liz looked up from the photo. He gestured with his hands, and she came over to where he stood. Without hesitating, he took her in his arms and hugged her tight. "Guess what? In less than ten minutes, they have a special guest appearance, who just happens to be Paolo's great-grandson."

Liz gasped. "I think Paolo was the fourth son."

And I'm the great-grandson of Giovanna. Connor shuddered, causing Liz to step back, her eyebrows shooting up.

"Are you cold?"

Their gazes locked. "No, not really." *More likely a ghost walked over my grave.* Forcing a grin, he said, "Promise me you'll let me hug you as much as possible, just in case."

Liz's laughter rang out, and without hesitation, he drew her in again for another drawn-out, breathless kiss. *She's driving me crazy, and it's only day one.*

The next ten minutes passed in a blur of touching and holding while they continued to view artefacts, paintings and carvings. They made their way back to the noticeboard where the special tour would start, while Connor tried to ignore the nervous churn of his stomach. *This man is my cousin, and no one in the room will know.*

The tour leader in his neatly pressed dark suit spoke into a microphone attached to his lapel. Struggling to keep up with his Italian dialogue, Connor's attention was distracted when the other tourists clapped their hands as a young man entered via a side door. Connor licked his dry lips, adrenaline rushing through his body. Riveted towards the special guest, his jaw dropped and he struggled to swallow. An intense desire to share his knowledge with Liz was slamming against his chest. *Damn.* He knew it wasn't the right moment to tell his secret, but he might burst at any moment if he didn't say something.

"Does every Italian male look like you?" Liz stared at the man with her mouth gaping. His reaction to her comment was to squeeze her hand hard. "Even his eyes are the same green."

He couldn't reply. His tongue was a twisted, useless appendage. Trying to make light of her comment, he winced instead, his smile cracking on his face like drying mud. Turning his attention back to the man, he desperately tried to follow the exchange between the tour leader and the special guest.

"They're speaking too fast for me. I think his name is Antonio." Connor pulled Liz along. The throng of visitors that had suddenly amassed from nowhere followed Antonio, walking towards the life-sized photo they had viewed earlier.

As individuals in the crowd asked Antonio questions, Connor concentrated harder, following their conversation. He whispered what made sense to Liz. "He's explaining that during the war, three of the brothers were killed in action, and Giovanna was murdered in southern Italy."

Liz nodded and pressed her hand against his. Snippets of Antonio's conversation were making him light-headed. *This entire situation is bizarre.* "He's now explaining how large the extended family is and how most still live in and around Rome." *I have all this family, and I never knew?*

He didn't have a chance to calm his racing heart or to understand the surreal feelings swimming around his head. Within a matter of minutes, Antonio was thanking everyone and making a speedy exit through the door he had entered from.

For a few moments, Connor continued to look at the closed door, his mouth gaping in shock. *So final.* He tried to bring some normality to his posture, so he straightened his shoulders and looked towards Liz when she spoke.

"I suppose when you're that rich, you dictate how long you talk for. Still, it was generous of Antonio to give up his time for a bunch of tourists."

But I'm family. The cogs in his brain were already in action with what he wanted to do once he told Liz the truth and sorted out the jewels. He'd draw on Phil's wealth of experience and work out how to contact his Italian relatives. This trip to Italy was certainly turning out to be a life changer on all counts.

Chapter 14

Liz stretched her legs, the new dawn's sunlight spreading slowly across the whitewashed bedroom walls. Ruby red paint trims surrounded the window architraves and the cornice around the ceiling. Lying on her back, she pulled the quilt up to her chin and snuggled deeper under the covers. Her thoughts wandered back to the day before and how there had barely been a moment when she wasn't touching Connor. She recalled the kissing, the blood rushing through her veins and how the air surrounding them vibrated whenever they touched.

They'd walked hand in hand after dinner through a small grove of olive trees and Liz wondered how it existed in such a city as Rome. The villa Connor chose for their one-night stay overlooked the olive trees. The small hidden restaurant they ate at was only a short walk away.

She smiled wistfully and sighed. The magnificence of the Frevannini Palace was out of this world, and the debt she owed Connor for everything he was doing to help research Uncle Ben's family continued to mount. *So why don't you tell him about the jewels?*

Rolling onto her stomach, she closed her eyes and clutched the pillow to her face. She couldn't explain why she wanted to keep it from Connor. It wasn't like he needed the extra money. So why the secret? She groaned into her pillow while her feet kicked the mattress like a toddler having a tantrum. Until she lost the desire to fight the niggle and forced her body to relax.

That wasn't hard to do as she hugged her pillow and relived the last kiss they'd shared the previous evening under a sultry Roman twilight. It drained every last inch of sustenance her body had taken in when she'd chosen gnocchi in Napoletana sauce for her meal. The kiss continued to deplete all the nourishment her body delighted in when she completed her meal with pistachio gelato. After dinner, they sat on an intricately carved lover's seat under an olive tree with the villa in sight. The tree's fragrance in the late evening air had trickled over her pores, soaking through her skin.

She hadn't considered the sleeping arrangements until they walked back to the villa, hand in hand, under the moonlight. For the first time that day, her heart had begun to pound frantically in her chest. It was hard to ignore the morals her grandmother instilled in her, her constant reminder to never rush things. She firmly believed that if it was meant to be, it would happen in good time. This sage piece of advice had avoided many a tangled emotional mess in the past.

But it was doubly hard to ignore the chemistry with Connor. It was a natural conclusion to end the day in his bed.

Inside their villa, Connor's eyes had followed her carefully, and he must've sensed her concerns. He reached up and gently massaged her forehead. "That's the first frown I've seen on your face all day." He drew her in close again to kiss her goodnight before showing her the two separate bedrooms. "Sleep well. Tomorrow will be just as hectic. Have a quick glance at the brochures I left on your bag, and let me know what you'd like to see."

Relief had coursed through her body, leaving her legs weak. She wouldn't have to decide that night, but heck, she wanted it. Right or wrong, rushed or not, she'd be lying if she hadn't already pictured two naked bodies slick with sweat.

By the time she was showered and in bed, she struggled to stay awake as she flicked through the sightseeing brochures. It wasn't long before she abandoned them, dropping them to the floor beside the bed. She must've fallen asleep immediately because the next moment of recognition was waking up the following morning.

She rolled to her side and questioned her actions. The last thing she wanted was for Connor to think she was prudish, but that was her reality. She wasn't Roberta who jumped into bed with the first gorgeous Mediterranean man to come her way. She wasn't Sally who took life with both hands and ran with it, not caring where it led. This might've been her if her responsibilities over the past few years hadn't crushed her spirits.

She'd taken this journey for a reason. The jewels. Then maybe her burdens might lift a little with the financial reward and she could find herself again.

This was the pep talk she needed. She was good to go. It was time to get her mind back on track and fulfil the purpose of this trip.

But then her shoulders sagged into the mattress and she sighed, suddenly finding it all too much this early in the morning to be a sensible adult.

Her eyes fluttered open, and daylight continued to seep into the room. She reached across for her phone and checked the time—6:07 am. There was still enough time for more sleep.

⁂

"Are you awake?"

The whispered words were spoken close to her ear, and she immediately recognised Connor's Canadian accent. Snapping her eyes open, it surprised her she'd gone to sleep again so easily. Crouched beside her bed, she fell into his sea-green pools. She reached out, inviting him to join her. So much for her pep talk.

Connor didn't hesitate. He slid in, facing her and wrapped his arms around her waist, immediately finding her lips.

"Mmm, I'd like to say I spent all night dreaming of doing just this, but I'd be lying. I fell asleep so fast and so hard it was morning before I took my next breath."

Liz giggled, his warm breath whispering along her cheek. "Same here."

Connor kicked aside the blue and white floral quilt and trapped her on the mattress with the pressure of his weight. He cupped her cheeks, and all thoughts of laughter vanished as fast as the night had.

Unable to move, she relished the flush of heat filling her body. Her gaze locked with his, and it took all her energy to control the tumbling in her stomach. The intensity in his eyes mirrored her desire, and his throbbing against her thigh left her trembling, unable to control the betraying signs of her body.

Slowly he lowered his face until his lips swept over hers with the barest of touches before withdrawing a fraction, letting his warm breath wash over her when he asked, "Did you sleep well?"

"Too well," she whispered, her voice coming out breathy. "I didn't get a chance to look at the brochures properly; I—"

"Ah ... we'll take a look at them soon, but for now—"

Seconds later, his mouth joined hers. Liz wanted it to go on forever, wondering how she would cope without this wake-up call *every* morning. She explored his naked chest while Connor brushed her skin underneath the flimsy top she wore, while the kiss went on and on.

Connor rolled on his side, partially taking her with him, and her slender limbs tangled with his. She lay with her eyes closed, her breath ragged, rubbing her leg against the toughness of his muscled thighs.

"You'll need to stop doing that unless you have other plans."

Her eyes snapped open. With his chest still heaving, Connor's quietly spoken words with a grin froze her actions immediately. Thanks to the bright daylight now showering the bedroom walls, she was certain Connor could see the blush racing along her neck and face. She dropped her gaze and inwardly groaned. Now was her chance to make a move if it was ever going to happen.

Connor rested his mouth against her hair and tightened his hold. "Are you ready to do some sightseeing?"

Liz lay back and looked up into his smiling face.

"Um ... Connor, I ..."

With his finger, he did a maddening tour of her face, finally resting it on her swollen lips. "Mmm?"

Her tongue darted out to touch his finger. Her eyes fluttered closed, the shock of desire leaving her dizzy for a moment.

"You were saying?"

Her shoulders sagged back onto the mattress as she opened her eyes. "Ah ... nothing ..."

"So ... umm ... just nothing?" His smile dazzled her, but his direct gaze sent other messages.

She shook her head to clear all the fuzziness and shrugged. She was finding it hard not to be distracted by his smile, which slowly vanished. With his hand cupped over her cheek, he said in a serious tone, "I promise this will do for now."

Liz couldn't drag her gaze away. She searched his face, sure any moment a giant wave would reach across and dump her underneath its power.

"I did, though, promise you a day of sightseeing. Ready for it?"

She nodded, frustrated yet relieved she didn't need to explain any further. Her body had other ideas, and the huge swell of disappointment was her doing. *Make the first move, damn it, and don't scare the guy away.*

It was too late. The moment passed. Connor reached over for the travel brochures still lying on the floor and settled on the bed again. He tucked her into the crook of his arm and settled comfortably beside her. She couldn't help noticing how perfectly they fit together, like two peas in a pod, as Nan would say, hoping she was keeping well on the other side of the world.

"So, what would you like to see today?"

She looked up, feeling a little bolder. "Everything ..."

Connor quirked an eyebrow, a fierce, intense heat radiating between them. "Wrong answer if you want to sightsee anything today."

Liz began to giggle. This was impossible but crazy. She wrapped her arms around his neck and squeezed tight. "Okay, one more amazing kiss, please, then let's get out of here and check this city out. Are we on?"

Connor's laughter rang out loud and beautifully clear. "What have I landed myself with here?" he asked as a smile crossed his face. "Hmm, some woman who's going to drive me crazy," he added as his mouth dropped to meet hers.

Oh, how she liked the sound of this warm and caring man, who wasn't put out by a weird Aussie giving out constant mixed messages.

Chapter 15

Connor pulled Liz up the last few steps before collapsing at the top of the Spanish Steps facing the Piazza Trinità dei Monti and the church of the same name. They had walked nonstop all day. Lunch, they ate on the run as they fought their way through the many frescoed walls and ceilings of the labyrinth of rooms making up the Sistine Chapel. They quickly learnt its appreciation required more than the one hour they'd allocated.

Liz shed her backpack and placed it on the lower step in front of her legs. The charm tinkled against the metal buckle, and it was a sound Connor was getting familiar with. Not hesitating, he settled Liz in front of his chest, wrapped his arms around her waist and rested his chin on her shoulder. He inhaled the citrus scent he'd come to love, enjoying some quiet time amongst the chaos of tourists. Young and old alike clambered up and down the ancient steps amidst calls for smiles, capturing lifetime memories on cameras and phones.

Connor eyed the colourful display of flowers on either side of the steps. Mixed colours of purple, dark red and pink wound their way down to the Piazza di Spagna at the base of the Spanish Steps. Their petals, wide open and facing the western sky, were a little wilted as the sun splayed its rays over them.

He pulled his travel bag off his shoulder and reached inside for the bar of chocolate and fresh apricots they'd purchased earlier. He smiled as Liz sat up to allow him easier access to his bag. She had a wicked sweet tooth and easily burnt it off as fast as she ate it.

"Am I sensing a food break?" Liz ran her hand through her hair, damp with sweat at her temples, and released the tie holding it. Shaking her head to free her shoulder-length hair, the afternoon breeze stirred it enough to tickle his face.

He couldn't resist. Dropping the food onto his lap so he could hold her hair together with both hands, he lifted it clear and nuzzled the base of her neck. She sighed with pleasure and sagged against him. His eyes closed of their own accord, and he soaked up the mild salty taste of her skin after a solid day of walking. His lips moved tenderly across her collarbone, and he imagined they were on a tiny island, separated from the rest of the world. *I could do this forever.* The startling truth had his eyes flicking open and his lips froze midkiss.

To cover his sudden withdrawal, he released her hair, letting it fall back in place, and passed the chocolate and fruit. A little breathless, he said, "I swear I've never known anyone who eats as much chocolate as you do."

Liz hoisted herself up and slid across the step until she sat level with him. With her hip sending sensitive pulses along his thigh, she snapped off a couple of squares, which he'd learnt was her favourite, creamy white chocolate. She handed him a piece and smiled boldly. "Well, without chocolate, you haven't really lived, have you?"

The truth of her statement bulldozed hard against his chest. *She's right, chocolate aside. All the money in the world and I've lived a sheltered and privileged life, working in high finance to placate the wealthy. Deciding which offshore deal will secure the best rates with the least tax. What do I know about the real world?*

To distract his disturbing thoughts, he reached into his travel bag for his water bottle and phone. When he returned home, he would rethink how he lived. His grandfather's reminder over the years that money would not necessarily bring him happiness kept flitting across his mind. Those often-repeated words prodded his head as he questioned the state of his well-being. *Am I happy?*

Taking another piece of chocolate from Liz's outstretched hand, he would need to dwell on the question and its definition. But for now, replenished with food and water, it was time to push it aside. This moment was a once-in-a-lifetime opportunity. Liz came from more than just different sides of the world. His incredible wealth, which he took for granted, played a huge role in his upbringing, which was so different from hers. Yet, this caring and generous woman, who'd given up a lot to care for her aging grandparents, had shown him, in such a short space of time, what it meant to be part of the real human race.

He drew Liz closer to his side, swiping through the photos they'd taken that day.

"The view onto the Vatican Garden is so amazing from up the top." Liz rotated the phone for a better look.

They had climbed the dome of St Peter's Basilica. The narrow spiral staircase led to a stunning view of the Vatican Gardens on one side and the huge square in front of the church on the other.

"Did we get a good shot of The Creation of Adam?"

Connor smiled as Liz swiped past the many photos of the one famous fresco. "I'm sure, of the hundreds of photos you took, there is bound to be one that turned out."

She playfully thumped him on the shoulder and chuckled. "I'm sorry. It's just that a friend of Nan came to the Sistine Chapel and returned home without noticing their most famous one."

Connor turned the phone to look at the next set of photos in front of the Trevi Fountain. He was so close to Liz that he couldn't resist turning and placing a kiss on her cheek. "You look so beautiful in this one."

Her breath hitched as she turned to face him. He didn't hesitate to lean towards her with another kiss, tasting of chocolate and sweet fruit, leaving his heart pumping wildly.

He pulled back, breathless. How was he going to exist without seeing her every day? His thoughts were disrupted when her shoulders shook as she continued to view their photos.

Confused that she would find the kiss funny when he was having a hell of a time controlling his erratic heart, a frown furrowed his brow.

"Oh, Connor, I'm sorry. I didn't mean to laugh. I can't help remembering when I thought we needed to get off the bus when the Colosseum loomed up so large in front of us." She continued to laugh helplessly, recalling their first sighting of the magnificent amphitheatre.

He slung his arm over her shoulder and laughed with her. "Of course, the bus was going to stop right in front of the world's most visited attraction, not three blocks back."

Connor squeezed her shoulder, finding it hard to believe fate delivered her to his side. When their laughter subsided, he swung his legs behind her and hugged her tighter, his lips drawn to that sweet spot on the back of her neck again. "It must be time to make our way to the airport?"

She nodded, turning in his arms and kissing his chin and neck. Her hand rubbed against his day's stubble, leaving every nerve ending on his face raw and ragged.

"Are you tired yet of slumming it on buses and trains?" she asked, turning back to the lower piazza.

As she cheekily mocked him, he entwined his fingers with hers, remembering his promise to change the way he lived. "Not at all, but we might need the use of a taxi to whiz us back to the villa for our luggage if we're going to make it to the airport in time. If you hadn't insisted on sitting and kissing so much, we could've made our way back earlier using the bus."

She turned back, grinning, her eyebrows arched. "In that case, I'm happy to use the expensive option."

Her eyes found his with a bold look, and he forgot about his promise. He leant in closer. "Same here." He latched onto the softness of her lips again. It pushed him below water level, leaving him unable to breathe.

When he did come up for air, she whispered close to his ear, "Thanks for an amazing day. I owe you big time, again."

His forehead dropped against hers as he fought to get his breath under control. "Another IOU? Brilliant! Just so you know, I'm keeping tally."

Chapter 16

Someone singing, a baby squealing, a car speeding by on the narrow road and the tolling of a church bell. She opened one eye. Roberta was tying back the curtains. Liz winced when the morning sun streamed into her room and onto her face. The window creaking open allowed this avalanche of noise to reach her. Rolling onto her stomach and pressing her face into her pillow, she hoped it was only an illusion that the night had turned to day so quickly.

Their plane had been hopelessly delayed the previous night, so by the time they landed in Lamezia Terme and driven to Falerna, it had ticked over to one o'clock in the morning when she finally made it to bed.

"You've got some explaining to do, girl." Roberta strode to the bed and whipped the pale pink quilt off her.

Shielding her face with her hands, Liz peeked through her fingers. "Is Marco still in the picture?"

Roberta flopped on the bed, her arms flailing out wide, one hand landing with a smack on Liz's thigh. "Yes, and it's been heaven."

Liz pushed Roberta's hand away and rubbed at the spot. "Why are you so cranky? A girl in love should have her head in the clouds."

Roberta laughed, staring at the ceiling. "Who said anything about love?"

Liz sat up with a groan. She wrapped her arms around her raised knees and rested her chin on top, eyeing Roberta. "Don't you have any feelings for this poor man? He's probably hopelessly in love with you."

"What? Like lover boy? I doubt it." Roberta rolled onto her side, shoving a pillow under her head. Once comfortable, she turned her full glare in Liz's direction. "Okay, so explain the note."

Liz ran a hand through her bed hair and sighed. This time, *she* flung herself back with her arms out wide. "I thought it was self-explanatory. We saw the most amazing palace owned by Uncle Ben's family, and one of the great-grandsons made a special appearance. Then we spent all day yesterday sightseeing. The Colosseum, Sistine Chapel, St Peter's Church, Trevi Fountain, Spanish Steps and ... and ..." She sighed dreamily. "Connor is so nice and we kissed so much, and I think the love word might be involved here."

Roberta made choking noises. "Excuse me for a minute while I gag over here. Are you serious? You've known the guy for what, about a week, right? He splashes his money on you, takes you away for a couple of days and *you're* in love. God help you, girl, you don't have a hope in hell."

Liz wasn't letting Roberta's mood affect her memories of the past two days. Instead, she focused on the curtains swaying in the morning breeze and the shadows dancing along the walls. Her fingers came up to rest on her lips, still swollen from two full days of kissing. A smile stretched across her face.

"So why isn't *he* helping you find the jewels?"

Liz sprang up out of bed and paced, sure all evidence of her smile was gone. "Oh, Roberta." She covered her face with her hands and groaned. "I've thought about it over the past couple of days. It's such a huge secret that I'm not sure I trust this information with just anyone. But I promised to tell Connor when we returned from Rome, and I will. I just need a few more days to work out what to say."

"So, you still want to look at all the fontana dei poveri options with me?"

Dropping her hands by her side, Liz's shoulders slumped. "Yes, and I would really appreciate your help. I *need* to attempt to find them or it'll be a wasted trip. I'll never be able to afford to come back anytime soon."

Roberta's face screwed up. "Okay, this is the deal. Marco has gone away for two days to work. I still kinda like you, but I didn't appreciate the hasty note left on the table. I don't trust lover boy, but I'll help you, starting in the next half hour. You're only allowed contact with lover boy after we've made a decent effort today. Clear?"

Liz winced. "We planned to meet up for lunch at the café." Twisting her lips, she added, "Would you like to come with us?"

Moaning as though in great pain, Roberta dragged her phone out of her back pocket and tapped in her PIN. "Okay, what's his number? I'll text him to meet us at 4 pm for a late coffee because I need your assistance. I'll also tell him, in a nice way if I can, that you're off-limits tomorrow morning, helping me do a favour for my aunt." She quirked an eyebrow. "Will that keep him off our back for the next two mornings?"

Liz rushed to the bed and sat beside Roberta, reciting his number. Then she wound her arms around Roberta's neck and squeezed tight. "Thank you so much. I knew you'd be angry after reading the note, but I have to make a decent effort to find the jewels. The last thing I expected was a man to distract me, but ..." She released her hold and rolled onto her back. She let the dreamy wash come over her. "He's such a good kisser, so hot, so good looking ..."

Roberta groaned. "Still right here being sick." She made more gagging noises before asking, "More importantly, was he any good in bed?"

Sitting up, she looked closely at Roberta, wondering how she'd missed how sensuous and ravishing she was. She oozed confidence that spoke volumes, and Liz wasn't surprised men were drawn to it. Her curves underneath her long cotton shirt and her ample breasts boasted all things women. There was no comparison to Liz's flat or slightly bumpy canvas. She looked down and shook her head. "I can't do it so soon after meeting someone, *and* as you pointed out, I've only known him for a week."

Liz put another cross on the page. "That leaves only two possibilities and even then, I'm not sure we've got it right."

They sat on a concrete ledge, their feet resting on a patch of soft grass. Using the building behind their back to shield them from the hot noon sun, they decided to have a breather and a snack. Liz sighed, raking a hand through her hair, her messy ponytail coming loose. "They just don't quite match Uncle Ben's diagram. I have this niggle telling me we haven't got it right."

Roberta pulled a chocolate biscuit from her backpack and crunched it. "Well, I say we use your story of wanting to plant a tree for your uncle. We'll start with the fountain near the cemetery because it's surrounded by lawn, not cement like the one near the town square. If we start early enough, we shouldn't have too many curious onlookers. What do you say?"

Liz rubbed the back of her neck and reached into her bag for water. "I don't really have a choice. We've looked at all the fountains in the whole damn town, and only two come anywhere close." Liz took a sip of water before she continued, "I suppose anything could have happened in seventy-odd years; not that much appears to have changed for centuries in this place."

"That's the spirit, my girl. Glad to see you've finally seen the place for the backwater it is."

Liz took the biscuit Roberta offered and munched on it. "No, I didn't say that. Falerna is beautiful in its own special way. You should've seen how spectacular the sunset was. I need to go back once more and get some good shots. I can't believe I took so few."

"I wonder why?" Roberta mused.

Liz chuckled and butted shoulders with Roberta. "You should get Marco to take you one afternoon."

Roberta leant back against the building. "Yeah, whatever. I still think you're seeing everything through rose-coloured glasses."

The coolness of the concrete wall seeped through Liz's shirt sticking to her back. The cemetery on her right ran parallel to the small park in front of the building where they sat. The breeze picked up and gathered a collection of leaves, sending them rolling and tripping over themselves along the recently trimmed green grass.

A breeze buffeted along the building and, closing her eyes, she enjoyed the small reprieve from the day's heat as it brushed her neck and shoulders. Her thoughts wandered hopelessly back to Connor as they had all morning. What was he doing? One hour to go before they met up, and already she had her arms around his neck and her lips against his. A smile spread across her face.

"Hey, guess what?"

Liz sat up. "What?"

"Something my aunt said this morning was really weird. I haven't said a word about the jewels to anyone, cross my heart," and she did the sign against her chest. "What I *did* tell my aunt was that your uncle requested in his will a tree be planted in his memory near a fontana dei poveri in this god-forsaken village. Anyway, she was talking to the owner of the grocery store and doing the usual gossip everyone does around here, and he happened to mention two different men at different times called in and asked some vague questions about water fountains, too."

"Ugh, that *is* weird." She swung around towards the edge of the building when a stranger's face peered around it and disappeared just as fast. Liz shot up and jogged to the corner but could see no one. A stir of wind brushed over her skin, leaving the hairs on the nape of her neck standing up on their ends. *Calm down, girl, it could be anyone curious to know who the strangers in town are.* No way was she going to dwell on the stolen letter.

Connor sauntered towards the café having spent all day roaming the streets. He rolled up the sleeves of his button-up shirt past his elbows, and the sun showered its rays over his skin. A slight breeze ambled along the narrow street where he walked, bringing welcome relief to the sweat visible on his arms. He folded the slip of paper with the list of fountains he'd obtained a few days earlier and slipped it into his pocket.

He struggled to match any of them with the detailed diagram his grandfather had left him. *What if Grandad got it wrong?* He scratched his head, trying to imagine how much development could have happened in Falerna that might've changed the place. His grandfather still had his wits about him five years ago when he'd recorded the details. If only they'd used street names back then, then he could've pinpointed it exactly, even if there were changes made since. Seventy-five years was a long time in some places, though it didn't appear so in this one.

Thoughts of the two days spent in Rome with Liz kept him occupied, and he was curious. What was keeping her busy? Roberta's text mentioned she might need Liz tomorrow morning too, which suited him. While he couldn't wait to get his arms around her tiny waist and feel the softness of her lips, the following morning would be a good opportunity to do some early morning digging before curious onlookers got in the way.

Looking up, he saw Liz and Roberta walking towards the café from the opposite direction. In the same instant Liz recognised him, his heart began to beat faster. *She does this to me.* He couldn't help the smile that stretched across his face when she passed her backpack to Roberta and came running towards him.

An unexpected burst of laughter surged past his lips as he swept her into his arms and spun her around before finding her lips in one fluid moment.

She held onto his neck in a vice-like grip, laughing and kissing before he gently placed her feet back on the ground.

"This is gross. Anyone else want to share coffee with me?"

Heated desire spread throughout his body as his hands moved over Liz's satiny skin. "Hello to you too, Roberta. Have you missed me?" He sent a mischievous smile in Roberta's direction as he gave Liz another solid hug. Hell, he wanted more than just a hug, but they were in a public place in a small village and it was time to show some restraint.

"We've been too busy to miss you, mate."

"Is that so?" Connor released his hold on Liz and stepped back.

"That's not true, Connor."

This response from Liz confirmed he wasn't the only one helpless against this incoming tide of unexpected pleasure, and he burst out laughing. "So, I can ignore Roberta for now?"

Liz grabbed his hand and gave it a squeeze. "Yes."

Roberta groaned and grimaced ridiculously. "I'm getting my coffee. All this love in the air is doing my head in."

Connor chuckled and tightened his hold. *Love?* The need to reach across and kiss Liz once more was maddening. It was crazy. Instead, he gently tugged on her arm and followed Roberta to the café. Coffee was not going to help him. It was a cold shower he needed. Right now!

Chapter 17

L iz left a grumbling Roberta with strict instructions to get to bed early because in less than twenty-four hours, Marco was back and she would need all her energy.

"Don't forget you're with *me* in the morning. The sooner I dig these damn jewels up, the quicker I can return to my holiday," Roberta complained.

"Yeah, sure, go on, admit it; you're going to miss the excitement," Liz threw right back at her.

"Go, girl, now. Get going. I don't want to lock eyes with lover boy when he's waiting for you at the front door."

Liz giggled and gave Fiorina a quick hug on her way out. With Fiorina gone from the house most mornings, it was usually the afternoons they crossed paths. "Thanks, Roberta; I'll see you at breakfast."

Liz was showered and refreshed, wearing a simple cotton dress in a swirl of colours with spaghetti straps and slip-on sandals. Cool, casual and comfortable. Her motto for most of her life.

It was getting close to dinnertime, and her rumbling stomach reminded her of this. She skipped down the narrow concrete steps and turned left to meet Connor next door. And ran smack into him, colliding with his solid chest.

"Ouch, did that hurt?" Connor tilted her face up with a worried look.

Breathless, she drank in his expensive aftershave and wrapped her arms around his neck. "No," and she didn't hesitate another second as her mouth latched onto his. This brash new girl was learning fast and from the best. Sally and Roberta. You only lived once, and it'd been years since she'd opened herself up to live at all.

She gasped when Connor's tongue touched the insides of her mouth, and she quietly groaned with pleasure.

Connor pulled back, chuckling. "Shh ... this might be illegal over here."

They touched foreheads, and she laughed softly. "Let's go then."

"If you're sure you want to see another sunset."

"I am," she hummed happily.

Liz stepped away, comfortably slipping her hand in Connor's and looked down at his exposed legs. "What the heck? What did you do?" she spluttered, eyeing off his cut-off denim shorts. "Did you cut those up?"

Connor raised a knee to show off his handiwork. "Sure did. I asked Zia Maria if she knew anyone who could do sewing repairs. It was going to take a week, so I borrowed a pair of sharp scissors instead."

"Why the heck did you do that for? My God, they're probably a thousand-dollar pair of jeans."

Connor took her hand and pulled her along. "Don't be ridiculous. Who in their right mind would spend that much on a pair of jeans?"

"Connor, they're Gucci jeans, and you cut them up," Liz wailed as they crossed the narrow street to his hire car.

"According to the laws of Liz, I need more sun on my skin and the need to feel grass with my toes."

Liz hadn't noticed his footwear, but they looked like village-bought sandals belonging to an old man. She wasn't over the shock of a ruined pair of Gucci jeans, but she began to giggle anyway.

"What's wrong now?"

"If I wore size eleven thongs, I'd loan you a pair."

Connor halted at the car and peered down at his sandals. "Can't say I've ever worn anything like this, but you know the saying, when in Rome—"

They burst out laughing. The contagious type with tears running down Liz's face. Connor unlocked the car, and she fell into the passenger seat, still doubled over. Connor was not faring any better. A fleeting glance in each other's direction and it set them off again.

"The sunset. We're going to miss it if we don't hurry up," Liz hiccupped through her continuing laughter.

"Well, stop harassing me over my footwear." Connor took the tissue she offered and attempted to wipe his eyes.

Liz took a big breath and declared, "Okay, deep breath, we'll get through this."

Which only set them off again for a few more minutes.

Eventually, they were on their way, and Connor surprised her by saying, "Do you want to continue the tooting game?"

"No," she groaned, "I can't even remember what we got up to."

Connor smiled broadly. "We got up to fifteen, if that helps."

Liz continued to mock-groan. "I'll never be the same person when I hear a car horn toot."

Connor chuckled beside her. "That day was a bit crazy, wasn't it? You know what? I've never laughed this hard in ages."

This sobered Liz quickly. "Don't you have much time for fun? Or is it all work, work, work?" She understood that. There were never enough hours in the day in *her* reality. Working to pay the bills, taking care of her grandmother, studying the one subject she allowed herself in the hope that one day she might finally graduate—if she wasn't middle-aged by then.

Connor tapped the steering wheel with this thumb, and it took him longer than she expected to respond.

"There is a lot of work involved, and meeting you has tempted me to change my ways."

"Oh, don't change anything based on my experience. I'm the last person you want advice from. Ask my cousin, Sally. She's always on my case about getting out and living more. If only it was that straightforward."

Connor reached across and squeezed her hand. "Ask Sally, hey? I might just do that."

The thumping in Liz's chest wound itself up. Did this mean extending this thing between them after Falerna?

"So, tell me, is Liz short for something?" Connor parked the car in the same place as last time and turned in the seat to face her.

"Elizabeth." Her head was still jumbled up from what he'd said earlier. "You don't get a choice in Oz. Your name is either shortened or changed about two seconds after you're born. For years it was Lizzy, but now that I'm all grown up, it's Liz."

"All grown up, hey?" Connor mused as he opened his door and got out.

Ah, yup, all grown up and with big people's feelings. Liz opened her door with a shaking hand and imagined all sorts of things happening that night. Already Sally was cheering in the background while Roberta was fist pumping in celebration.

Liz had to do everything in her power to stop her knees from wobbling. With despair, she stepped out. How was she supposed to get past the next awkward stage? Kissing, hugging, that was easy. It was the next step where she faltered every single time.

Liz looked up. Connor was watching her with a wicked grin. Could he read her mind? An embarrassing flush raced across her neck. She gave him a lopsided smile and caught the first cushion Connor threw her way.

With both cushions tucked under her arms, she carried the same picnic blanket while Connor carried the food esky.

"Where does all this stuff come from?"

"It's Zia Maria's. I think she likes me."

I think I like you too. Liz chewed her bottom lip while she spread out the blanket. A rush of earthy smells reached her nose, and she inhaled it slowly, hoping to steady her crazy beating heart.

"So, if I was born in Australia, would I be called Con?"

Huh? "Oh, the shortened name? Nah."

The fierce sun shone directly across from them. Visually, it was only a couple of metres away from touching the horizon.

"I'll get your backpack from the car. We'll need our sunglasses."

With her thongs flicked off the side, she sat cross-legged, nestled a cushion on her lap and pictured the photos she would capture on her phone, which was also in the bag. She needed to get some decent shots.

It would hurt terribly if she left Falerna without a passable picture of this magnificent spectacle. She also wanted a photo of Connor. Good idea or bad, jewels or no jewels, she wanted some reminder of these magical two weeks.

Connor discarded his old-man sandals and flopped down beside her. She winced at how much his jeans cost and reached across and fingered the frayed edges while he squished his toes on the grass at the edge of the blanket.

This she could smile about.

"That's better. I wasn't sure if you'd ever forgive me for cutting up my mother's Christmas present."

"You did what?"

"You heard, Lizzy."

Muscles tightened around her chest. It had been years since anyone had called her that. Even Sally and her grandparents had deferred to the grown-up version of her name without fuss.

She liked how it rolled off his tongue in his sexy-as-hell accent. But missed it at the same time. It reminded her of more carefree times. Before responsibilities had banked up, making her feel old before her time.

She didn't mean for the moisture to build up, and she blinked rapidly, knowing full well that Connor was watching her like a hawk. It only took seconds, but he abandoned his position at the edge of the blanket and slipped in behind her, pulling her against his chest, his long legs cocooning her. "Did I say something wrong?"

"I'm sorry and no. Sometimes I miss the carefree Lizzy, that's all."

Connor's mouth found many places to be, and her eyes flickered closed while she enjoyed the sensations. Gradually the pain around her chest dispersed. She would worry about Nan later. Daily messages from Sally confirmed she was doing okay. Dwelling on her grandmother while this hot guy was paying her all this attention was not the smartest thing to do.

When she opened her eyes, moaning softly, she spotted the sun. She sprang up, Connor's arms dropping away reluctantly. "My phone, damn,

I'm going to miss the good shots again, and I doubt you'll come a third time."

She dug around in her backpack for it and almost missed Connor's words.

"I'd just about do anything for you."

She spun around and locked gazes with his amazing misty green eyes. The eyes or the sun. *Quick, make a decision.* He rested his arms on his raised knees and watched her. A splay of red rays stroked his profile, and she had trouble breathing normally. It made him look like Adonis, and she wasn't so sure she deserved all this male beauty. Considerate, thoughtful, kind and a body like any Greek god to go with it. Was it too good to be true? Roberta didn't hesitate to tell her often.

With a smirk, he said, "Get your shots, Liz."

She dropped her gaze and concentrated on her phone settings. With shaking hands, she doubted the photos would work. Connor took out his phone and was taking shots too, and the sounds of other people broke through into her jumbled thoughts. The area was quite busy again; kids kicked around a football, others were already eating and laughter mingled. It was a happy place, and she'd look back at these photos with just that sentiment.

Once the sun broke past the horizon, she sat back down and, with steadying hands, continued to take shots. Within seconds, Connor was draped around her again. This was fast becoming her happy place, and she sank against his chest while his stubbled cheek rested against hers.

"Should we eat before it gets dark?" Her rumbling stomach wasn't letting her forget.

"Not on your life and miss a single shot? I'm not coming back a third time."

She turned to face him and didn't miss the glint of amusement in his eyes. She reached across and kissed him. When she tried to pull back, he wouldn't have it until he remembered the sinking sun and moved away in alarm.

"Sorry, get your shots in before it's too late. Zia Maria loaned me a torch. We'll eat after it sets."

Liz took more photos, each one as spectacular as the last. Connor rose and went to the car, returning with the promised torch.

With the sun almost gone, cars were disappearing and the park was rapidly emptying. Not completely, though. Other couples and small family groups were still gathered on the lawn, some wearing fluorescent glow sticks around their heads, arms and ankles. Further along, a youngster ran in circles holding a sparkler aloft.

When she glanced behind, Connor had spread their banquet out. "What did Zia Maria provide us with today?" This woman was a superb cook. The last picnic was a party on her tastebuds.

"Something with melanzane was all she told me."

"What's that?"

"A traditional eggplant recipe."

"Oh, yum. I want this woman in my life forever."

Connor chuckled. "Did you get enough photos?"

Happy she'd satisfied her sunset fetish, she put her phone away and turned towards the food. "Sure have, Conno."

"What was that?" Connor asked with a smirk.

"You asked what your name would be shortened to if you were an Aussie. You know, there's Davo, Jacko, Robbo, Micko"—she shrugged, doing her best her hold her laughter in—"and now there's Conno."

Connor groaned as though in agony but reached across and pulled her into his arms. She fell awkwardly against him, laughing before Connor pushed the picnic to the side, shoved the cushions under their heads and wrapped her up in his arms. "I'll take Conno any day. It might just grow on me."

The melanzane dish was forgotten for quite some time as darkness encroached on their space and hid them from the rest of the world. Nothing could wipe the smile off Liz's face, but when they eventually ate, the exotic meal left her groaning all over again. Delicious and to die for.

Chapter 18

"Okay, two shovels, one bucket, one tape measure, one compass, one native tree my aunt gladly offered from her backyard and a cup of coffee to go. Anything else we need?"

Liz tied her hair back in a ponytail and, in a weary voice, said, "I've got the food, drinks and enthusiasm covered."

Roberta eyed her warily. "I bet you do. What time did you rock on home last night?"

On the kitchen table, Liz rested her head on her arms. The coffee machine whirred in the background, filling the sleepy spaces in her head like a comforter. She shrugged. "I don't remember. We watched the sunset, we ate, we talked, we ... ah ... well, never mind, it was just very late before we drove back." She lifted her face and massaged her eyes. "I'm going to regret letting a man interfere with what I came here for."

"You'll have to try harder to look like you regret anything," Roberta joked.

The kitchen chair scraping forward had Liz wincing, her tired head absorbing the sound. Roberta sat across from her, alert and eager to dig up the infamous jewels.

"I'm making you a strong coffee."

Liz retaliated with a moan. "I hate the stuff."

"Too bad. You've got to do your share of digging. I need you wide awake."

Roberta rose and busied herself in the kitchen while Liz reconciled with the fact that she'd only slept a couple of hours. Oh, but what a night. They'd lain wrapped up in the picnic blanket until the early hours of the morning. He had told her about his sister living in London and a little about his parents. She got the feeling there was more to talk about when it came to his parents. He also regaled tales of his grandfather and the things they used to do together, a subject he talked about for ages. As he spoke, she sensed a streak of sorrow and loneliness running rampant through him. Since the death of his grandfather and with his sister on the other side of the world, Liz wondered if anyone took care of him.

She'd wrapped her arms around him when he'd gone quiet, wishing she could be there when he needed someone. He might have more money than she did, but it didn't appear to bring him happiness or that strong sense of family she'd grown up with.

Liz had told him things, too. About her desire to finish her degree and how every adversity in the world was holding her back from doing so. Her number one priority was her grandmother.

When they weren't talking, they were kissing and touching in all the right places. Liz's thin cotton dress was no barrier to Connor's inquisitive hands, and in any other place, she might've flung it off to make his job easier. She undid his shirt buttons and, towards the end of the night, slowly unbuckled his belt to give him some space. Her stomach still fluttered that morning, recalling how he had laughed when she justified her actions.

Finally, they parted on the street outside, and Liz had raced up the narrow concrete stairs to get some much-needed sleep. She didn't quite make it to open the door when Connor pursued her and ravished her all over again, leaving her breathless. Sleep was the last thing on her mind.

She sighed when Roberta placed the steaming cup of espresso coffee near her nose and demanded she drink.

The only thing they didn't discuss was what would happen after Falerna. Jewels or no jewels, one large part of Liz would remain in this small village.

She sat up and rubbed her face vigorously before reaching for the coffee cup.

Taking a sip, she knocked back her chair and ran to the sink to spit it out. "Disgusting! How do you drink it every day?" She rinsed her mouth before reaching for a paper serviette to press against it. "High sugar soft drinks will have to do. I'll grab a couple out of Fiorina's fridge and replace them later today. Will that be okay?"

Roberta leant against the kitchen bench and chuckled. With her coffee finished, she turned and rinsed her cup. "She buys them for me, so have as many as you need. I don't want you slackening off today."

Liz shook her head but couldn't stop the smile. "I can see why fate dragged you here to help me." She reached into the fridge for the drink. Popping one, she took a long swig, then took a couple more before being satisfied the sugar was working.

As her face levelled, the coolness tickled her throat. Roberta twirled the rinsed coffee cup on her little finger. "Thanks for putting your holiday on hold for me."

Roberta returned her habitual evil eye. "Only until Marco gets back."

Liz smiled. This was the Roberta she was getting to know. "Still, I want to thank you. Not only am I trespassing on Fiorina's hospitality, but I'm also depending on you to help me find these damn jewels. You know the language, and your aunt is a wealth of information. By the way, where does Fiorina go every morning?"

Laughing, Roberta pushed herself off the kitchen bench and placed the cup on the table. "She helps an old couple most mornings. Does their cleaning and cooking, that sort of thing."

But Liz wasn't finished yet. "Look at you; this must be the first morning you're wide awake and alert before lunch. You've made your own coffee for a change, and I believe you might be enjoying my company for once. When we dig up the jewels, I have every intention of sharing them with you."

Roberta shook her head. "I think you'll need every cent if what you've told me is true. You can put your grandmother into proper care when it gets too tough and have some me time. Now I don't want to give too much away, but this has been my best trip to Falerna so far. I know I'm a spoilt brat and a real bitch sometimes, and for once, I don't mind someone being honest about it. Having discovered Marco also helps *a lot,* but if we manage to find the jewels, what an amazing historical discovery."

Liz stood staring at Roberta, sure her mouth was gaping. "Is this the same Roberta I met less than two weeks ago? Since when did you change? My God, you might actually be a very compassionate nurse when you finish your training. Either that or a history enthusiast?"

Roberta chuckled. "Hey, I didn't say you had to be honest all the time." She arched an eyebrow and tilted her face. "I like you. I'm still not sure about lover boy, but *we* might just be friends after this if you continue to rub your goodness onto me."

Liz's laughter rang around the small kitchen as she clipped the top of the food cooler on and followed Roberta outside. Still shaking her head, she marvelled at how the decision to come to Falerna had brought her into contact with two completely different people, certain they would profoundly change her life forever. Not to mention how finding the jewels could change things, too.

◈

"Hold this end." Liz passed the end of the tape measure to Roberta and ran it away from the wall of the building, exactly five feet facing west.

"There can only be one west, right?"

Liz laughed. "Last I heard." She was very handy with a compass, having spent many years with Sally in the Girl Guides. She held the copy of her notes in one hand while scrutinising the diagram drawn from Uncle Ben's letter. There was only one building in his drawing, but she wished he'd mentioned it was close to the old cemetery. A quick glance at the plaques and it was obvious to Liz they were older than seventy-five years. She bit her bottom lip, looking out past the cemetery. *Damn. I would have felt certain we were at the right spot if he'd added that vital piece of information.*

Frustrated at the uncertainty, she laid a twig on the spot before reeling in the tape measure. "I'll mark an area about one square metre around the twig, and I suppose we start digging. The letter said at the two-foot mark, we should find rocks they placed around and over the jewels. A further two foot of digging should reveal the jewels."

Roberta brought her arms up near her face with her fingers crossed. "Here goes. I hope we don't need a permit for this. How about I do round one of digging?"

Liz didn't argue, and wanted to be out of there with the jewels before any official person came looking.

Her lack of sleep was catching up with her and her legs collapsed underneath her as she landed on the soft grass. The early morning sun dappled her skin, and she shoved on a wide brimmed cotton hat she'd borrowed from Roberta. A couple of cars drove past on the road a hundred metres away, but no one else disturbed them.

Liz's thoughts roamed back to the previous night with Connor; she was losing the battle. She needed to put a stop to her wayward heart because there was no foreseeable future after Falerna. But it was hard to push aside the brush of naked skin, the insatiable pleasure when his lips traced a path from her lips to her shoulder and the way he hardened and throbbed against her body.

She sighed at the same time as she whipped around to something in her periphery. A flash of movement, a blur of clothing. She shot up and ran to the side of the building but saw nothing. She jammed her hands under her armpits, the hair on her nape lifting. *This is so weird. I did see someone. How could they disappear so fast?*

With jerky movements, she used her hat to wipe away the beads of sweat on her upper lip and walked back to Roberta. Peering down the hole, she was surprised to see Roberta had dug down about one foot. "Man, have you done this sort of thing before?"

Roberta stopped for a minute and reached for her water bottle sitting on the grass. She splashed some water on her face and used her hat to wipe it dry. "My mum has a huge garden. Say no more. By the way, where did you run to and what's with the frown?"

Liz explained how she thought she'd seen someone watching them.

Flexing her fingers as she drank, Roberta said, "Don't stress; probably some of the local kids spying on us, or," she said with a grin, "maybe it was a ghost."

Liz wasn't so sure, but she wanted things to move faster, so she reached for the shovel and took over the digging.

Within a matter of minutes, a blister formed on her palm, but she ignored it and gritted her teeth. She made slow, steady progress, determined to do more than her share. Using the sleeve of her shirt, she wiped her face as beads of sweat rolled down her back. Pooling at the top of her shorts, she reached back to flap her shirt and released the sweaty moisture.

"Here, let me do some more." Roberta playfully shoved Liz out of the way and snatched the shovel. "I'm eager to see some rocks, and we're not too far from the two-foot mark."

Liz used the bucket to remove some of the dirt away from the hole as Roberta continued to dig. "What will you do with dirt under your nails?"

"Hold you accountable, of course." They chuckled despite the humid conditions. Watching Roberta's arms strain under her sleeves, Liz couldn't believe how one single letter had sent her halfway around the world in search of lost family jewels. You wouldn't read about it.

She leant over for another bucket full of dirt when she heard a loud thud. Roberta groaned as she lay sprawled across the hole, face down near her feet.

Confused, a movement blurred her vision. A second blow. Something hard smacked against her head.

Chapter 19

Connor spied the time on his phone, showing nine am, and couldn't believe how long he'd slept in. Wide awake, he lay on his back with his arms crossed behind his head. He had long since flung off the quilt, the loose cotton sheet tantalising his body, blood rushing to his lower half.

With eyes closed, he enjoyed the moment, wishing Liz was beside him. He wanted to stretch his length along hers, hold her in his arms and kiss her long enough to leave him in that mindless space where time meant nothing. *I should be out digging.*

Instead, his thoughts were stuck on the previous night and how he'd opened up to someone for the first time. He couldn't tell Liz everything. He didn't want to spoil the night with talk of his father or his family, which was well and truly coming apart at the seams. There was still so much he wanted to say, but not all at once.

He rested his hand on his chest, his heart beating faster than normal. The ease with which he opened up to Liz had his body on full alert, his heart doing extra time. But time was precious and fast running out. The more of it he spent with her, the more he craved it.

Later that day, when Liz was free of Roberta's clutches, he would tell her. It was time she knew of their connection, time to let her know he knew of the jewels. For some reason, his confidence didn't waver. She would understand his reasons for not saying anything earlier.

With a racing heartbeat and all, he swung his feet to the side of the bed, eager to get up and start the day.

He made his way to the old cemetery after borrowing a shovel from Zia Maria. His motives for needing one were vague. It was a flimsy excuse of being interested in plants and shrubs and keen to take some samples back home. He hoped his broken Italian conveyed the right message and his reasons were plausible enough not to warrant too much gossip throughout the small village.

He checked his pocket for his grandfather's letter, anticipating he could estimate by eye well enough as he was not prepared with a compass or measuring stick.

The old cemetery was a good ten-minute walk from the centre of the village. With the sun well on its way to midday, he shifted his cap to angle it against the hot rays.

As he approached the only building near the fontana, he hoped it was the same one his grandfather had sketched on the letter. When he was nearly there, a man was peering around the corner with his back to Connor. He slowed his steps, suddenly suspicious about the man's behaviour and whether he should turn tail and return later.

Liz and Roberta's laughter in the air had his voice jamming in his throat when he tried to shout a warning. Dropping the shovel, his walk turned into a run when the man, unaware of his approach, sidled up the building with what looked like a piece of metal in his hand.

Confused about what the man was doing, he forced his feet to move faster. With fifty metres still to go, the man disappeared around the corner of the building, holding the metal bar as though ready to strike.

Nearing the building, Connor's nostrils flared. *Don't you dare, you bastard*. With noisy breath and his heart pounding against his ribcage, he reached the corner of the building and heard Roberta's scream. Running at full pelt, the blow to Liz's head left a sickening taste in his mouth. Only after she dropped to the ground did a piercing scream sear his throat as a rage so totally out of his control had him ramming his body into the man. The man fell with the impact and grunted. The offender's foot became trapped in the partially dug hole, and Connor threw a punch in the general direction of his nose. Blood spurted out.

His arm froze midair when Roberta screamed beside him. Connor's other fist was still hanging onto the man's shirt, clenched tightly around his top left-hand pocket. In the space of seconds, his hand came into contact with something in it. The criminal roused himself, shoved Connor off and fled the scene. Connor looked down at his hand, holding what looked like a folded letter.

He shoved it in his trouser pocket and fell to his knees beside Liz. He should have held the man in a tight grip and bound his arms and legs until the police arrived, but Roberta's screams had given him other priorities.

"Oh, my God, Liz, oh my God," Connor repeated, cradling her in his arms. Unable to comprehend why they were attacked, he looked up. Roberta rose on unsteady legs with tears coursing down her face.

"We need an ambulance," she cried. "My God, what just happened?" She fumbled with the pocket of her jeans as tears streamed down her face. "Where the hell is my phone?" With shaking hands, she finally retrieved it from a mound of soil and contacted her aunt.

He drew Liz closer, rocking her back and forth, speaking incoherently. Blood pooled near her left ear where a bluish bruise was forming. He lost sense of all time until the paramedics prised him from her body. They took control of the situation, wheeling Liz and Roberta on gurneys to awaiting ambulances.

Connor remained rooted to the ground, too dumbfounded to understand the violence he had just witnessed and the reasons behind it. He barely managed to register the flashing lights of the departing ambulances and the two police officers approaching him. On shaky legs, he rose as they came closer, using every ounce of strength to curb the well of emotion that butted against his chest and threatened to spill over into tears. *Liz is badly hurt.*

As he straightened his back, the overhead sun glinted on a piece of metal about a metre away from where he stood. Instinctively and without a thought, he walked towards it. He stooped down, picked it up and gasped. *Liz's lucky charm.* Thrusting it into his jeans pocket, he had every intention of fixing it back onto her backpack.

⌒⌒⌒

Four days later, Liz continued to lie in an induced coma in the hospital. Four whole days where Roberta declined to speak to him, adamant he was somehow responsible for what happened. Connor refused to let Roberta's suspicions stand in his way, and he drove the distance between Falerna and the hospital at Lamezia Terme every day. When visiting hours permitted, he held Liz's hand and begged her to come back to him, hoping his words were decipherable through a throat constricted with fear that she might not recover.

His stiff body rose from the uncomfortable hospital chair, and he stretched the kinks out of his legs. Nothing could release the bunched-up muscles around his chest. This situation reminded him too much of sitting beside his grandfather's bed in his final days. Liz was too young, and they'd only just connected. Was he cursed?

He bent to kiss her cheek and gave her hand a final squeeze. "I'll be back tomorrow," he whispered.

On his way out, Connor left the hospital his credit card details and instructed them to cover all her costs. With weariness pressing down on his shoulders, he approached the sliding entrance doors as Roberta entered.

"Roberta, wait."

She tried to sidestep around him, but his arm came out and halted her progress.

"What?"

Anger spurted through his chest. "You've got this all wrong."

"Leave her alone, Connor. I'll handle this, thank you very much."

"What about her family?"

"I'll sort it out."

He didn't know enough about Liz to be able to contact her family, and this didn't help his state of mind. He only had her phone number. Breaking into the house next door to secure contact details from Liz's belongings had crossed his mind for a fleeting moment before he flicked it away. It wouldn't help the situation.

He straightened and folded his arms. "Blackening my name with the police won't help. You've got no idea why I'm here." She tried to move on, but he gripped her shoulder, unwilling to end it this way. "The thief who stole her letter in Rome is behind this."

"And you know how?" She ripped his hand off her shoulder and made to walk off. "There's too much going on here that's sus. I didn't trust you the first day we met, and I still don't. Go away. Go back to wherever you came from. I'm taking care of Liz now, and I'll get her home in one piece."

"I'm not leaving, and the police were more than happy with my version of events." He'd decided not to show them the letter he had secured from the thief. He knew only too well how it would appear once Roberta learnt he had the original one the thief stole at the airport. He was under no illusion that the thief had followed the instructions in the letter to a tee and had followed Liz to Falerna, hoping to unearth the jewels himself. What concerned him, though, was that the thief was still out there, somewhere.

"Yeah, you use whatever power of persuasion you like. Throw all the money you can at the police and corrupt them too, but I know something smells off here. You're connected somehow, and I don't like it."

Roberta had no idea how connected he was, and he wasn't about to enlighten her. She stalked off towards the elevators, leaving him frustrated that she should view him this way when it was so far from the truth. But he had to tell Liz the truth first. Roberta would have to wait.

Back in Falerna, the breeze rustled both letters he held in his hand. His heart twisted as he studied his grandfather's style of writing and Uncle Ben's. For the years they had spent apart, their handwriting appeared identical.

Reading them again, it amazed him that their memory of that night was identical when it came time for them to record it. He looked up from where he sat on an old concrete pillar on Il Ponto, the old bridge in Falerna. He watched old men with pipes hanging from their mouths, their hats askew, playing friendly hands of poker between friends. He took in the weather-beaten buildings, some a testament to the hundreds of years they had withstood time. With a start, he realised his grandfather was once here with these same buildings.

He rose and meandered along the bridge. Inquisitive eyes followed his every step. He smiled and acknowledged their curiosity with a slight wave of his hand. Stopping to appreciate the half-mooned tiled roofs in a sea of sunburnt orange, his gaze drifted towards the endless horizon of the ocean in the distance, tears pricking his eyes. The memory of watching the sunsets with Liz was as vivid as the day itself.

When he looked down towards the meandering river under the bridge, wild prickly pear grew along its banks. Immediately, he was reminded of his grandfather's love of the exotic fruit and the lengths he would occasionally go to obtain them. Fico d'India is what his grandfather called the fruit, and Connor had often enjoyed their soft, sweet flesh.

For the first time since arriving in Falerna, his chest constricted at the connection between the grandfather he had loved and the young boy who was raised in this small village.

"Benito. Benito."

Connor swung around at the familiar name. An old, stooped man approached him in what looked like an agonising effort to walk the short distance. Each step an Olympic hurdle. Connor rushed closer to the hunched man and helped him towards a concrete seat near the bridge's rail, all the while his heart thumping against his chest.

Looking into watery, red-rimmed eyes, gnarled hands gripped Connor's arm. He used every scrap of energy his tired brain had left to make sense of what the man was telling him.

"You remind me so much of Benito. We were good friends."

Connor recalled his grandfather's words on his last night and, in an instant, knew this kind, old man was talking about his grandfather's missing twin. Connor seated him as gently as he could, the old man refusing to release his hold on his arm.

The man took a few moments to rest, his breathing laboured. "You're looking in the wrong place for the jewels," he revealed.

Connor gripped the edge of the concrete seat with his spare hand. *Oh my God, someone else knows about them?* In halting dialect, he asked, "How do you know about the jewels?"

The old man smiled with missing teeth, those remaining, blackened with time. "I was there that night. I watched them dig the hole in the rain, but I hid well behind Fetuletti's old house."

Seeming to relax, the old man released his hold and reached into his jacket pocket. With tobacco-stained fingers, he pulled out his pipe and lit it before taking a couple of puffs. Connor inhaled the strong smell, curbing the need to cough it out of his lungs, waiting patiently for him to continue.

After a couple more puffs, he asked, "Who are you?"

In dialect, Connor replied, "I am Nicolo's grandson, and on the night he died, he asked me to come to Falerna and retrieve his mother's jewels."

The old man nodded, continuing to smoke. "It was a tragedy when their parents were murdered. I was so scared the same people would murder my family. I never told a soul about seeing Benito and Nicolo that night." He paused and turned his wrinkled face towards Connor. "I'd forgotten the memory until I heard strangers in town were looking for an old fontana dei poveri. When I saw you today, the memory rushed back to me, and I knew I had to finally tell someone."

Relief swept through Connor. Something hadn't clicked when he'd compared his grandfather's diagram to the water fountains he'd inspected. *But why is there no record of this other fountain?*

He snapped back to attention and concentrated on the old man's next words. "The fontana where they buried the jewels was already old and disused back then. Fetuletti's old house was eventually used as an orphanage after the war. If you didn't know about the fontana, you'd never recognise it today. The building is now used for childcare during the week, and the old fontana faces the outdoor play area. On weekends, there is no one around."

The old man patted his hand. "I missed my friends after they disappeared, and nothing was ever the same. Do you know if Benito survived the war?"

Connor smiled. "What is your name?"

"Saverio."

In halting dialect, he told Saverio what he knew about Benito and a little about his grandfather's life.

When he finished, Saverio rose to leave. In a panic, Connor quickly asked, "Where is the old orphanage building?"

"Four streets back from the café on the corner."

Not wanting Saverio to leave, Connor asked if he needed help walking back home. Saverio waved him away as though insulted by such a request.

Saverio took a few slow steps, then stopped as though already puffed and turned back with a smile. With the skin around his eyes sagging and wrinkling down onto his cheeks, he said, "Benito was a good friend, and in his memory, I will not tell anyone what I have told you." His hands shook by his side. "God can take me now. My duty is done. I hope you find the jewels your family deserves to have. I know they are still there. Benito and Nicolo never came back for them. People assumed the parents were killed for them. I hope they bring you good luck instead of the bad luck that destroyed their family."

When he turned away again, Connor only just caught the rest of what Saverio said as he waved goodbye. "It does my heart good to learn they both survived the war."

Chapter 20

As Saverio painstakingly walked back across Il Ponto, Connor's legs grew suddenly weak. Lowering himself onto the concrete seat, he knew he'd never forget Saverio's genuine, kind face. *I know exactly where to find the jewels. I have to tell Liz.*

The doctors had told him they hoped she would come out of her induced coma today. Would he find her awake if he left to visit her now? He jumped up with every intention of having a quick look at the childcare centre before racing down the mountain to Lamezia Terme.

He barely reached the other side of Il Ponto when his mobile phone vibrated in his top pocket.

His frown deepened when Phil's number flashed across the screen. "Phil, hello, how are you?"

"Connor, I'm glad you answered immediately."

A flash of fear moved across his chest. There was no reason for Phil to call unless something was wrong. They'd exchanged messages during the past two weeks about business, so it didn't bode well that he was phoning.

"What's up, Phil?"

Despite the thousands of kilometres between them, Phil's deep sigh sounded like he was right there. "It's your mum, Connor. She ... she overdosed on tablets. She's in a bad way, and I think you should come home now."

Connor's heart froze despite the searing heat beating down on him. His legs buckled, and he sank against the old bridge, grateful it was only used for foot traffic. He ran his free hand roughly through his hair, the usual anger at his father frothing at the edges, an unstoppable wall of rage slammed against his chest.

"Connor? Connor? Are you still there?"

At the sound of Phil's voice on the other end, he sucked in a deep breath to calm his temper. "Oh, Phil, why? Why did she do it?"

"Look, Connor, we'll sort it out somehow and help her work through it. I'll take care of her until you get back. I've already booked your flight out of Lamezia Terme to Rome. It leaves in less than three hours. Do you think you can make it?"

The phone dropped into his lap as hopelessness assailed him. After a few moments, Phil's worried voice was still audible, and Connor gritted his teeth to stop the flow of tears trying to escape. He didn't have time for that. Wiping his hands on his jeans, he picked up the phone. "Of course. I'll be on it and thanks, Phil. I just wish ... I ..."

"I'm at the hospital now. I won't leave her side until you get here, I promise."

I wish I had a father like you. After Phil ended the call, Connor rested his hand on his chest, pain piercing it from all sides.

On the other side of the Il Ponto, Saverio and a group of similarly aged men looked sympathetically towards him. Did something show in his body language? He shook his head, not wanting to believe what Phil had just told him. What made a person sink to unimaginable depths and do something as drastic as his mother had? *Thank God for Phil.* Connor would easily make it to the airport in time.

His body jolted back in alarm. *Three hours!*

Three hours and he needed to be onboard. Three hours to hope Liz was conscious again so he could explain his sudden absence. *Oh my God, what a mess.*

He straightened, and with a final swipe of sweat over his face with his sleeve, put his head into thinking mode and took off.

In less than half an hour, he was packed and ready to leave Zia Maria's Casa. As he tore down the mountain, his hand rarely left the horn, tooting every corner on that damn treacherous road. Outside the hospital, he joined the best of the Italians and parked the hire car half on the footpath with the other half askew on the road. He didn't give a damn about parking fines, if they existed. His mind was already a hundred paces ahead of his feet, hoping Liz was out of her coma.

He ran towards the front entrance. The modern glass doors slid open to reveal Roberta leaving the hospital. Her hostile glance tore at his insides. He failed to understand the injustice of her accusations and her unwillingness to talk.

This time he was determined to make her listen. She couldn't avoid him as he walked directly towards her. "Roberta, can I talk to you for a minute?"

Roberta made to walk past and threw back, "She's awake."

She's awake. Elation sent a tremor racing through his body. He reached out to stop Roberta from walking past. "Will you listen to me, *please?*"

With his hand firmly clamped on her shoulder, he spun her around. She crossed her arms and tilted her face. "No, *you* listen to me. I haven't trusted you from the first moment we met. There were too many coincidences for me to believe you were genuine. So *you* explain to me how an innocent girl from Australia travels to Italy and gets attacked twice, and both times *you* just happen to be in the vicinity?"

His hand fell as they stared at each other. "You can vilify me all you like, but you're wrong. You don't know a damn thing about me and thank God it's not you I have to convince."

Roberta reached into her bag for her car keys. Jiggling them in her hand, Connor recognised them as her aunt's. "In the two weeks I have known Liz,

I have learnt she's a kind, trusting soul. Too trusting and *too* naïve for the suave likes of you. You splashed your money around, wined and dined her and made her feel loved when we both know what you were really after." Her lips twisted into a sneer. "You can't fool me, Connor. I know why you're hunting Liz's every move. I know what you're after."

With his hands clenched by his side, he shouted to her departing figure, "I'll prove you wrong, Roberta." He had no intention of telling her he was Nicolo's grandson. It was Liz's right to be the first to know and Roberta could go to hell.

He took a couple of steadying breaths, turned and approached the front entrance of the hospital. A relieved smile broke out, remembering Liz was awake and he was wasting precious time on Roberta. *Liz is the one I have to talk to, not Roberta.*

The lift seemed to take forever to arrive; his fingers nervously rubbed against his palms as visitors and medical staff exited. When the lift doors finally opened on her floor, he squeezed his way through them, not wanting to waste a single second for them to slide apart fully.

The first thing he noticed when he stepped into her room was how pale her face was now that the bandages were gone. Her bruised side still had a blue tinge, but the swelling didn't look so bad. Her eyelids opened to reveal her beautiful hazelnut eyes. She smiled hesitantly when he embraced her, drawing her close against his chest.

He spoke against her hair and immediately missed the smell of citrus he loved. Instead, he tasted hospital antiseptic that clung to her body and clothing. "Liz, oh, Liz, you're going to be okay. Thank goodness you're awake; I have *so much* to tell you."

Her fingers clutched his shirt, and he gently eased himself away and slid into the chair next to the bed. With the beeping of the hospital equipment beside them, he took hold of her slim hands and wrapped them between his. They were cool to touch, so he gently rubbed them, hoping to infuse them with warmth. His gaze never left her face, wanting to absorb as much of her as possible. *I can't believe I have to leave her so soon.*

"Liz, are you okay to talk?"

She nodded, but her eyelids fluttered and struggled to stay open. He squeezed her hand a touch harder, desperate to do anything to ensure she stayed awake a little longer. "Liz," he whispered, leaning closer, "I need to leave Italy very soon. There's an emergency at home."

Turning to face him, her eyes opened fully as though his words had sent a shot of strength through her. "I trusted you, Connor," she said with a croaky voice, "but I'm a fool."

His heart dipped.

"You're involved with the thief from the airport, yet you promised me you had nothing to do with him. How could you lie to me all this time?"

Her hands slipped free of his and she turned away. It was clear Roberta had poisoned her mind. "Liz, look at me."

She warily turned back when he reached out to cup her face. "That's not true."

Tears ran down her cheek, and he used his thumb to wipe them away. "I've been meaning to tell you the truth for a couple of days. I've always known about the jewels, and now I know exactly where to find them. After the attack, I put the pieces together and figured out that you and Roberta were looking for them. I was going to that exact place too, but we've got it all wrong."

She recoiled as though another tower of strength surged its way through her. She swept his hand away. Gasping for air, her eyes bored into his. "You've known from the start? How do you know this if you claim you have nothing to do with the thief? Who are you?"

Connor sat back, his heart thumping. Any minute now, his phone alarm would start beeping, reminding him he needed to leave within five minutes to make the flight on time—and he still had a lot of explaining to do.

"Liz, listen to me. I have about ten minutes before I have to leave and make my flight. Will you wait until I've had a chance to tell you everything? I'm not sure how long it will take to sort out the problem back home, but if you give me your contact details in Australia, I promise I'll contact you and explain everything."

She tried sitting up but struggled. The insistent beep from the machine beside the bed sounded as though it were beeping louder and faster. Quickly standing, he grabbed a couple of pillows to support her. She collapsed back onto them. He groaned out in frustration when more tears poured down her face. "Liz, *please* listen to me."

"Stop it," she said with more venom than he expected.

Connor reached for the box of tissues on the stand beside the bed and held them out to her.

She pushed his hand away. "Roberta was right and damn you, the last thing I'm going to give you are my details in Australia so you can organise a third attack. For two weeks, you've led me on, knowing I was looking for the jewels, hoping I'd lead you very nicely to them. Which I did."

He jerked back as though she'd slapped him. "What are you talking about?" He dropped the box of tissues and paced the small room. "Do you honestly believe I tried to win you over so I could find the jewels? You seriously think I need the money that badly?"

Her hand flapped weakly by her side. "You make out as though you have a lot of money, but I don't know anything about you. How do I know you're not working together with the bastard who tried to kill me only days ago? He obviously knew something about the jewels, too."

Of course he did. He had the damn letter he stole from you, he wanted to shout back, but her breathing was laboured and Connor was concerned it would hinder her recovery. He walked back to the chair and sat down. Reaching for her hand, she snatched it back.

Desperate to change the path this conversation was taking, he asked, "Did you *not* feel anything between us?"

Snapping back, her arm made a sweeping gesture. "I know what *I* felt, and I also know what it feels like to be taken for a fool. I can't believe I was so stupid and naïve. I nearly lost my life because of it."

Connor rose abruptly. The chair scraping on the tiled floor reverberated along his skin. The minutes continued to tick in his head, his time fast running out. This exchange had gone so far off the path he had planned.

Panic was starting to set in. "What about you, Liz? You're no better than I am?"

"And what's that supposed to mean?" she asked, angrily glaring back.

He crossed his arms, a throbbing pain jabbing at his stiff neck. "For two whole weeks you kept it a secret. Why didn't you say something about the jewels you were looking for? We were kissing, holding hands, doing all the things two people in love might do, but it wasn't enough for you to open up to me."

"Love?" she scoffed. "Taken for a ride, more like it. And why would I have any reason to tell you about a private family matter? It was none of your business."

His phone's alarm beeped. *Hell*. His legs wouldn't budge, and his eyes closed for a moment. He tried to steady his breathing. *Five minutes, that's all I've got left.*

He opened his eyes, only to be faced with a hostile stare in return. The seconds continued to escape his capture, the alarm ringing louder and louder. "I thought I'd finally met someone different." His mouth twisted in a wry grimace. "Guess I was wrong."

"Why are the jewels so important to you if you don't need the money?"

With time running out, those words scrambled his head.

He stared at her. He had so much to explain. Where did he start with only seconds left? All he could think to say was, "Because they belong to my family," before he turned on his heel and left the room.

Chapter 21

Exiting the Toronto Pearson International Airport, Connor rubbed his tired eyes. A private vehicle organised by Phil or the office would normally be waiting for him, but he'd told Phil before leaving Rome that he'd make his own way to the hospital.

The ten-hour flight had droned on endlessly, and the cramped conditions, even in first class, left his muscles stiff and sore. Sleep had evaded him for most of the overnight trip, while frustration and anger churned his insides. He regretted his hasty suggestion. All he wanted was to slip back into the country unannounced and without the usual fanfare. Would his luck hold out?

He grimaced as he wheeled his suitcase outside to join the throng of travellers lining up at the taxi rank. Keeping his face averted, he shoved on a wide-brimmed hat he'd picked up in Rome. With his mussed-up hair, creased clothing and everyone around him as exhausted as he was, he hoped no one recognised him. A permanent scowl resided on his face, and he didn't need anyone taking a snap and then plastering it over every Canadian newspaper within hours.

As the queue inched closer to the front, a thousand what-ifs swam around in his head. He reached up and pressed against his temple where a throb twitched. He closed his eyes briefly, hoping to stamp it out before it worsened.

Phil had been able to keep the news of his mother out of the media. With his father out of town for a few days, Phil had sounded relieved he was not around to create any extra hassles. *Why isn't the bastard at work?*

He stifled a yawn, refusing to dwell on his father longer than necessary. The primal need to throw a punch that might land neatly on his nose was a scene he'd pictured often.

Instead, Connor stretched his back and took a lungful of crisp, early morning air, longing for it to revitalise his head and keep him awake for the rest of the day. His tired brain couldn't help comparing the early morning summer temperatures between Falerna and Toronto. Of course, this led to thinking of Liz ... again.

Yep, much of his confusion throughout the flight centred on how he'd misjudged her completely. He rubbed his chest where a constant ache lodged itself uncomfortably. Would he ever see her again?

Suddenly impatient to see his mother and ensure she was okay, he ground his bottom lip between his teeth and questioned again why he'd chosen to stand in an ordinary taxi queue. Frustrated, he rubbed his palm against his thigh. If it wasn't for the promise to rethink how he lived, he could have been halfway to the hospital by now.

In the span of two short weeks, Liz taught him one simple fact: all the comforts and advantages of a life laid out for a person could still leave them unhappy. His mother was the perfect example. It didn't matter how much money she had, the eternal happiness everyone looked for, was missing.

He sighed with relief when he finally reached the front of the queue. After instructing the driver to take him to the Toronto East General Hospital, he switched on his phone and sent Phil a message to let him know he was on the way.

Relaxing his exhausted body against the back seat of the cab, he closed his eyes and rested his head against the headrest. The hospital was a good half-hour drive, so he took a few steadying breaths and trusted his mother was out of danger. Trying to ignore the stale smell of cigarettes in the vehicle, he turned his mind to attacking his stupid actions. *How did I get it so wrong?* He cursed his reluctance to tell Liz earlier about their connection.

It would have all been sorted out days ago, and I would have been there to protect her when the thief showed up. Damn!

Annoyed with how he'd botched his final moments with Liz, he shook his head, opened his eyes and took in the Toronto downtown skyline in the distance. The sun was rising for yet another day, but not even the anticipation of a beautiful Toronto day could lift his dampened spirits.

Tired and with a heavy heart, he eyed the dark brown interior of the cab. His stare seemed transfixed on the security mesh that separated him from the driver, and it wasn't long before the small diamond shapes of mesh blurred.

He blinked a couple of times to clear his sight and head. Then he dug into his jeans pocket to retrieve his phone, ready to pay the cab driver on arrival at the hospital. He touched something else smooth and frowned, not recalling putting any coins in there. Dragging his phone out, he gasped when Liz's charm fell onto his lap.

With another reminder of Liz, his heart began to thump. He picked it up between his fingers and ran his thumb over its engraved surface. *A shooting star. Isn't this supposed to be a lucky charm?* He grimaced, retracing his days since picking up the charm at the scene of the attack. He couldn't think of a single lucky thing that had happened to him since picking it up.

He rolled it between his fingers, reminded of his grandfather's pride and hard work ethic, but most of all, his stubbornness. With these thoughts, the muscles in Connor's face tightened, his jaw setting. Lifting his chin and looking out of the moving vehicle's window, he vowed to find Liz in Australia. He knew the name of the town where she lived. If he had to doorknock every goddamn house in that town to find her, he would. Then he would return her charm and explain everything he should've done a week ago.

He swallowed past a streak of stubbornness caught in his throat. He refused to go back to Falerna without Liz. If she didn't want to return to dig up the jewels, he would leave them there forever. If it took a lifetime to find her, then so be it. Just like his grandfather and his missing twin brother, their vow not to return alone for the jewels had never wavered.

With his finger continuing to smooth over the charm, he realised he wasn't being completely truthful. The chance encounter with Saverio was a massive stroke of good luck, and he carried the charm in his pocket that day.

The charm survived a washing and ironing when he'd requested his laundry be done at Zia Maria's Casa, and he hadn't worn the jeans again until the day he met Saverio.

He pulled across his soft leather travel bag and sat it on his lap. Locating the concealed zipper, he tucked the charm inside with the two original letters already hidden.

As the cab neared the hospital, he squeezed Liz into that private place where his grandfather's memories rested, concealed behind his heart. He needed every spare ounce of energy and mind space to concentrate on his mother. She needed him now, and he had to be there for her.

These thoughts sustained him for the remainder of the trip. On the kerb outside the hospital, the driver retrieved his suitcase and set it up on its wheels. Connor thanked him and began wheeling it towards the main entrance.

When he hoisted his suitcase onto the footpath, a white flash struck his periphery. The squeal of brakes alerted his tired head just as a white van careered around the corner in a disorderly fashion.

In that split second, as Connor watched the van approach, he knew it was too late. His scream was muted by the sound of the van hitting the kerb and driving into his right side. The impact threw him onto the concrete footpath, his head crashing against it. There was a stinging pain in his right arm. Then there was nothing.

Chapter 22

A tiny wedge of guilt tugged against Roberta's chest as she looked down at a distraught Liz crumpled on her bed.

"Remind me again. What exactly did he say?" Roberta knew it was hopeless to get her to sit up in the state she was in. Discharged from hospital the day before, she'd lost all interest in eating, sleeping or anything else. And on top of all that, she was supposed to fly home the next day.

Roberta shoved a wet towel under her nose. Liz took it and covered her face instead of wiping off the sheen of tears running their course. Roberta only just made out her words as she hiccupped back a sob. "He said the jewels belonged to his family."

Roberta's frown deepened. "Then who the hell is he?"

Liz's long and mournful groan grated along her nerves, so Roberta climbed onto the bed and sat cross-legged in front of her, pulling the towel away. "Look, it's been a week since he left. Don't you think he might have phoned you?"

Liz shook her head. "You didn't hear me. I was adamant I wouldn't give him my contact details in Australia. I certainly wouldn't ring anyone after what *I* said."

Roberta was finding it hard to control the angry words she wanted to scream out. "Why the hell didn't he tell you sooner about the jewels?"

"Why didn't *I* tell him I was looking for the jewels?"

Roberta had done some online stalking of Connor while Liz recovered in hospital. Zia Maria provided her with his surname and she'd used free internet in Lamezia Terme. Within a matter of minutes, knew the accusations lashed out at him the day he left were unfounded. Article after article detailed the death of his grandfather and the empire he built up from scratch. Write-ups abounded on how he arrived in Canada penniless from war-torn Europe and worked hard to achieve what he had in his lifetime.

She also found stories and pictures of Connor, and there seemed no reason why he would need the jewels for their monetary value. *Why doesn't his grandfather's surname connect any dots?* Nothing she read answered why Connor was in Falerna, so possibly his grandfather *was* born a peasant in this place with no record of his birth.

Then how did the jewels belong to his family?

If only she'd listened to Liz each time she'd discovered a new piece of information or another link in Uncle Ben's past. Hadn't she mentioned a cousin they'd seen in Rome? Hell, there was a good chance a cousin was crawling out of every crack in every continent and chasing the same jewels.

To Roberta's way of thinking, it was *very* odd someone attacked Liz twice. It was also strange how her aunt's gossip had revealed others were asking the locals vague questions about water fountains.

Liz grabbed the spare pillow and hugged it. "He even paid all my medical costs. So now I'm feeling worse."

Roberta's guilt tripled. She was the reason Liz turned against Connor. If she hadn't been so pissed off at the world and so frightened after the attack, she would never have levelled all the blame at Connor without checking the facts. It was time to tell Liz what she'd learnt about him.

She rose and paced the small guest room. An idea was forming, and she was keen to sort this mess out. It only clicked a few minutes ago that she had Connor's mobile number from the afternoon they planned a late lunch. With the number already in her phone, she wouldn't have to ask Liz for it. *I'll call Connor. Apologise and sort it all out.*

Mulling over the conversation she would have with Connor, she suddenly staggered back from the window when something snapped inside her head.

"Oh my God, Liz ... I've got it. OH. MY. GOD."

"What?" Liz lifted her head from the pillow and awkwardly sat up.

"How come you didn't connect the dots earlier? Were you so blinded by love you couldn't see what was right in front of you?"

"What are you talking about?" Liz snapped.

"Connor's grandfather, you dill, *is* the missing twin brother. He must've changed his surname too, just like your Uncle Ben did."

Liz's eyes widened bigger than saucers. She stumbled off the bed. "Oh, my God, Roberta, it all makes sense now. His eyes. His perfect green eyes."

Confused, Roberta scratched her head.

Liz swallowed a laugh, smoothing down her creased shirt. "Every time I looked into Connor's eyes, something kept niggling. I get it now. They are the exact colour of Uncle Ben's. How often do you see that colour? He *has* to be the missing twin. Connor's grandfather would've given him instructions about the jewels before he died as they were very close, but—"

Liz flopped back onto the bed, looking spent; gaunt face and tired eyes. With a sigh, she asked, "Do you think Connor had any idea who I was when we first met in Rome?"

Roberta's brow creased in concentration. "Maybe it was just fate when he saved your stuff in Rome, but"—her finger tapped the side of her face, ideas running riot—"do you remember when we were in that stuffy room with the priest?"

Liz nodded. "He was acting kind of weird as though the air in the room was stifling."

"Exactly," Roberta pounced on her words. "When he heard the real surname of Uncle Ben, he would've recognised his grandfather's original surname. Remember, he fell back or something. That's when he would've made the connection. Christ! And I questioned him as to whether he was mixed up with the thief from Rome." Roberta laughed despite the seriousness of the situation.

Liz turned towards the window. The late afternoon sun slanted into the room and spread across her pale face. Gloomily, she said, "Still doesn't help me. I sent him packing with strict instructions not to make contact."

Roberta let her wallow in her dejected state. She wouldn't tell her of her plans to phone Connor. First things first. "Right, I'm changing my flight plans. I'm leaving with you tomorrow and going home to Melbourne via Cairns. Since this mess is my fault, the least I can do is get you home safely."

Without looking up, Liz replied, "It's just as much my fault. The second attack terrified me, and I was ready to blame anyone."

"Hey, you're not excited I'm coming with you?"

Liz attempted a half smile, but Roberta could tell she wasn't ready to be happy yet.

"What about Marco? Why would you leave a few days early and deprive yourself of his company?"

Roberta knew she had a point there, but she sank to the floor beside the bed and shrugged. "There are Marco's everywhere in the world. I'll find myself another one—and do you know why?"

Liz shrugged and sat up again.

"As much as I hate to admit it, you and Connor had something special. I'll be honest and say I was jealous of you both. Your skin glowed, your eyes shone and all I was getting was a decent shag."

This elicited an almost smile and half a chuckle from Liz.

"I'm going to be even more honest and tell you a couple of days ago, I decided to cyberstalk Connor."

Liz's shoulders stiffened.

"I know, I know, calm down, I know what you're thinking—haven't I done enough damage? Well, let me tell you, girl, you only have to type his name and Toronto on the same line and thousands of responses come up. Loverboy is super famous in his hometown and dirty, filthy rich."

Roberta expected some reaction from Liz but got nothing except for an enormous sigh. "It's probably better this way. There's no point in trying to say I'm sorry. If he's rich, he can have anyone he wants. He's probably already forgotten I exist. I was a quick fling he was trying to fit in. Don't rich people marry and divorce as a pastime?"

We'll see. Despite all the sense Liz made, Roberta was still intent on phoning Connor and apologising. She set her mind to do just that once they arrived in Australia. But first, her travel itinerary needed to be changed fast, and Liz needed to be in a condition to travel the next day.

Good luck with that.

Chapter 23

Belinda Levorico sat beside her son's hospital bed, holding his left hand. She eyed the flower arrangements scattered around the private medical ward and had the desire to throw the pretty pinks, yellows and whites out the window. They looked too cheerful and healthy. Connor's heavily bandaged torso proved that he wasn't.

Not anymore.

She didn't need reminding that Connor was no longer healthy and whole. Bowing her head, the machine beside the bed beeped in time with her heavy heart. God only knew how he would take the news when he woke up.

The doctors told her he was heavily sedated and that it would take a couple of days before they weaned him off the drugs, enough for Connor to be conscious.

They had waited a week before making their decision, giving the bump to his head time to heal. The operation was a success, but they had no idea how the news would shatter her active, hardworking son.

She eyed the official report from the police lying on her lap. It stated the driver of the van suffered a heart attack. When it jumped the kerb, the vehicle dragged Connor against a concrete wall and, with the driver's foot stuck on the accelerator, had rammed his right side for precious minutes, tearing at his arm.

Gritting her teeth, she picked up the sheet of paper and shoved it in her bag.

It's all my fault. With the back of her hand, she wiped away the moisture building under her lashes. When she'd learnt of the accident, she discharged herself from hospital, finally realising she needed to be the mother her adult children had gone without for many years. *I've already lost Lucia.*

She refused to leave Connor's side. With single-minded determination, she refused every single drop of alcohol since leaving her hospital bed a week ago. Her prescription medication, always on hand in her handbag, went out with the garbage.

As the fog lifted from her head where it lay for many years, she gave thanks to a God she had long since forgotten. Grateful for her second chance at life, she was now desperate for Connor's forgiveness.

She laid her head on his arm, ignoring the dizziness and muscle spasms resulting from stopping her medication. She didn't care if she had trouble sleeping, suffered anxiety attacks or had mood swings. Seeing her son in hospital because he'd rushed from overseas to help *her* was the push she needed. *But why at such a high cost to Connor?*

No longer would she pander to her husband, nor would she live in the same house. Apathy had shielded her feelings for many years, while a small part had waited and hoped it could all be healed and fixed. With incredible alacrity after so many years of uncertainty, she knew better now. He would never change. If he did, she would find acceptance of him hard after all the years of emotional abuse. *He can go to hell.*

There was a touch on her shoulder, and she straightened her back. Through blurry eyes, she looked up into the kind hazel eyes of Phil.

Whispering, he said, "Come, I'll buy you some lunch."

Shaking her head, she said, "I can't. What if he wakes?"

Phil reached for her hand. His tall, lithe body was still generously fit for a man in his late fifties. "I just spoke with the nurse. He's not going to come out of this fully for a couple of days. You, on the other hand, need to have something to eat and drink."

Exasperated but grateful, she couldn't understand why Phil refused to leave her alone since she had tried so pitifully to end her life. "Why, Phil? Why are you doing so much for me?"

His intense gaze didn't leave her face. As she rose from the chair, he engulfed her hand, bringing it up to his chest. "Belinda, I promised Connor I wouldn't leave your side until he arrived back. Until he's completely back with us, I'm hanging around." Smiling that beautiful, cheeky smile she had witnessed for years, he continued, "So, if I'm going to have something to eat, so are you. Come on, you'll have plenty of time to talk to Connor in a couple of days."

Belinda hesitated. The sudden warmth of his hand sent a ripple through her body. Refusing to believe it was even possible at her age, she hoped the blush heating her neck wasn't too obvious when she reached for her bag hanging on the chair. Leaning down to kiss Connor, she promised him she'd be back very soon.

Belinda used a serviette to hide her shaking hands. Phil's gaze rested on them as the waiter delivered their coffee and lunch orders.

Phil reached across and took one of them in his. Their food and drinks remained untouched for the minute. Hell-bent as she was and determined not to cry in front of Phil again, God himself could not have stopped the trickle flowing down her cheeks. Out of the blue, someone was being kind and generous, and she couldn't understand why she deserved it. With her free hand, she fished inside her handbag for a packet of tissues, the tears silently dripping onto her pale lemon skirt covering her lap. She bit on her bottom lip, striving to control her emotions. Embarrassment lent a slight flush to her skin.

"You're a very beautiful woman."

Her hand froze, and her face snapped up.

"But I'm married, Phil."

"To someone so unworthy he doesn't deserve you."

"But"—she coughed to clear her throat and to get a stranglehold on her tears—"but … you're like family. You've been with us for so long."

Phil released her hand and indicated she should make a start on her lunch. "Connor and I have spoken over the years. He's a good son, Belinda, and he'll get through this. He's the reason I'm here. I was ready to throw the towel in when Trudy died. My children and family tried to help me heal, but it was Connor and Nicolo who did all the hard pushing and coercing. It wasn't until my beautiful grandson came into the world that I realised I had to keep living and force myself out of bed each day for my family, my friends and especially for Connor since Nicolo's passing."

She lifted a cucumber sandwich and took a bite, her gaze fixed on Phil's strong, angular face as he concentrated on his food. Trying to swallow past the lump in her throat, she said, "I don't deserve my children. I've been neglectful for so many years. I certainly don't deserve you."

Phil put his fork down and looked up. "You've been in a bad place for too long without the strength to pull yourself out."

With shaking hands, she lifted her coffee cup to her lips for a sip. "This shaking is a side effect of not taking my medication." The cup rattled as she placed it back on its saucer. "I should have thrown them out years ago and seen my life for what it was."

Phil reached for her hand again and gave it a squeeze. "Connor will be very proud of you."

"But"—she massaged her forehead, wanting to lay her head on the table to relieve the pressure pulsing behind her temple—"will he forgive me when he learns the truth, Phil? Why did you ask him to come to me? If he was still on holidays, none of this would've happened."

Phil leant back in his chair and, for the first time, she took a good look at him. Rubbing his hand through his greying, dark hair, she noticed the dark smudges under his eyes. They glazed over with moisture. "You don't think the same thought hasn't run through my head a thousand times already? *I* know how hard it's going to be on him, but you're his mother, and he would never have forgiven me if something happened to you and he wasn't told."

Pleading, he continued, "We can't turn back the clock on the last week, but we can be right here for him when he hears the news. Connor is like a second son to me. This time I'm going to be the one to push and encourage, and I want *you* right beside me, helping."

Belinda tried to speak, but no words would form. She struggled to make any sound as she dabbed at her eyes with her serviette.

"When is Lucia arriving?"

She fumbled for a tissue, pulled one out and blew her nose. "Tonight, late."

Phil nodded, picked up his fork and continued to eat. "The doctor will tell us when he is lucid enough to understand. It'll be good to have Lucia here."

She picked up a second sandwich, and they both ate in silence. When she finished, she asked, "Phil, do you know why Connor went to Italy? I asked Lucia, and she didn't know. She said he promised to tell her one day."

"We both know he needed a break, but the only thing he told me was that he was doing something for his grandfather. You know Connor, he's a very private person, and there was no way I would pry."

Belinda reached into her handbag and retrieved Connor's phone. She looked at the screen to check she hadn't missed a call before returning it. "I haven't got his pin number, but I'm keeping it charged and answering all his calls. I'm asking each caller if they were with Connor in Italy. So far, I've had no luck. Why would he choose to travel on his own when he has so many friends who would jump at the chance?"

Phil shrugged. "I don't know. Does he have a girlfriend?"

"None he's told me about. It was only a couple of months ago I made the remark that talk of any women was noticeably absent in our conversations. If he does have someone special, they certainly don't communicate by phone."

Belinda decided she was too exhausted to finish her lunch and sat back, trying to ignore the feelings of depression gnawing at her insides. *I can't even tell Phil if he has a girlfriend. What sort of mother am I? My beautiful son, what have the years done to you?*

She took another sip of coffee, but even that left a bitter taste in her mouth. With sheer determination, she pushed all depressive thoughts away and let her gaze linger on Phil's face. She'd known him and his beautiful wife, Trudy, for many years and had liked them as dear friends. Her heart had gone out to Phil when Trudy was killed, but she never delved any deeper after the funeral. If anything, since Trudy's death, she'd retreated further into her misery and rarely had occasion to cross paths with him. Looking across the table at him now, it was hard to view him in this different light.

Phil's gaze slid across to meet hers, and her heart gave an extra jolt. His dimples, she noticed, were visible when he smiled.

"I'll keep you company this afternoon; then I'll drive you home."

She was ready to object, but he raised his hand to stop her before she had a chance to utter a word. Changing her mind, she said, "This week, I've been staying at our inner-city unit. I won't be returning to my home."

She drew comfort from him as he reached over and covered her hand. The shaking was barely noticeable as his warmth soothed her anxieties.

With his face tilted, he eyed her with a gentle brush of kindness. His mouth transformed into a cheeky grin. "Good. You can come to my place and keep this old man company." A single eyebrow rose as though in warning, just in case she planned to object. When she remained silent, he continued, "I have plenty of spare rooms you can use. You don't need to be alone."

The tension in her shoulders loosened at the same time she let go of the breath she wasn't aware was trapped inside her lungs. She closed her eyes for a moment, thanking whichever angel was looking over her. Phil was a fine man. Together they could go a long way to help each other reconnect with the world and help Connor through the blackest moment of his life.

Chapter 24

onnor lay with his eyes shut; a constant beep was close by. Fluttering them open, he was shrouded in darkness. *It must be night.* He tried to shrug from where he lay, but his right side was trapped under bandages, and the effort was too much. At least his mind was clearer compared to his previous attempts to wake up.

Flashes of the white van flickered behind his eyes, and he was certain it had hit him. While he couldn't recall the vehicle's impact, relief swept across his chest when the sudden rush of memories of that day filled his mind. *If I can remember everything before the hit, at least my head is okay.* Raising his left hand, he felt the bandages wrapped around his torso and right arm. *Broken bones?*

When his eyes adjusted, soft light filtered in from the nurse's station outside his room, revealing his mother sleeping on the settee against the far wall. The dark tracksuit she wore was the type usually reserved for Sunday mornings. She used to say it was her excuse to dress down on one day of the week. As she rested with a cushion under her head, Connor took in her contented look, reminding him why he had to leave Falerna. *Is she okay?*

He licked his lips to moisten them, making every attempt not to move. He was reluctant to wake her while she slept.

He relaxed back onto the pillow and wondered what time it was. With his mind alert, he noticed for the first time an underlying pain on his right side, a throb pulsating to the end of his fingers. He tried to wriggle his right hand but soon realised the bandages restricted his movement.

Ignoring the pain, his thoughts slipped back to Falerna ... and Liz. The two days they had spent in Rome made him sigh, and his penis twitched under the sheet. *Hopefully, no damage down there.* He took his mind back to the Spanish Steps and when he'd wound his arms around her chest. He smiled, remembering how his lips had drunk her exquisite taste as they played along her shoulders and neck. In the darkened room, his eyes fluttered closed again, and he imagined doing more than just kissing. In his mind, his hands gently kneaded her silken skin on a soft bed of lush, green grass, her body taking him to places he'd never dreamt of.

I will find her again.

⁕

Connor resisted the temptation to wake, strangely satisfied as the effect of his dream lingered. With his eyes still closed, he tried to shut out the early morning bustle of the nurses outside his room. In vain, he tried to hold onto the images of Liz, suddenly worried they would disappear forever once daylight intruded.

Quiet footsteps entered his room, followed by his mother and the nurse whispering. The nurse picked up his left hand and held her warm fingers over his wrist. A minute later, she placed his hand back on the sheet. Half opening his eyes, he watched as she wrote details on his patient chart hanging on the end of his bed.

"Connor, you're awake?"

He turned to his mother and her worried smile. She must've left during the night because she looked freshly showered and made-up. The dark circles under her eyes, though, told him she still had a way to go with her recovery.

Wanting to reassure her he was feeling fine, he tried to speak but only managed a croak. She reached for a drinking cup and straw and placed them within his reach. He took a couple of sips, the coolness of the liquid coating his dry mouth. Never had water tasted so good.

"That better?" his mother asked.

Nodding, Connor managed to say, "Thanks."

Suddenly feeling exhausted, he relaxed and closed his eyes. His mother fingered his hair, pushing it away from his forehead as only a loving mother had permission to do. He heard the chair slide closer to his bed and smelt her lavender fragrance, as familiar to him as the citrus scent he craved. It felt good, and the small boy in Connor revelled in the attention he was getting. Its soothing effect had his mind drifting back to sleep, remembering the bedtime stories she would read to him and the goodnight kisses she had bestowed as he clutched his favourite childhood toy.

Cramps attacked his stomach. Waking, he quickly realised they were hunger pains. Dozing in and out of consciousness, he couldn't remember the last time he'd eaten. He craved slabs of freshly baked bread with all sorts of Italian delicacies between their heavenly crusts.

Wiggling his toes, he stretched his legs under the sheet, the soft murmur of voices penetrating his head. *Lucia?* His eyes snapped open, and a sound must have escaped his lips. All talk stopped, and three pairs of eyes swivelled in his direction.

"Lucia?" His voice sounded husky, but she was beside him in an instant.

She half clambered onto his bed and wound her arms around his neck. "Oh, Connor, how dare you scare the living wits out of me?"

Her tears fell onto his face, but he only had smiles for his overexuberant sister. Looking past her, his mother and Phil approach the bed. He couldn't help noticing Phil's hand resting protectively on his mother's waist.

He winced when Lucia yanked on the sheet to wipe her eyes.

"Oh my God"—her eyes widened in apology—"I didn't mean to hurt you, Connor; I'm so sorry." Dropping the sheet quickly, she nestled her face against his chest, tears soaking into his hospital pyjamas.

Raising his left arm, he tucked her hair behind her ear to stop it from tickling his nose. He coughed to clear his throat, knowing it was dry from lack of use. When her tears subsided a little, he asked, "What's the problem, sis? It's only broken bones."

She sat up with alarming speed and, with an incredulous stare, turned to his mother and Phil.

Silence echoed around the room. A strained look passed between the three of them. There was an extra blip of his heart, and he wondered what it all meant.

"What's wrong?" he whispered.

Lucia turned back and squeezed her length alongside his, resting her face on his shoulder. His mother took the chair and held onto his left hand while Phil remained at the end of the bed.

For an instant, claustrophobia threatened to overwhelm him at their closeness. Biting on his bottom lip, nerves churned inside his stomach, obliterating any hunger pains he might have had.

It was his mother who spoke. "You were hit by a driver who suffered a heart attack."

Connor nodded.

"Your right arm was severely damaged. Three days ago, the doctors had no choice but to amputate it."

What? Amputate? No longer there?

Dizziness brought on nausea, and he swallowed a few times to calm it down. He tried to raise his head to look closer at his bandaged torso but couldn't see a thing because of Lucia. He could still feel his right hand. How was it not there?

A tremor ricocheted around his body at the disbelief that all the money in the world was not enough to save his arm. Then it turned to shaking.

Grief and a myriad of other emotions bubbled inside his throat and exploded with a single word.

"Leave!"

His mother's mouth fell open, and Phil's body stiffened. Lucia raised herself enough to look him straight in the eye. "No way, Connor. If you think we're leaving you to deal with this on your own, think again."

His thoughts scrambled to understand what it all meant. All he could conjure up was his inability to ever hold Liz again in both his arms. He shook his head, fighting the tears that clouded his vision. No longer able to contain them, they burst forth. Wretched sobs escaped his throat, muted only by Lucia's shoulder as she wrapped her arms around him.

When the doctor arrived, Lucia reluctantly prised her arms back and climbed off the bed. She reached for a handful of tissues and thrust them at him. He took them and wiped his face, noticing there wasn't a dry eye in the room.

"Hello, Connor."

Connor only nodded, a hollow cavity opening in his chest, bigger than any meteorite could ever make.

The doctor turned to his mother and asked, "Has Connor been told of the situation?"

His mother nodded, wiping her eyes. Phil now stood behind her with his hand resting gently against her neck.

Turning back to Connor, the doctor's features softened. "You're very lucky, Connor. The operation was a success, and you're recovering remarkably fast." The doctor gave his shoulder a gentle squeeze. "I know this will take a lot of getting used to, but you're young and healthy and you shouldn't let this stop you from living a full and normal life."

He tried to focus on the doctor's words but couldn't shrug off the blanket of despair determined to shroud his body. He only half heard his words about 'occupational therapists' and how they would teach him to adapt. He heard 'prosthesis arm' and 'amazing advancements in technology' and retreated inwards.

Jesus, I'm right-handed. I can't even write. What about finding Liz? My god, I had it all planned out so perfectly ...

His thoughts zigzagged from one side of his brain to the other. *How will I escape my father's loathing presence? How can I prove I can do things on my own? Forget about the jewels. What's the point? And what about Liz? She won't want me now that I don't have both arms.* He almost cried out in despair but clamped his jaw tight just in time. *I'll now be the one-armed bandit in Roberta's books. But ... I want to leave and start afresh. Hell, driving a car, wiping my backside ... who will have me now?*

His head spun, bleakness threatening to trap him in a dangerous vortex. Not unlike the water spouts he'd watched with Liz, ready to suck him underneath, unable to breathe. His breathing turned shallow, and the beep of the machine near his bed began a rapid tattoo beside his ear.

"Nurse!" the doctor shouted, and a flurry of footsteps rushed to his side. Within seconds, he felt the prick of a needle and instant relief as blackness descended.

Chapter 25

L ying on her bed, Liz shook off the last of her jetlag and stretched her legs under the doona. Sally had met them at the airport the previous night, driven home to Malanda and frog-marched them both to bed. Neither Liz nor Roberta had argued. Forty-eight hours of travelling since leaving Lamezia Terme had left them bone tired and weary, with sleep the only cure.

Looking at her alarm clock, she noted the time and snuggled further under her covers. Ten o'clock meant she'd slept really well, and it wouldn't be long before Sally returned with her grandmother in time for lunch.

She missed her grandmother and hoped she hadn't felt lost and confused without her presence. On the drive home, Sally had reassured her she had been feeling better the past few days after suffering from the flu for most of the time away.

Liz had winced when she heard this, guilt steamrolling across her chest. *I shouldn't have left her.* With the long flight to mull over her time away, she'd landed at the Cairns International Airport, regretting going.

She balled her hands around the edge of the doona and pulled it up under her chin. She sighed, keeping this all to herself. How could she tell Roberta she regretted meeting her? Try convincing the other half of her brain she wished she'd never met Connor.

The least she could do was not go into too much detail when she shared her holiday stories with Sally. The less Sally knew, the more Liz could wallow alone in her misery.

Roberta lamented the entire flight back, taking the blame for how it had all gone wrong. Liz was in two minds. Had Connor left in a hurry due to a family emergency, or was it only an excuse for ending what they had started? In hindsight, she was grateful Connor was gone. Now that she understood the extent of his wealth and fame, she had no desire to live that sort of lifestyle. How could anyone be happy in the public eye and at the mercy of the paparazzi and media? Maybe one day she would look him up on the internet and learn some more. For now, she wanted to put it all behind her.

What she really regretted, though, was not finding the jewels. At least she'd returned home with most of the money she'd left with. It was small consolation, but her chances of returning to Falerna any time soon were slim. She was just thankful she wasn't worse off.

Try telling your heart that.

She shivered, letting go of her doona and hugging her pillow instead. She wasn't sure if it was because of the two attacks that seriously scared the hell out of her, how events conspired to end her liaison with Connor or the acutely cold winter morning Malanda was having. While North Queensland wasn't renowned for its severe winters, it was chilly enough to feel the difference from the Falerna summer mornings.

And, of course, being reminded of Falerna brought her straight back to Connor. Had he already moved on? Try as she might to forget it happened, she desperately missed how his arms felt around her. Her chest ached when she recalled how it felt when his lips pressed against hers. The memories of how her body had crackled with awareness whenever he was close only added to the anguish. She would miss his humour, their conversations and how gazing into his sea-green eyes transported her to another place. A place she wanted to return to.

With her guard up, she was confident she could keep the memories and experiences with Connor at bay. But after a few minutes of being determined, her shoulders relaxed and her mind slipped back, proving how traitorous her body really was.

Damn! She groaned into her pillow, not wanting to admit she had somehow managed to break her heart again. There was no recourse but to mend it. Slowly. Day by day.

Tears trickled down her face. She lay on her side, using the pillow to stop them from dripping onto her nightshirt. She let them run their course before closing her eyes and falling asleep again.

⁕

Roberta wrapped her hands around a hot mug of coffee and tucked her feet underneath her. She sat on the chocolate-brown lounge facing Sally. "I tried to make contact with you, but I had no idea what Liz's passwords were to her phone or laptop. I could've used the Australian Embassy, but when the doctors told me she would fully recover, I figured it would be easier to tell you in person. She was attacked twice."

"What?" Sally ran her hand through her hair, tugging on it. "I haven't had a chance to talk to her at all. Her grandmother was barely back five minutes and started to have trouble breathing, so I called the doctor to come."

Roberta had dragged herself out of bed and fumbled to this end of the house only minutes ago. She'd found the kitchen and everything she needed to make herself a strong coffee. Still in her pyjamas and hair in perfect disarray, she asked, "Is Liz with the doctor?"

Sally nodded and sat up. "Do you want to tell me how you met and what you know about the attacks?"

Taking small sips of the hot beverage, Roberta asked, "Did she send you any messages about Connor?"

Sally's eyes widened. "Connor? No. Does this mean there's a man involved?"

Taking a deep breath, Roberta plonked the mug on the coffee table and queried, "How much time do we have?"

Sally shrugged. "I haven't got a bloody clue, but I know Liz will bottle this up for months until it eats her insides out and she falls, paralysed. By the time I realise something is wrong, it'll be too late." Scrubbing a hand over her face, she added, "Trust me, when Liz falls, it's a long road back."

"Shit." Roberta reached for her mug again, stretched her legs and settled against the soft, comfy lounge chair. "This might be one of those falls."

Sally chewed on her fingernails. "Okay, you better tell me what you can so I know what I'm in for."

"Well, the first attack happened at Rome's International Airport. I met her shortly after on the train heading down to Falerna …"

⚜

Half an hour later, Roberta sat up and leant forward, resting her elbows on her thighs. "The truth is, Liz won't have a bar of it. It's my fault she was so nasty to him. I kept accusing him of being the thief's accomplice. You know how you get a gut feeling something isn't right, or things are too coincidental?"

Sally nodded.

"That's how it came across to me. It seemed too much. You know … he just happened to be in the same place, at the same time and, as we learnt too late, looking for the same jewels. Falerna is off the beaten track. You don't accidentally pass the place; you choose to go there. So, what was he really up to? He kept using the excuse he was researching his late grandfather's birthplace and, of course, Liz's kind and trusting nature fell for it. Me"—she pointed her thumb at her chest—"I wasn't so convinced, so I made accusations without checking the facts. Once Liz confided in me about the buried jewels, I was even more suspicious, but I was wrong."

Sally rubbed her chin and asked, "What made you change your mind?"

Roberta relayed the events as she knew them on the day Connor left for Canada. "It wasn't until he left and Liz was recovering in hospital that I searched his name on the internet."

Sally impatiently gestured with her hand. "And?"

"Well"—Roberta paused for a moment—"he's one of Canada's richest men, that's why. According to what I read, he is a successful businessman without a single word to tarnish his reputation. He certainly doesn't need the jewels for their money."

Sally let out a long breath. "Holy shit."

"Exactly my thoughts, but it was his last words to Liz that had me intrigued until it finally sunk in."

Still gesticulating, Sally hurried Roberta on.

"His parting words were the jewels belonged to his family. We can't be certain, but I reckon he's the grandson of Uncle Ben's twin brother. His grandfather must have changed his surname, too. We're also pretty certain we know the moment Connor realised there was a connection."

Sally nodded, absorbing all the information as Roberta continued to share it.

"And you know what else?" Roberta lifted her knees and wrapped her arms around them. "Liz and Connor looked good together. When two people gel like that, you get to wondering why it never happens to you. Their eyes shone whenever they looked at each other, and they glowed."

Sally smiled.

"He looked great, dressed in the best, smelt of money, but …"

"Is he Liz's type?" Sally asked.

"I don't know. To a stranger, he was just another cute, rich guy. He never gave away that he was some mega-wealthy, successful businessman. As to whether he's Liz's type, well—there was definitely chemistry there, but a person like her doesn't survive the glare of a camera in your face every day. Don't get me wrong, but I'm not sure she could handle that sort of pressure."

Taking a deep breath and releasing it slowly, Sally concluded, "You know what, Roberta? You're spot on, and thank God she met you over there. But, damn, I'm not sure how comprehensive her travel and medical insurance was. Her hospital stay will cost her a fortune."

Roberta sat back and spread her arms wide, resting them on the couch. "No need to worry. Connor took care of it a couple of days before he left."

Sally's eyes bulged. "Really?"

"She was still in a coma when he instructed the hospital to charge all the costs to him. We didn't find this out until he left, which only made Liz feel worse. So yes," Roberta confirmed, "really."

Roberta rose and picked up her coffee mug. "There isn't much more I can share. Obviously, the jewels were never found and Liz has no intention of going back to try again."

"Damn! I had to convince her for ages to go over in the first place. I went on and on about how finding the jewels might make a difference to taking care of her grandmother."

Roberta sighed dejectedly. "I get all that. She said as much to me." Making for the kitchen to rinse her mug, she added, "I wish things had gone differently, but it's too late now. How about I have a shower and make myself presentable, then give Liz a hand with her grandmother?"

Distracted with her thoughts, Sally gave a quick nod.

And think about the phone call I should make before I chicken out.

Chapter 26

"You've finally left him?" Connor looked at his mother from where he lay on the hospital bed.

Moisture glazed her eyes as she nodded. She used a tissue to dab at their corners, tears threatening to overflow.

Whispering, he could barely hear her say, "Connor, this is my fault. If I wasn't so selfish, blind, and stupid, none of this would have happened to you."

His chest ached with so much sorrow. He wanted this so badly for her, the freedom to live her own life and find some solace. Now she would always feel guilty. Somehow, he had failed again to take proper care of her.

Two blows in such a short space of time. He had to grit his teeth and take it on the chest. *Man up and deal with it.* A catchphrase his father had often used, and God help him, how he'd hated to hear it when he was growing up.

He dragged his attention back to his mother when she spoke again. "You're being discharged tomorrow morning, and I'm taking you to our inner-city unit. That's where I've been staying since your accident. When Lucia returned to London, we decided you'd be better off out of hospital. I know it's only been a week since the operation, but you'll have twenty-four-hour nursing care, and I've been given a list of therapists and specialists to help you rehabilitate. Phil insists we set up an office, too."

Connor swallowed, trying to keep the emotions at bay. He hurt all over: his mind, his body and even his missing arm. "I'm glad Phil promised to take care of you until I returned," he managed to say.

Nodding, with her eyes threatening to spill again, she said, "He's been very good to me."

Phil? He never once entertained the thought that anything could happen between them. Now that it had, it felt right. It seemed the logical solution. He loved his mother unconditionally, no questions asked. As for Phil, he was a loyal and hardworking member of the company. Someone he completely trusted.

Keenly missing his sister and aching deeply for Liz's touch, he turned away from where his mother sat, certain in the semidarkened hospital room she would see the pain etched on his face. This was the price he had to pay for not taking care of her sooner. A tear dribbled down his cheek. The moisture dropped to his pillow, the wet spot touching his skin. He had lost so much ... but at least his mother might have finally found her way again.

The phone ringing penetrated the thick blanket of despair threatening to overwhelm him. He didn't move when his mother rose and said, "I'll take it outside."

It was well past visiting hours, so he closed his eyes and tried to embrace the pain telling his brain his right hand was still attached. At least it took away from the pain tearing at his chest.

⁂

Belinda's pulse raced when she realised it was Connor's phone ringing in her bag. She hadn't told him she was fielding his phone calls; he probably assumed Phil was taking care of them. There had been plenty, if the collection of 'get well' messages she was saving was anything to go by. She wasn't keeping the accident a secret either, hoping his friends would rally around and help him get through the months ahead.

As she sped away from his room, she fumbled in her bag, wanting to get around the corridor corner before she answered and not wanting to miss it.

She spotted the comfy bench-style seat in the wide corridor and swiped the screen as her legs buckled and her backside landed on it. "Hello, Connor's phone." Her hand came up to her chest as she concentrated on catching her breath without sounding too breathy. Shocked to realise how unfit she was, she grimaced, determined to change that. Once upon a time, she used to be a star on the tennis court.

When it took a couple of seconds for the caller to respond, she sensed the phone call was coming from overseas.

"Hello, Connor?"

"No, it's Connor's mother." She took a deep breath and let it out slowly, hoping to sound clearer. "Connor has had an accident, and I'm taking his calls for a few more days. May I ask who's calling?"

"It's Roberta."

"Roberta, are you calling from overseas?"

"Yes, Australia. Um ... is Connor okay?"

"He will be eventually. A vehicle hit him, and things didn't go well for his right arm. They ... made the decision to amputate." Belinda's bottom lip quivered as she said the word. It was still too close to home, and she wondered if she'd ever forgive herself. Sound burst through her eardrum when Roberta replied.

"Flamin' hell! Oh my God, oh shit. I am so sorry; I had no idea."

Despite her quivering lip and roller coaster emotions, Belinda smiled at the language coming from the other end and wondered how this person had come to cross Connor's path. "Was there a message you wanted me to give him?"

The woman's response took more than a few seconds to transmit back. It was as though she had to rethink what she planned to say.

"Could ... could you please tell him Roberta apologises for the accusations she made in Falerna?"

Belinda shot up from the seat, recognising the town's name from something Phil had said. "Roberta, were you with Connor in Italy? Please don't hang up."

"Did I say something wrong?"

"No, no, it's just that no one can tell me why Connor went to Italy. He wasn't able to speak for nearly ten days, and a week ago, we told him he no longer has an arm. He's not saying much to anyone. I wasn't sure if someone in Italy should know what happened to him."

"I said terrible things to him. It caused a rift between Connor and Liz on the day he left in a hurry. He shouldn't hold it against her."

Liz? "Is Liz someone I should contact?"

"I don't know. You should probably ask Connor."

"Can I have your phone number, Roberta, just in case I need your help?" Belinda fumbled in her bag for a pen and notebook, holding the phone between her neck and shoulder. "Connor's feeling very low at the moment, and if there's anything that can help his recovery, I don't want to lose the opportunity."

"Sure." Roberta rattled off her mobile number. "Now, just so you know, I live in Melbourne, which is right down the bottom of Oz, while Liz lives way up in the north. We arrived back a week ago, and I'm currently with Liz. I saw her home first. She was only discharged from hospital herself a day before we left Falerna. I hope Connor sorts something out with her because they had something going, and I might have spoiled it for them."

By now, Belinda was more than intrigued. "Roberta, do you know why Connor was in Italy?"

"Er ... I do, but I'd rather you asked Connor. It was something to do with his grandfather."

"So, what happened to Liz, and why was she in hospital?"

"Look, it's a long story, but Liz was attacked and knocked unconscious. That's when I really threw the blame on Connor and accused him of being involved with the thief that seemed to be following Liz."

Belinda pushed her shoulders back and leant against the white corridor wall. "A thief? What could Connor possibly want to steal?"

"Yeah, yeah, I know. He's filthy rich, but I had no idea at the time."

Belinda fingered the corner of a poster hanging near her head and studied the tiger in an African jungle scene, confused as ever about this woman. "Um, do you know if Connor met Liz in Italy?"

"Yeah, he did. He saved her passport and money when she was attacked the first time in Rome. The next thing you know, Connor's in Falerna, of all places. It didn't take them long to become an item and, in my books, it only made him look more suspicious. Too many coincidences, know what I mean?"

Belinda's frown deepened at Roberta's words. She didn't know what she meant. "Are you saying Connor and Liz were special together?"

"Yes, I am. They only had eyes for each other, but look, you should ask Connor all about it. I'm sure he'll tell you once he's feeling better."

Rolling her shoulders to relieve the tension, Belinda rubbed her tired eyes. "I will, Roberta, and thank you very much for calling. He's going to have a tough couple of months ahead, and I want as many of his friends around if possible. I promise I'll call you back and let you know how he's going."

"That would be great. Tell him not to hesitate to call Liz because she's feeling bad about the whole thing."

Pushing away from the wall, Belinda started to walk back to Connor's room. "Thanks again, and I'll stay in touch."

Belinda tapped the 'end' button and slipped the phone back into her bag. Swinging it over her shoulder, she made her way back down the corridor. *How much of this phone call do I tell him?* She pushed his door open with her foot and decided to talk it over with Phil first. Tiptoeing to the side of the bed, she heard his deep, even breathing. Relief washed over her that he had finally fallen asleep. The doctor warned them the pain would be a constant factor until the nerves at the end of the amputation healed and knotted together.

She leant over and kissed his cheek, touching the moisture still drying on his cheek. *Oh, God. I have to be so strong for him.*

Chapter 27

S ally stood at the kitchen sink, looking out the window at the darkening sky while Liz helped her grandmother with the last spoonful of her soup. She inhaled a deep lungful of the cool evening air wafting through the fly screen, filling her expanding chest, taking in the heady scent of freshly cut grass. Holding it for a moment, she closed her eyes and released it slowly. As though on cue, goosebumps rose on her skin, sending an involuntary shiver along her arms.

Trying not to worry about Liz and the tough stretch she and her grandmother had in front of them, she dropped her hand into the soapy water and returned to the dirty bowls and coffee mugs.

Behind her, Liz used gentle persuasion to encourage her grandmother to eat. The time was nearing when her care requirements would exceed Liz's capabilities. Placing her grandmother in an aged-care facility would hit Liz hard, but Sally and her family would be there to support her.

Roberta had spent the week with them, leaving for Melbourne that morning when Sally drove her to the airport. With Liz busy adjusting to her grandmother's rapidly deteriorating health, Sally and Roberta had indulged in further private conversations about Connor. Sally had read about his grandfather's empire on the internet and had studied Connor's dark, good looks with care. Something about the vulnerable look in his eyes had Sally questioning why she didn't write him off as unsuitable for Liz.

Roberta talked about the phone call she wanted to make, and they had discussed the benefits of it all week. Convinced it was the right thing to do, the shock news of his accident had left them both speechless. That had been the day before, and neither could decide if the time was right to tell Liz.

Sally sighed and picked up a tea towel to start the drying. She would stay in touch with Roberta, but they decided not to interfere unless Connor's mother called first.

Overnight it seemed Liz's grandmother had become fragile, with Liz intent on spending as much time with her as possible. Sally's heart contracted, watching her cousin's attempts to make up for going to Italy and not being there for her. With Liz's emotions raw and exposed, Sally witnessed, with each passing day, how her anxiety etched deeper into her brow.

Turning back to the table, she plucked up a smile for her great-aunt. She struggled to speak much these days, and Sally patted her hand as she reached for the freezer containers on the table. With extra soup cooked, Sally prepared to freeze them in meal-sized portions, providing easy meals for Liz to rely on.

Keeping their conversation light, Sally asked, "Hey, Liz, have you had a chance to print off your timetable for next semester?"

Liz prodded her grandmother for the last bit of soup, her eyes not leaving her grandmother's face. "Not yet. I'll have to do something soon."

Sally placed the containers in the freezer and spoke over her shoulder, "If you need a hand with anything, let me know."

Back at the table, Sally pulled out a sturdy kitchen chair, one she'd sat on a thousand times before. She looked around the room that had served as a second home. She'd been in and out over the years with her memories as full as her stomach. Sharing countless cups of tea, biscuits, cakes and meals, all served with love as she and Liz had weathered life together.

The same old kitchen clock marched time on, and even the sungold kitchen bench tops appeared faded as though their colour lifespan was nearly up in time with her great-aunt.

"Actually, Sal, I've been seriously thinking of deferring the next six months. I'm not sure if my head is in the right space at the moment, and I have a feeling I'm going to be busy with Nan."

Sally turned her attention back and took in the sad lilt to Liz's mouth, her reluctance to look up and the moisture building in her eyes. There had been no time for a heart-to-heart between them; she hoped they might talk about things later that night.

⁕

"I thought I'd stay the night. I've just made you a hot Milo. Ready for it?"

"Thanks." Liz nodded, towel-drying her hair. "I'll just hang this in the bathroom and comb my hair. I'll be back in a sec."

Sally rested her legs on the chocolate-brown footstool matching the lounge suite and let her head fall back. She faced a wall of photos as she took sips of her hot drink and counted the years. The many photos, of her too, progressed from infancy to just a few years ago.

Liz returned and picked up her mug before sitting opposite with her feet resting on a matching stool. "Mm." She took a sip and stretched her legs, her head resting against the softness of the lounge chair. "This is just what I need. Thanks, Sal."

Sally let her enjoy a few moments of solitude before she intruded. "Do you want to talk about anything?"

Liz remained how she was with her eyes closed. "Like what?"

Sally placed her mug down on the small coffee table to her right. "Um ... about your grandmother's health, your holiday to Italy and ahh ... maybe Connor."

Liz lurched forward, her eyes fully opened. "Did Roberta say something?" Hot drink spilt on her shaking hand. At the last minute, she licked it off before it landed on the couch.

"She's worried about you and blames herself for what happened."

"Yeah, I know all that." A worried frown returned to Liz's brow. "How much did she tell you?"

Sally reached across for her hot drink and took a sip. "I know about the attack that left you unconscious, I already guessed you didn't find the jewels, and she mentioned you might have fallen in love with a Connor, who could be the grandson of Uncle Ben's twin?"

Liz put her mug down and sighed. "We're not sure about that, but if the jewels belong to his family, then who else could he be? And Sal"—she groaned painfully—"I said some horrible things to him before he left, and it's not Roberta's fault. I know the second attack scared us both, but the more I think about it, the dumber my accusations were. God, how I wished you were there. You're always so clear-headed in any situation."

Sally smiled at the compliment. "Are you sure he wasn't involved?"

Liz sat back, her lips twisting into a wry smile. "I presume Roberta told you she's stalked him on the net and done some reading?"

Sally confirmed her answer with a nod. "So have I done some looking. Have you?"

Picking up a cushion, Liz shook her head as she fingered its embroidery, her gaze unseeing. "I'm not sure I'll ever be able to."

The clock in the kitchen chimed the hour, dragging her out of her trance. Sighing, she dropped the cushion to her side and reached for her mug. "It was his eyes."

Trying to make sense of her answer, Sally asked, "What do you mean?"

"It never dawned on me. Not once. But when Roberta connected the dots, it was suddenly *so* obvious. His eyes are the exact colour of Uncle Ben's. You don't see that shade of green often, and I still beat myself up that I didn't see it the first time I saw them." Liz rolled her shoulders as though trying to ease their tension before taking another sip. "Was I that blind to something staring me in the face? Freakin' love, it turns a person's brain to mush."

Sally chuckled. "So, you did fall in love?"

Exchanging the mug for the cushion again, Liz wrapped her arms around it. She squeezed her eyes shut for a moment before opening them.

"I don't want you panicky, Sal. We both knew the rules. We agreed to help each other with the research and do some touristy stuff, no strings attached. I just wish he'd said something about the possible connection. But as nothing was discussed, it should've been 'end of story'. Except I'm left feeling like the bad person. Not only did he spend a lot of money on me, including paying for my hospital stay, but I also went and accused him of being a thief, or his accomplice, when down deep"—she squeezed the cushion tighter—"I knew it wasn't true. He was so good and kind to me. I can't believe what I said."

When she looked up, she said reflectively, "As for falling in love, it wasn't hard to do. He swept me off my feet, and I loved every minute. But let's face it, what does a mega-rich guy like Connor want with the likes of me? I need to accept our time together and relegate it to a happy memory somewhere at the back of my mind. I'll send him a letter of apology and a 'thank you' for paying my medical bills, end of story. His business address will probably be all over the internet. Surely someone will pass it on."

Sally knew it was easier said than done for Liz and wondered how many months or years it would take her to achieve that, if ever. As for Connor's accident, when was the right time to tell Liz? Hopefully they heard from Connor's mum soon.

Determined to keep her talking, Sally threw another question at her. "Did the doctor talk to you about the care your Nan needs moving forward?"

The mention of her grandmother was all it took for Liz to crumble. Sally raced over to her and took her in her arms.

"Oh, Sal," Liz cried, "she ... she went downhill so fast while I was away. She must've sensed I wasn't around." Liz's tears soaked into her own shirt as she held her against her chest. "The ... the doctor says there's a vacancy at the nursing home, but ... but I know as soon as she leaves here, it's ... it's like I'm putting her to death. I ... I know she won't last long in a place like that."

Sally tried to console her, holding her in her arms and offering words of encouragement, but knew she spoke with a grain of truth. "Hey, if you're planning to take some time off from uni, there's no reason why you can't visit her every day and make sure she's being properly taken care of."

Liz nodded against Sally's chest. "I... I know." She sniffled and pulled away, reaching for a tissue in the box sitting on the coffee stand. "That's my main reason for deferring." Drying her eyes and blowing her nose, she hiccupped. "I know it's getting harder to look after her, but ..." She sank against the lounge, looking miserable. "I love her so much, and I miss the old Nan. I don't want to be without her."

Sally took hold of her hands and squeezed them. "You'll always have me and Mum and Dad. We all care about you. Got it?"

Liz struggled to smile, more tears trickling down her face. "Oh, Sal, I'm such an emotional mess. Too much has happened in a short space of time and damn it, I didn't even come close to finding the jewels. It would've made it so much easier to pay for the best treatment for Nan. Now I'll be running on a shoestring budget as usual and she'll miss out."

And so will you. Sally's heart constricted at Liz's money worries. She wanted so badly to rally against the injustices of the world, where more money meant you could die in a dignified manner.

Chapter 28

Connor rubbed his bleary eyes, willing them to open. The knock on his bedroom door confirmed the morning nurse had arrived to help him wash and change. She would do some chores first, but by about the third attempt to rouse him from bed, she would enter regardless.

He didn't want to get up. Reaching for the bottle of scotch near his lamp, he cursed when he saw it was empty. *Christ, I just want one more mouthful.* Anything to ease the pain that kept him awake most of the night.

Twisting onto his stomach, he burrowed his face into his pillow, determined never to get out of bed again. In the four weeks since being discharged from hospital, every morning was a struggle. He didn't envisage it ever changing.

He must've dozed off again because further knocking penetrated the fog clouding his brain.

Reluctantly rolling onto his back, he scratched his chin. The three days of stubble pricked his softened, pale hand. He reached across for the remote on his bedside table and activated the button to open the blinds. When he threw it back, it missed and landed on the carpeted floor. His gaze remained riveted on the translucent skin of his hand and the bluish veins protruding. With the full force of the morning sun now shining through the wall of glass on the tenth floor of their inner-city unit, his veins resembled a street map gone wrong. In disgust, he thrust his hand down onto the sheets. How would any woman ever want to hold such a weak-looking hand?

Without warning, his mind overcame the phantom pain that attacked him in bouts when he least expected it by remembering a pair of sun-golden hands laying protectively in his once strong ones. His thoughts floated gently across his mind for a few blissful moments before he groaned out loud and willed his head to forget about her. Sometimes the pain of losing Liz eclipsed the pain of losing his arm.

The door to his room opened, and the matronly nurse his mother employed strode in. "Good morning, Connor."

His response was unintelligible and not worth the effort. He had no intention of attempting to be friendly or helpful. He had to get past the Berlin Wall of pain that copious amounts of drugs only managed to control before he could contemplate looking life in the face again. Alcohol was his second-best friend.

"I believe you have some friends dropping in for lunch today." The hefty-sized nurse manhandled him into a sitting position like some floppy mannequin. No sooner was he up and standing than the usual bevy of cleaners waltzed in to change his sheets, vacuum the carpet, tidy his room and generally irritate him.

His mother's guilt catered to his every whim. Every friend he knew from kindergarten had been to see him, but she couldn't help him with the one person he really wanted to see, unless he told her about his time in Falerna.

Phil would drop in later with work-related questions and issues while therapists and specialists would teach him to write again, brush his hair, eat his food, tie his shoelaces and the hundreds of other things any normal two-handed person did without thinking.

"Would you like a shave today?"

Connor scowled. "No!" He didn't speak much these days, and if the nurse thought he was rude and didn't like it, then she could leave. He couldn't have cared less. *The money Mother pays her must be good because she puts up with a lot of my shit.*

"Well, go have a shower. You have to be ready by ten. You're being fitted for your temporary prosthesis."

It had already been explained that his stump would continue to shrink for months, and a temporary prosthesis was a start until he was fitted with his final one. Without an elbow joint, it would take longer for him to master its use.

The nurse gave him a gentle nudge from behind. Connor gritted his teeth and made his way to the bathroom. It was the mental block that was holding back his progress. He was adapting okay to doing things one-handed, but learning to write would be his biggest challenge. He wasn't ready to face that yet.

Once out of the shower, Connor made for the kitchen and spotted his mother sitting on a stool alongside the dark granite kitchen bench, drinking a coffee. She never failed with a smile and was the only person who ignored his grouchiness. Instantly he would recall her years of hell, and as much as he wanted to shut her out of his life, a small part of him couldn't do it.

Her newfound love for Phil had completely overhauled her. No longer dependant on alcohol and antidepressants, her vitality for life was in direct contrast to Connor's lack of it. While being around him didn't give her much inducement to laugh, somewhere lurking in his head was this need to hear it again. If he ever stopped being a total arse.

"Your phone is flat. I've put it on charge." She took another sip of her coffee and pushed one towards him.

He didn't take any interest in answering his phone, often letting the calls go to voicemail. Without fail, his mother always ensured it was charged. "I've also brought all your mail from the office. You might want to go through it and send out thankyou notes."

Connor twirled the kitchen stool before sitting down. "Burn them. I have no intention of reading their sympathy or sending any thankyou's back."

His mother prepared his cereal, ignoring his comment. He ignored her worried frown.

"Did you sleep well last night?"

"Sure," he replied sarcastically. Sitting down, he pulled his breakfast closer to his chest and clumsily attempted to eat with his left hand.

Out of the corner of his eye, he could tell she didn't want to watch him, but her gaze flicked across sporadically whenever he snuck a glance. Taking the occasional sip of coffee, she tapped the bench top with her fingers.

She looked deep in thought, and her next question momentarily surprised him.

"Were you holidaying in Italy, or was it business related?"

Christ. The last thing he needed was to be reminded of Liz. "Forget it, Mother. It's none of your business."

She swallowed, hurt wavering across her face, but he didn't acknowledge it and continued eating.

"Would you like a hand going through your mail?"

Exasperated, he dropped his spoon, splattering muesli and milk across the counter, and shouted, "No. I also don't need you around all day. Sure, you blame yourself for what happened to me, but I'll deal with it. Go home. Go back to Phil and forget about me for a few days."

He slumped over his breakfast and steadfastly refused to look at her. She slid off her stool, shoes clacking on the tiled floor as she grabbed her handbag off the end of the bench. "I hope you enjoy your friends at lunch; I'll see you tomorrow, maybe?"

Shoving his breakfast plate away, then slamming his palm on the bench, he looked up and barked, "And stop sending every goddamned person I know to try and cheer me up!"

His mother straightened her skirt and avoided looking at him. His heart lurched when he suspected they might be glazing over, but he ground his teeth together in a futile attempt to hide his own pain.

She reached the front door, opened it and stopped. With one foot outside, she turned back and said, "Oh, by the way, Roberta apologises for the accusations she made. She knows they were wrong."

The door slammed shut.

There was no way she would've seen his jaw drop and his eyes pop out.

In haste, he nearly fell off the stool as he veered around the bench to grab his phone. Finding enough charge on it, he quickly searched the calls received until he finally found the one he was looking for.

Damn, damn, damn. A bloody month ago and she only tells me now.

Fumbling with the phone, he swiped the screen until his mother's number came up; she would barely be at her car. When she didn't answer, and his call went to voicemail, he swore and slammed the phone on the bench.

Changing his mind, he slid the phone closer and awkwardly sent a text with his left hand, a skill he would need to perfect.

Within a matter of seconds, her reply beeped.

Two can play this game.

What the hell?

Connor leant over the kitchen bench on his only elbow and raked his fingers through his drying hair. He knew what she meant. If he didn't tell her his reasons for being in Italy, there was little chance she'd share her news. *Does she know about Liz?*

He spun around and stormed off to his room to change. This was something he was getting better at. While he dressed, his mind continued to torment him until he slammed his hand against the wall. *Get a grip!* There was no use getting all worked up. It was only one phone call. *One lousy phone call.* There had certainly not been any others and none from Liz.

As he pulled a Lacoste shirt over his head, one thought jabbed at the outer reaches of his brain. He tore out of the room in search of the box of personal mail his mother had spoken about. Finding it still on the kitchen bench, he poured the contents out and hastily checked the sender addresses. Discarding the ones that didn't interest him onto the floor, his gaze finally landed on the one envelope showing an Australian stamp in the right-hand corner.

With his heart beating exceptionally fast, he turned the envelope over and gasped, reading Liz's name. Fingers tightening around the envelope, he used his teeth to grab and tear it open and struggled to remove the card from inside. He made his way towards the lounge and dropped into its softness, releasing the breath he wasn't aware he was holding.

He closed his eyes and brought the card up to his chest. His head was playing tricks on him when he smelt her citrus scent, as though his nose nuzzled her hair.

Slowly, he drew it back and opened his eyes, holding the card open.

Dear Connor. I hope this finds you well. I wish to apologise for my behaviour on the day you left and want to thank you for taking care of my hospital costs.

Thank you, Liz.

What? That's all? Bitterness welled in his throat when he reread the note. Not a single word of love or missing him. Not a single word to convey her feelings in any way matched his.

So why the hell did Roberta bother to phone? Was she after some financial gain now that she knew who he really was?

He scrunched up the card, his heart plummeting. This was it; he'd never recover. Didn't care anymore. He angrily brushed at the tears daring to roll down his face. He was living in a dream if he thought he'd ever see Liz again, and it was time to give it up.

Chapter 29

Belinda drew strength from Phil. They sat on his beige leather couch in his home, its softness drawing them in.

"Make the phone call, Belinda. You're hurting, and your guilt is going to crush you." Phil pressed his lips against her cheek, and Belinda turned to receive the kiss better. She absorbed his love and concern, cloaked around her like a thick winter jacket.

Her voice wavered, agitated at how her interference had made matters worse. "Oh, Phil, I don't get it. Since the day I mentioned Roberta's phone call, instead of motivating him out of the slump he's in, it's had the exact opposite effect." She raked her hand through her hair. "It's been two weeks, and he rarely showers. He hasn't shaved and is showing no interest in the business, as you well know, and"—she cleared her throat, her emotions tangling up—"what if he tries to take his own life? I know how it feels when you reach that point. I'm so petrified, but I can't seem to get through to him ... ohhh ..." She whimpered, tears beginning to gather around her eyes.

"Shh." Phil placed his hands on either side of her face. He gently kissed her on the mouth and used his fingers to wipe away the tears. "Find out if Roberta thinks involving Liz is a good idea. You'll never rest if you don't. You know something happened in Italy between this woman and Connor, and it sounds like there was some misunderstanding when they parted. She might be able to help him face life as an amputee."

Belinda leant in and rested her forehead on Phil's. Sighing, she said, "I honestly don't know what he does all day. He drinks too much, but apparently, I'm not qualified to suggest he stop. I'm not even certain if it's the phantom pain he's trying to dull anymore. He's popping too many painkillers, and he's not eating properly. He's lost so much weight he looks gaunt and unwell."

She looked up into Phil's worried face; he was carrying her burden and Connor's. She clamped down on her teeth to stop any further tears. It was well past the time for crying. It was time for action and Phil was right. *Thank God.* She met his gaze and let the usual rush of gratitude flood her body, reciting a quick prayer to the angel responsible for taking care of her.

"It should be early morning in Australia if you phone now." Phil roused himself from her gaze and rose. "We'll use the phone in the office." He took her hand, clasped it firmly and smiled. "We'll get through this, Belinda. I promise you."

⁂

Liz flicked through the midweek paper, relaxing over breakfast after a good night's sleep. Her grandmother had been exceptionally well since being admitted to the aged-care facility. Surprised, Liz barely contained her tears when her grandmother chatted with her numerous times the previous day as if dementia had never come between them.

Chewing another mouthful of cereal, she mentally ran through the list of things to do that day and still be at the nursing home by ten. Her chores all clear in her mind, she hunched over the paper again. With her hair hanging loose around her face, she idly tucked it behind her ears, continuing to read the day's news. She looked up when her mobile phone rang.

For a couple of heartbeats, she wondered if it was the nursing home. She stumbled out of the kitchen chair in haste to reach it before it ended.

"Hello."

There was a distant clicking in her ear—the usual telemarketer calling from overseas. Rarely did she give them a chance to speak before ending the call. She was about to tap the red 'end call' button when a woman with an accent, much like Connor's, spoke.

"Hello, is this Liz?"

Hesitantly, she answered, "Yes, who's calling?"

"I'm Connor's mum, Belinda, and I was hoping I could take a few minutes of your time to chat with you about Connor."

Her heart thumped. "Is Connor okay?"

"Not really …"

Liz sunk to the kitchen floor as Connor's mum told her the news, her free arm hugging her chest. When it seemed that Belinda had told her everything, Liz winced, lamenting the loss of Connor's arm as though her own had been ripped from its socket. "How did you get my phone number?"

"Roberta," she said, pausing for a split second before continuing, "and you're not to get angry with her. She rang about six weeks ago when Connor was barely conscious to apologise for what she'd said to him."

Sitting up straighter, resentment speared through Liz's chest. "So, she already knows about the amputation?"

"Yes, and that's why it's important you don't take it out on her. She knew you would feel this way, but at the time, both Roberta and your cousin Sally thought it was best to wait until I made contact again before telling you anything."

Sally, too?

"I'd also hoped Connor might've said something to me, but he's been very tightlipped about his trip to Italy, and I've only learnt a little from Roberta."

Cracking her knuckles against the tiled floor, Liz snapped, "Well, what am I supposed to do?"

"Well … I was hoping …"

Across the thousands of kilometres between them, Liz sensed she'd hit a raw nerve with her abrupt words and knew the quiver in Belinda's voice was not because of any interference on the line. Cringing, she blurted, "I'm sorry. I didn't mean to say it like that. I'm sorry for what's happened to Connor, and I would like to help."

And see Connor again?

"Thanks, Liz. I'd appreciate anything you can do. You're the last straw. I need someone to help him out of the dark hole he's buried himself in. Roberta told me about your grandmother and how her health is deteriorating rapidly. If you feel you cannot possibly do what I am about to ask, I will understand. But ... I just need someone who can make Connor realise his life is worth living. Roberta said he fell in love with you and ... and I'm desperate, Liz ... really desperate to get my son back. I'll do anything."

Love?

Belinda's voice wavered on the last sentence, and she let out a small cry followed by a sniff. With her bottom lip caught between her teeth, Liz dug her fingers back and forth across her scalp and squeezed her eyes tight, preparing for the request she knew was coming.

"All you need to do is name a day and turn up at the airport. I'll have everything organised from my end. You don't even have to stay long." Belinda sniffled, and Liz dropped her head back, looking up at the ceiling.

Do I open Pandora's Box and expose myself to all those feelings again? Sighing, she closed her eyes again, and a pair of sea-green ones framed by dark hair and a gorgeous dimple sat right before her. If she concentrated hard enough, she could feel the graze of his fingers on her cheek and smell his expensive cologne. But what about Nan? Could she risk being away from her again? She opened them again when Belinda continued speaking.

"Liz? Liz? Are you still there?"

Taking a deep breath, she answered, "Yes, I'm still here."

"I know it's a long way for you to come, but I'm hoping your presence might jolt him out of his depression. He's not in a good place."

And where will it put me? Somehow, she'd relegated Connor's memory to the deep recesses of her heart, taken out on special occasions where she could relive them alone.

"Liz ... are you okay? I don't mean to upset you, but from what Roberta said, you might've parted on a misunderstanding?"

Liz couldn't help the groan she sent hurtling down the line. Her face dropped to her raised knees while her eyes burned with unshed tears. "You could say that."

"Oh, Liz, I'm really sorry this happened. Will you think about my request? Can I phone you tonight, your time? I promise, whatever your answer is, I won't force you to do anything you don't want to do. I'm desperate because ... because he's such a mess."

When Belinda's crying became audible again, Liz sat up and waited, giving her some time.

After a few moments, Liz ventured to say, "Are you okay?"

"Oh, Liz, it's my fault he flew back to Canada that day. If it wasn't for my stupidity, none of this would've happened."

Liz had no idea what she meant, and it wasn't her place to ask. She remembered Connor saying he had to return for a family emergency. Her heart went out to Belinda who, after all, was a mother doing the best she could for her son. "Belinda, ring me later tonight, and I promise I'll have an answer. I have to see if I can make arrangements for my grandmother. I can't promise more than a few days if I agree to come."

The rush of relief flowed down the line to Liz, who had now risen and was pacing the kitchen floor.

"Thank you, Liz, thank you so much. I'll ring you at about eight tonight."

Liz dropped the phone onto the kitchen table after the call ended. Shock set in. *Connor without an arm?* She rubbed the back of her neck, her muscles twitching under her skin. Trying as hard as she could, her mind was determined to remember Connor with both arms. Especially when they'd been wrapped tightly around her.

She leant over the kitchen sink and stared out into the yard. There was a lot to process. Belinda had said it was his right arm, so that meant a lot of life-changing adjustments for Connor to accept. Could she help him? All this time since leaving her in Falerna, he'd been dealing with this, and she'd had no idea. Should she phone him? His number was still in her list of contacts and she'd been so close to deleting it many times. She pushed the thought away. If Connor was in a bad way, she would wait until she was there in person. *Oh, Connor, I'm so sorry for doubting you.*

She moaned into the quiet of the house and wearily rubbed her eyes. *First things first.* A phone call was necessary to Roberta and Sally to blast the blazes out of them for keeping her in the dark. She would hold Sally to ransom for keeping this a secret, and she and her mum would have no choice but to take care of Nan for a few days.

Thank God she's been really good lately. A weight lifted from her chest.

She pushed back from the sink and began to laugh. So much so, happy tears streamed down her face. Sally and her mum would jump at the opportunity to help her out, so there was no decision to make.

She was going to Toronto to see Connor.

Crazy piano accordion music started playing in her head, and she erupted into a dance—alone—in her kitchen, twirling and spinning wildly until she spun out of control and stumbled to the floor. There she sat for ages, with a grin from ear to ear and her arms wrapped around her knees. Was it possible seeing Connor again might make her happy?

Chapter 30

L iz stood in front of the elaborate dresser combing her hair and trying to ignore the butterflies swirling in her stomach. She put down her comb, reached for her lipstick and dabbed some on.

She'd arrived in Toronto late the previous evening and was whisked away from the airport by Belinda's personal driver, Adrian. She'd slept very little on the flight over. Once she was seated on the plane, with the two hectic days of preparation behind her, she'd had trouble settling. With too much time to think, her thoughts seemed intent on invading her personal space. *What if Connor is too messed up?* She pictured his dark hair falling across his vibrant eyes. Heard his witty laughter. Recalled the beating of his heart when he held her in his arms. Felt the touch of his lips as they brushed against hers.

She couldn't picture a troubled man with one arm.

Sighing, she ran her fingers through her hair, deciding not to tie it back. After her arrival and introduction, Belinda had organised a chamomile tea and a toasted sandwich before insisting she went to bed to allow her body to sleep away the jetlag.

Making a weird face at herself in the mirror, she almost laughed but instead allowed a small smile to emerge. She'd had a good nights' sleep and was feeling refreshed.

Reaching for the jug of water on the dresser, she gulped down half a glass before grabbing her handbag. She opened it and checked her phone was switched on. Sally promised to send her daily updates on her grandmother, and she didn't want to miss any of them.

She took one last glance at herself in the mirror and hoped her snug jeans and comfortable cotton shirt were appropriate. Then she dismissed the thought. What did it matter how she dressed? Grabbing her jacket from the back of the chair, she made for the door. She took a deep breath, held onto it for a few seconds, then released it slowly before turning the handle. *Breakfast first, then I get to see Connor.*

Adrian held the car door open, allowing her to step inside. "Morning, Miss Liz."

Liz put on her sunniest smile, returned his greeting and thanked him for his help. The weather resembled a perfect autumn morning, but she buttoned up her jacket to keep that little bit warmer. Belinda followed her, turning to wave goodbye to Phil, who was leaving shortly to go to the office.

It was hard to miss the dark circles under Belinda's eyes. Worry was etched on her face as her hands smoothed and re-smoothed her soft, aquamarine skirt.

"We're only a few minutes' drive from where Connor is staying." Belinda absently pinched the skin at her throat as she turned to Liz. "I hope he's had a restful couple of days. I haven't seen him since the day I phoned you." She turned back towards the car window and muttered, "He wanted a bit of space."

Liz reached across and squeezed her hand. "I hope I can make a difference." When Belinda faced her again, Liz smiled, saying, "Let me guess, stubborn as a mule?"

Belinda tried to smile, but it was a hard-fought war between wanting to smile and wanting to cry, and it wasn't long before tears trickled down her cheeks. "Just like his grandfather." She sniffled into a tissue.

Liz held onto her smile. Where did Belinda's husband fit in? She understood enough to know Phil wasn't her husband. Connor had told her his parents were married. Was that conversation only two months ago? Had so much changed for Connor in that time?

She had little time to think further as Adrian turned into an underground car park. The sudden lack of sunlight dampened her spirits and left her pulse floundering in the dark. *What if I can't make a difference? What if Connor doesn't want to see me?*

⁕

Connor lay awkwardly with his left shoulder digging into something hard. He wasn't lying on his bed, but he couldn't remember why. His mouth tasted papery, and slowly, the memory of how much alcohol he'd drunk the previous night slipped into his memory bank. Absently, he ran his tongue over dry, caked lips and moaned. Pins and needles pierced his skin when he shifted on the couch.

As though stuck together with glue, he struggled to prise his eyes apart. The bright shafts of light streaming through the windows aimed straight for his pupils, and his reflexes slammed them shut again. *Shit, I forgot to close the blinds. Where the bloody hell is the remote?* There were three remotes somewhere, and he didn't have the faintest idea where any of them were.

With his eyes firmly closed, he heard noises coming from his bedroom. It didn't sound like the usual noises his nurse would make. He shifted his head to hear it better. His teeth clamped down hard when he recognised the sounds consistent with two lovers in bed. *Is this why I'm sleeping out here?* He had the urge to cover both his ears with his hands until he remembered he only had one hand. The usual blackness descended on him, coating itself around his heart, leaving him hopelessly depressed and wanting to bawl like a small child.

His father had insisted on organising a party with a few old friends. Connor had gone along with the suggestion, not caring. He'd lost count of how many arrived and how few were his friends. The easy flow of drinks had dulled his mind.

Shifting to a more comfortable position, he half suspected a couple of empty beer bottles were digging into his skin. If he rolled away, he'd only find pain of another sort. Choosing the lesser of the two evils, he stayed put. He would try sleeping again and not wake up for the rest of the day. His sore head could use more sleep.

He tried shutting out the muted groans coming from his room while his nose twitched at the smell of cigarette fumes punctuating the air. For some reason, he couldn't tolerate its stench that morning, and its odour pressed down, heavily coating the clothes he wore from the previous night. *Bloody hell, I must've flaked out right here.*

The sound of a key turning in the front door lock interrupted his attempt to nod off; it would be the nurse. *She'll sort out the pair in the bedroom, whoever they are.*

Unintentionally listening for the sound of the nurse's flat work shoes, he frowned when he heard the clack of heels and what sounded like a second pair of shoes. *Mother?* She hadn't been to see him for nearly a week, but he'd been too stubborn to ring and apologise. He was no better than his father.

The footsteps sounded closer, which meant they were past the kitchen and heading towards the lounge.

"Connor?"

His heart did a triple beat at his mother's anguished voice. When his eyes snapped open, his world tilted when he stared into the tormented face of his mother and the hallucination of Liz standing beside her.

With his hand trembling and dizziness a threat, he struggled to sit up. Rising to face his mother and Liz, his weakened legs shook in his jeans. It only worsened as he surveyed the full impact of the previous night's disgrace.

Disappointment was written across his mother's face, and it oozed from every crevice of her body. Her shoulders drooped and, for once, her make-up didn't hide her weariness. She looked around the room, and Connor followed her movements, not daring to look at Liz. *What is she doing here?*

There were empty beer and spirit bottles strewn everywhere. Ashtrays overflowed with cigarette butts, and trays of partially eaten food were scattered around the room. Chairs lay toppled on the floor.

His bedroom door opened, and Connor's jaw dropped when his father walked out wearing a white, long-sleeved shirt with one button done up and nothing else, his crotch visible. A young woman clinging to his arm and giggling wore a thin slip that did nothing to cover her nakedness.

His father stopped midstride, taking in his audience. To Belinda, he said with a sneer, "Belinda, my dear good wife, I hope Phil is keeping you warm at night?" He reached for the young women's bare buttocks and gripped one half. Pulling her close to his side as they sauntered off, he remarked, "We're going to enjoy a shower together. It was nice to catch up with you."

The bathroom door closing was the only sound for many awkward heartbeats until his mother whispered in a broken voice. "Why?"

Connor didn't have the energy to shrug, and he couldn't turn to acknowledge Liz. He willed himself not to look at her golden, honey skin. If he did, he would want to run his lips along its smoothness to taste how sweet it used to be. He clenched his jaw to keep from taking the few necessary steps so he could wind his fingers through her silky hair. And he didn't dare look into her soulful eyes.

The persistent sound of a mobile phone punctuated the quiet air. No one moved. The phone stopped ringing. After a few seconds, it began again, and Connor snapped his gaze in Liz's direction when she exclaimed, "Oh, it's my phone."

⁕

The sound of her phone ringing finally penetrated the shock that shrouded her from the first moment she walked into the room. Connor looked so sick and unwell that it was hard to believe he was the same man. She stood beside Belinda, gaping, embarrassed and finally understanding how Connor's father fit in the picture.

Whipping her bag off her shoulder, she unzipped it and reached for the phone. Sally's name flashing on the screen sent alarm bells clanging against her chest. She half turned away from the others, swiping the screen to answer the call.

"Sally, I'm here. Sorry I didn't pick up the first time." Her last message from Sally the previous night confirmed all was well with her grandmother.

"Oh, Liz, it's your nan. She's had a bad turn, and it doesn't look good. We need you to come home straight away."

Liz shut her eyes and inwardly groaned. Nan had been so good for nearly a week. *Why? Why now, damn it?* Why had she decided to leave? Her grandmother must've sensed she wasn't there. Tears welled up behind her lids, and she gripped the phone tighter as Sally desperately tried to get her attention.

"Liz, Liz are you there?"

Taking a deep breath, tears brimmed on the edge of her lashes. "Yes, Sal, I'm still here, and I'll make my way back immediately. I'll ring you as soon as I'm organised."

Ending the call, she took a moment to focus on what she needed to do when an unexpected shaft of anger zapped her on the shoulder and coursed its way along every muscle in her body. She straightened and dashed away her tears with her jacket sleeve. Turning to Connor, she unleashed all the anger and hurt she felt for not being by her grandmother's side in her final days.

"Look at you," she spat, her eyes tiny slits. "Every damn service at your side, all the money in the world to help you overcome your disability, and *this* is how you do it?" She flung her arms wide to take in the disgraceful mess around her. "I would've done *anything*"—she stomped her foot as though the shaft of anger earthed on that spot—"to have some extra cash to make my grandmother's final days a little better, but *damn you*, I didn't have anything spare, so I could give her the extra care she deserved. And you!"—she poked him in the chest with her pointer finger—"I come all this way to try and help you when you can't be bothered to help yourself!"

Connor stared, unmoving.

Her fist whacked the side of her leg. "Look at this ... it sickens me."

Gulping a couple of times, knowing she would soon unleash more than anger as her vision blurred, she warned, "God help you, Connor, if my grandmother dies before I get the chance to return, I promise I will *never* forgive you."

She spun on her heel and grabbed Belinda's arm. Only then did the tears come tumbling down her face. "Belinda, I am so, *so* sorry, but I need to go home now." She didn't try to check or wipe them away.

Belinda showed regret and sorrow, with moisture building up around her eyes, too. Immediately she said, "Of course. You make your way downstairs to Adrian. I'll phone him now. By the time he collects your luggage and drives you back to the airport, I'll have everything organised."

Belinda embraced Liz and said, "Thank you so much for coming and good luck with your grandmother," before walking her to the door.

⁘

Connor hadn't moved an inch and couldn't remember drawing breath the entire time Liz hurled her accusations. He choked noisily, trying to draw air in through his nose after the door closed loudly behind her. At the same time, his heart gave an enormous thump, the shock nearly causing him to stumble back onto the couch.

His mother leant heavily against the wall, talking on her phone to Adrian. With effort, she straightened her body, even though she looked drained of every drop of blood. Then she opened the door and left without a single glance in his direction. At the same time a door slammed hard against his chest, holding in new hurt he never knew existed.

Left alone, with only the sound of the shower running, Connor staggered back the few steps to the couch, and his body fell into a crumbled heap. *Liz was here, in this apartment, in Canada.* He replayed her words over and over, the bitter tang in his mouth spreading to the back of his throat. A burning sensation spread along his veins, and his flesh crawled at his unclean and rank body.

Wishing to be anywhere but where he was, he knew he was defeated, and his dam finally burst. Wracking sobs tore at his body. Grief was a tidal wave that washed away every shred of normality he hoped he might still have. He cried as he'd never cried before, falling into an exhausted sleep fuelled by despair.

The sun was already beginning its descent when he woke many hours later. He stumbled to his feet and looked in awe at the now spotless unit. He'd had a dream and desperately tried to hold onto it as he made his way to his room. There was no sign of his father or anyone else, and he didn't expect there to be. Opening his wardrobe, he shifted things aside, certain he'd seen it somewhere.

The phantom pain shooting through his missing arm as he shoved aside shoes and boxes, having no idea what they contained, almost sent him to his knees. After a few seconds and many deep breaths, relief swept through him. When he caught sight of the travel bag he'd used in Falerna, he sagged against the wardrobe wall.

Holding it tight against his chest, he carried it back to the couch, too scared to part with it again. He found the concealed zipper and the shiny lucky charm he remembered placing there for safekeeping. He fingered it as he had done before, mesmerised by the shooting star.

He knew what he had to do.

Rising and making his way to the kitchen, he found his phone, scrolled through the numbers, stopped at the one he needed and made the call.

When the person picked up, he said, "I need your help."

Chapter 31

L iz never made it.

She raced through the front entrance of the Cairns Base Hospital
with Sally one step behind. Ignoring the lift, she tore up the two flights of
stairs. The moment she saw the curtains drawn, she knew she was too late.

Whipping aside the screen, she spotted her aunt and uncle speaking
to the nurse near her grandmother's bed. With enough updates during
stopovers to indicate it was close to her grandmother's time, her raw
emotions had already spilled over numerous times on the flight.

Already blubbery, nothing could stop a fresh torrent from pouring out.
The sight of her grandmother looking like she was only asleep broke all
her leftover reserves. Her wail echoed around the room. She threw herself
at her grandmother and rained tears over her still-warm body. She shook
while sobs racked her tired and exhausted body, and her arms draped
around her grandmother, unwilling to let go.

Minutes, or it could have been hours, she lay there drawing in the last of
her nan's warmth. She had no idea of time. Eventually, gentle hands prised
her from the bed. Frozen in that position, her uncle picked her up and
cradled her in his arms. Only then did her muscles move, and she collapsed
against his chest.

"Honey, it's time we let them take care of your nan," her uncle said,
carrying her away.

She must've fainted because her world turned black, and she gladly
embraced the darkness.

Chapter 32

F *our Months Later*

Connor sat on the timber picnic table under the arching branches of a tropical tree he didn't recognise. His feet rested on the long, bench-style seat bolted to it. It was spotted with bird droppings and bits of leaves and berries from the branches above, that had long since dried and weathered to its surface.

With his elbow resting on his thigh, he swung a water bottle in his hand and it hit the insides of his knees with a soft tap. Sweat dripped down his back, the dense humidity threatening to crush his lungs each time he took a breath of hot air. He tilted his face up, holding the water bottle between his knees, pushing his sunglasses up his nose again. As hot as it was, he was relieved the tree was doing its best to shade him from the worst of the day's heat, even at four o'clock in the afternoon.

Digging into the pocket of his cut-off jeans for a handkerchief, he used it to wipe the sweaty sheen off his face and took another sip of water. He smiled when he recalled Liz's horror when he'd cut his Gucci jeans. He still relied on memories of those two weeks to get him through his days.

He glanced at the time on his phone. The nervous beat of his heart picked up, leaving him slightly nauseous. He looked across the car park to make sure he hadn't accidentally missed Liz's exit from the Cairns campus of James Cook University. Sally had described her white Mazda and quoted her number plate. It remained in his peripheral vision the entire time.

He'd only spoken with Sally twenty minutes ago, and she assured him Liz would finish shortly after four, as they had arranged to meet in the city later.

Connor sighed, keeping a watch on the sliding glass doors she'd be exiting from. His thoughts returned to the last time he'd seen her. The harsh words she'd spoken about never forgiving him if her grandmother died without her by her side still tormented him. Roberta had called to tell him she'd never made it in time. The fear that she would not talk to him gnawed away at his insides.

Seeing her that day worked its magic, though. Waking up and finding a spotlessly clean unit and no sign of his father was all the encouragement he needed to dig out the lucky charm and phone his mother, begging for help.

This time around, he embraced the specialists, took an interest in the business again and told his mother and Phil his reasons for travelling to Falerna.

Together with Phil's help, he contacted his relatives in Rome. The Frevannini relatives were stunned at the news that the twin boys had survived the war, and they planned a reunion soon. The jewels' existence was the only thing they didn't discuss. Connor was adamant it was kept a secret until he was certain they were still buried.

Two weeks ago, he dropped the bombshell. Taking another drink from his water bottle, he smiled, recalling their reaction. He told his mother and Phil he was selling his share of the business, offering his share to Phil, and moving to Australia.

Phil had sat stunned for a full minute before bursting with laughter. "You're not going to believe this, Connor, but I've already been thinking of selling my small shareholding. I have a couple of interested investors." Phil had reached across, taken his mother's hand and brought it to his lips. "Your mother and I are not getting any younger and would like to do some travelling. With the divorce finalised, we have more than enough money to see us through, and I think it would be good for both of us."

Connor looked at them and envied what they had found together, but his heart lurched at Phil's next words.

"Now, Connor, if we were to add your share of the business and mine together and the same investor buys all of it, that would make it a controlling share, and I think your father would have to toe the line or get out." Phil had tilted his face and quirked an eyebrow. "So, what do you think we should do?"

After Connor picked his jaw up from the floor, a smile had stretched beyond the confines of his mouth. He was also certain that if he'd looked in a mirror, his eyes would have been twinkling. "Now, Phil, I think that's a brilliant idea, and we should act on it immediately."

Looking across at the building's exit, Connor continued to smile. The sale of the business was being dealt with at present in the strictest of confidence. By the time they advised his father of the change of ownership, it would be too late for him to save his controlling share. He rarely turned up to work, and Connor had only seen him twice since the day he decided to turn his life around. His father played such a small role in his life these days, it was Phil he went to for guidance and advice.

Swatting a fly away from his ear, his thoughts returned to his decision to come to Australia. There was no guarantee Liz would have anything to do with him, but there was no turning back. Grimacing, he hoped it wasn't this hot all year round.

But first, there was the need to return to Falerna for unfinished business. Everything was in place to finally unearth the jewels—and he needed Liz there.

A burst of chatter alerted him to the crowd of students exiting and walking towards the car park. Liz stood out in the group of about six or seven students with her bright yellow tee and multicoloured scarf. He placed his water bottle on the tabletop, rubbed his hand down his thigh and bit into his bottom lip. Taking a deep breath and willing his heart to stop beating so fast, he waited for the group to approach, with no idea of how he planned to get her attention.

When they were only metres away, one of the male students put his arm around Liz's shoulder, and she laughed at one of his jokes. Connor hoisted himself off the table and stood rigid, close to the path they would pass, when Liz turned in his direction and stopped midstride. She went through the shock of stunned recognition before masking her features with iciness, enough to cool the intense heat of the tropics. His body shivered at the disdain permeating her face.

Another student tripped when Liz suddenly halted. As they continued to eye each other warily, someone asked if she was okay.

When she wrenched her gaze away, she said to them, "It's all good, guys. I'll see you tomorrow."

The same male student asked her, "Do you want me to hang around?"

Liz shook her head and smiled at him. "Honestly, it's all good. You go on home. I'll see you tomorrow." Her knuckles shone brighter as she clenched her carry bag tighter against her chest.

The group continued to walk towards the car park, and the male student shot glances back, looking uncertain whether he should leave Liz alone.

When they were far enough away, Liz's face fell. Her shoes scuffed at the loose stones near the path and her arms stayed wrapped around her bag. Connor ached to reach out and hold her, even with one arm. Instead, his heart did double time with each awkward moment that neither spoke, until he finally blurted, "I have a proposition."

Her face whipped up, wary.

Shifting from one foot to the other, he said, "I want you to come back to Falerna with me to unearth the jewels. They belong to you, too."

She gave a slow, disbelieving shake of her head, stumbling back a step. "You knew all along Uncle Ben was your grandfather's twin, didn't you?"

Connor's shoulders drooped at her accusation. "I planned to tell you everything the day you were attacked."

"But—" her strangled voice choked, anger spilling from her mouth, "—but the whole time we were together was a farce. How can I trust you again?"

Their gazes seemed intent on staying locked together. Connor swallowed before speaking. "Fly to Falerna with me. Get your share of the jewels. Come back home, no strings attached. If the jewels are not there, so be it. You'll have just wasted some time, that's all. I'll take care of everything else."

Muscles twitched on her neck. "It's easy for you, isn't it? I don't want the damn jewels anymore. I could've used them to take better care of my grandmother, but she's no longer here." Crimson flushed her face. Her jaw tightened as though trying to reel in her anger.

She looked past him towards the backdrop of rainforest-covered mountains fringing the campus while he feasted on her face. He absorbed everything, hoping it wouldn't be the last time.

Sighing, she straightened her shoulders and turned her gaze back. "I can't go anywhere for three weeks. I've got an exam to sit."

"Fine." Connor almost choked on the word but managed to sound normal. He grabbed at his shorts to keep his hand from shaking. *So, she isn't ready to forgive me yet.*

Her eyebrows rose.

"I plan to travel to Brisbane, Sydney and Melbourne. I need to decide which city I want to live in."

"Oh." Her mouth dropped open as she mulled over his words.

"I'll be back in three weeks with everything organised. A week is all we need in Falerna." *Now turn around and walk away. Just do it before she undoes everything you're trying to hold in.* "Goodbye, Liz, and I'm really sorry about your grandmother."

Connor turned and strode towards the street at the university's front entrance. From there, he would phone for a taxi. After a few steps, he stopped and turned back. "If you'd like to catch up with my mother and Phil, they're staying at Palm Cove. Sally has the details."

Using every bit of willpower, he turned away again. Not before the image of her stunned face was cemented into place. He left her gaping at his final words and probably at his audacity for leaving. He'd give her time to think. Three weeks was long enough. He had no intention of giving up on her yet. Crossing his fingers, he hoped his mother worked some magic while he was away.

Chapter 33

Liz kicked at a branch on the footpath as she made her way to her car. *No bloody strings attached. Yeah, sure.* Her body was still shaking after the unexpected meeting with Connor. With shoulders hunched forward, her gaze followed her feet. Those damn green eyes were the only thing she saw.

A cyclist whizzed past, causing her heart to slam against her chest. When he shouted in the breeze, "you're on the wrong side," she winced and scrunched her eyes shut, giving herself a chance to get her breathing under control.

Focused back on the footpath, she realised she was walking on the cycle path and veered quickly to the left side for pedestrians.

At her car, she opened the driver's door. The oppressive heat from inside quickly escaped, slapping her in the face with its intensity.

She couldn't hold back the tide of anguish sweeping over her at seeing the healthy Connor again. She burst into tears and hunched down on the kerb in the car's shadow, all the confusion of the past few minutes working its way out.

Tears rained on her bag resting on her knees. She thought she'd pushed aside the memories of Connor and Falerna but seeing him again brought it all back. *Why the heck is he moving to Australia?* Her tears continued, and the pain surrounding her heart strengthened. That news certainly put everything in a new perspective, but Australia was a big country. There was room enough for both of them.

When her tears abated, she yanked her shirt up and wiped her face dry. She pulled out her ponytail and retied it into a bun on the top of her head. The sweat pooling behind her neck now had a chance to escape. Rivulets trailed down her back as the hot breeze brushed past, creating an unnatural coolness her head was certainly *not* feeling.

She rested her chin on her palms, her elbows on her knees. *Did I really agree to go to Falerna? Did I say I was free in three weeks' time?*

Then she remembered she was supposed to meet Sally after her lecture, and her muscles tightened around her chest. Sally and Roberta were involved in this three-way conspiracy. No, make it a five-way gang of treachery if she included Belinda and Phil.

Liz lifted her shirt again, not caring if anyone else was close enough to see, and wiped her bag dry before digging around for her phone. She sent a message to Sally.

Going home.

She rose from the kerb and stretched her legs. Just as she was about to throw her bag onto the passenger's seat, there was a ding with an incoming message. Rummaging for her phone again, she swiped it open.

Thought you might. I'll be an hour behind you. See you soon.

Liz switched off the phone and shoved it back into her bag. She slumped onto the driver's seat before flinging her bag onto the back seat. It could stay there forever. She was in no mood to talk or see anyone that night.

Slamming her car door shut, she revved the motor and sped off, leaving skid marks in her wake.

⁘

Liz was still sitting in the dark, hunched against a lounge chair, when Sally's car drove up to the carport. With no house lights on, she hoped Sally would take the hint and turn around. With another good hour of blubbering on the way home, she didn't need to look in the mirror to know she looked a mess.

With a key to the front door, Sally had used it on many occasions; no doubt she'd do so today, so it shouldn't have alarmed her when the door opened, except she heard other voices.

Moments later, the lounge room light flickered on, and Liz squinted when the sudden glare pierced her eyes.

"Oh, Liz." Sally dropped her bag and keys and rushed over, flinging her arms around Liz's shoulders. "I knew when you messaged things didn't quite go to plan."

Sally's arms tightened and Liz stiffened. "At least you knew about the plan. What sort of mean trick was that?"

Sally's arms loosened as she fell back onto her bottom. "He swore me to secrecy. Wanted to surprise you."

Liz's tears prickled, and she sniffled to keep them at bay. "I hope that's not him in the kitchen. I look a mess."

Sally bit her lip and tried to look apologetic. "Actually, it's Belinda and Phil, and they're shouting us a pub meal tonight."

Liz groaned. *That is the last thing I feel like doing.*

"Come on, Liz. Connor said you got on well with his mother. She's thankful you flew to Toronto because, apparently, it did the trick. After you left, Connor realised the mess he was in and sorted it all out. This is her way of saying thank you."

"So, where is Connor tonight?"

"I have no idea, except he was catching a flight somewhere."

Her scowl deepened. "Nice try, Sal. Don't try and put that one over me. I'm sure everyone knows Connor's whereabouts except me. I assume Roberta is in on this, too?"

Sally couldn't hide her smile. "Come on"—she stood and held out her hand. Liz grabbed it, and she pulled her to her feet—"go have a shower and make yourself decent. I can at least promise you Connor won't be dining with us tonight, even though I thought you'd like that." She pulled Liz into one last hug. "Just promise me one thing ... when he's had enough of you, please send him my way? He's super cute and rich to boot." She pulled away and seductively worked her hand around her neck and down to her breasts. "I don't mind catching him on the rebound."

Astonished, Liz burst out laughing.

"That's more like it. For goodness' sake, girl, hold onto him. Why the hell do you think he came all this way? To see me?"

Liz sobered up. Just before Sally left the room, she looked back and said, "We leave for the pub in half an hour," then disappeared into the kitchen where Belinda and Phil waited.

Pulling her hair free of the bun, she ran her fingers through it, hoping to relax the start of a headache throbbing at her temples. An hour of crying was a good way to bring one on. Making her way to the bathroom, she knew Belinda and Phil meant her no harm. They had been very kind and understanding the whole time she'd been in Toronto, and the least she could do was be civil in return.

Twenty minutes later, feeling almost human after a cool shower, Liz entered the kitchen. Belinda rushed over and embraced her. Her motherly hands rubbed her back, giving Liz time to inhale the exotic smell of her perfume and to wish her Nan were still around to hug her like this. She'd missed that human touch. *And Connor's.*

Belinda pulled back. "Liz, it's so good to see you again." Then she frowned. "What has that darn son of mine done this time to upset you?"

Liz attempted a lopsided smile and tried to reassure Belinda she was okay. "I'm not sure if it's what he did say or what he hasn't. I assume you know why we were both in Falerna?"

Phil came up to stand behind Belinda and answered, "Yes, we do. He wants you to return with him to dig up the jewels."

"If they're still there."

"Oh, they are," Phil stated, squeezing Belinda's shoulders. "Connor has a lot to tell you, especially how he found their exact location."

Belinda reached across and held Liz's cheek. "Please give him a chance, Liz. I know you had no idea who the real Connor was when you first met him, but he's had to change and adapt so much since returning from

Falerna." Belinda dropped her hand as moisture built up around her eyes. She swallowed a couple of times before whispering and holding back her tears. "I'm so ashamed of what I did, Liz. I tried to commit suicide by overdosing on my medication. This is the reason Connor rushed back home."

Liz released the lung full of trapped air. *Suicide?*

"I know there was a misunderstanding between you and Connor on the day he left. I also know he has a lot of regrets about things he didn't tell you sooner. Our family situation hasn't helped either. You've met Connor's dad ..."

Nodding, Liz bit her bottom lip. She recalled the embarrassing encounter with Connor's father as though it had been tattooed behind her eyes.

"I'm just thankful every day for the love and support I receive from Phil. Without him, I never would have made it through that hell. But I'll always feel guilty for the price Connor paid."

All this information overwhelmed Liz; if she was alone, she might have cradled her head in her hands and shut her eyes for a long time. Instead, she reached out for Belinda's hands and squeezed them. "I'm not sure what's going to happen, but I've decided to return to Falerna to find the jewels. I'm sure you already know this, as it seems I'm the last person to learn anything." At this, she turned and raised her eyebrows in Sally's direction. "While we're at it, is there anything else I should know?"

They all laughed.

"If there is, I'm sure to remember it over dinner." Belinda relaxed as Phil wrapped his arm loosely around her shoulders.

"I take it we're ready to sample Malanda's local cuisine?" Phil quipped.

"Only the best pub fare for special guests," Sally joked, walking outside to the car.

Two weeks later, Belinda and Phil left Palm Cove in a luxurious Winnebago motorhome to travel around Australia.

On the same day, a package arrived for Liz with Connor's name on the back. She carried it into the lounge with shaking hands and prised it open. The contents fell on her lap. The first page was a shaky handwritten note that read:

Dear Liz

Attached are the details of your flight to Lamezia Terme. I need to leave a few days earlier than planned to tidy up some loose ends. I'll meet you at the airport. Sorry I couldn't be there to fly with you, but I promise I'll be waiting at the other end. At Roberta's and her aunt's insistence, you will be staying at her place, and I will be next door at Zia Maria's Casa.

As it will be the middle of winter, I have organised a suitcase of warm clothing and footwear for you. Sally will drop it around to your home.

Take care till we meet again.

Connor

Liz brought her knees up to her chest and rested the letter on top. *The same arrangements as last time, but nothing is the same.* She flicked through the attached pages, spotting the business class ticket and all the arrangements in place for a one-night stopover. Her head fell back against the couch, and she closed her eyes. *He said no strings attached.* Was this what she wanted?

She sat this way for countless minutes, despair shrouding her body, her misery too etched to even bring on tears. She could count the number of days on one hand where she hadn't woken up with puffy eyes red from crying. This gloom shadowed her from the day Connor left her in the hospital at Lamezia Terme. Seeing him so sick and gaunt in Toronto and the death of her grandmother snowballed her unhappiness into a massive lump constantly shoved against her heart. Sleeping soundly at night seemed a thing of the past.

She was miserable, only getting through each day on autopilot. *And I told Connor I would never forgive him if Nan died before I reached her. What a great speech to hurl at someone in his situation.* Her tired body crumbled inwards, her face falling towards her knees. She didn't know what she wanted, but she had to apologise to Connor.

Chapter 34

Liz prepared for landing by putting her book away as the plane commenced its descent into Lamezia Terme. This time her trip included a stopover in Hong Kong. She made the most of it, enjoying a refreshing night's sleep in a five-star motel for a change. She also carried earplugs and an eye mask and slept on the last leg.

Her stomach, though, continued to flutter with nerves, more so now she was fully awake and so close to the end of her flight. With her tray cleared and clicked back in place and her hand sanitiser and tissues packed in her blue and grey backpack, something occurred to her. Frowning, she picked up the bag and rested it on her knees. Turning it over a couple of times, she checked all the zippers, looking for the shooting star charm that used to hang from it. On one zipper, she found a lonesome ring and couldn't for the life of her remember when she might have lost it. Worse still, she had completely forgotten about it and couldn't recall seeing it on her return trip home with Roberta.

She placed the bag near her feet and pushed it under the seat in front. *Oh well, I suppose all my luck vanished when it did.*

Zipping up her worn leather jacket and doing up her seatbelt, she visualised the suitcase full of clothing Connor provided and recalled the shaft of anger that assailed her that day. She suspected the gaping abyss between her life and Connor's was at the centre of it. So used to having to scrape through every day with her meagre finances, this splurge of expensive clothing made her nervous and angry. She'd never be able to repay him.

"I'm not going to be made to feel any guiltier by accepting any more from him," she had retorted to Sally, who sat opposite in the lounge room, gaping, while her hand smoothed over the Versace electric-blue jacket. Sally would've scaled a high-rise building just to wear it once.

Appalled, Sally pleaded, "What about the boots? Come on, Liz. They're soft and sensible and warm."

"And they're Fiorentini boots. The money spent on those would cover the cost of my rates and insurance on this house and the old shop for a good two years."

Sally was close to tears as she held the boots to her cheek and inhaled the smell of their leather. "Oh, Liz, what's wrong with having money?"

Liz eyed the winter underclothes sitting on her lap and retorted, "Nothing, except I don't have any to waste."

"Come on, girl, you'll have your share of the jewels soon. You'll be able to splash out and treat yourself."

Standing, Liz had tossed the clothes back into the suitcase. "*If* the jewels are there."

Sally was fast chewing her nails back to the quick. "Oh, man. I really, really hope you have a huge fallout with Connor. I've got his phone number in my contacts, and I'm putting it on speed dial when you're finished with him."

"Please yourself." Liz snatched the boots from her and shoved them in the suitcase on top of the clothing. The cost of the suitcase alone could feed her for a year. "Look, I'm grateful for what he's done, but I can't afford this. He's already spent a small fortune on me, and my conscience won't let me accept anything else. *Please* don't utter a word to him about not accepting any of it. I'll sort it out when we return from Falerna."

Sally had raked her hands through her hair, her face full of despair. "But it's going to be cold over there. What are you going to wear?"

Huffing, Liz had sat down again and pushed the suitcase into the corner of the room. "I know Nan has some thermal wear somewhere, and I'm sure

I can scrounge up some thick socks, gloves and beanies. What the heck else will I need?"

Sally had groaned and left without even saying a goodbye.

Liz smiled as she replayed the conversation and watched the lights of Lamezia Terme twinkle through her window. Sally had returned an hour later with a bag full of winter wear smelling of mothballs. She dumped them on the kitchen table and, still shaking her head, left without another word.

The suitcase full of expensive clothing was not spoken about again.

Now with only minutes remaining before she confronted Connor again, her head began to argue with her heart. Why had she experienced such anger over the suitcase of expensive clothing? Why couldn't she just accept his gift? She looked down at her drab clothing. Would Connor be embarrassed by how she dressed? *Damn.* They had been so right together. How she dressed hadn't seemed an issue before. Did it change everything knowing who he really was?

The wheels screeched on the tarmac, flinging her forward in the seat, raising goose bumps along her skin. She fiddled with the belt, waiting for the seatbelt light to switch off, wanting to race off the plane and run into his arms.

Except he only has one now.

Her head swam with recriminations, reminding her he wasn't the same person anymore. More likely he was looking to get the ordeal of the jewels out of his hair as soon as possible so he could move on with his life, make a fresh start. *Would it be with her?*

While other passengers stood and reached overhead for their belongings, she held back the urge to race off the plane, and asked herself the hardest question. What if his feelings have changed? At this intrusive thought, her heart dropped a notch. It was time to face the music; either way it would hurt.

Connor sat in the arrivals lounge and ran his thumb over and over the shooting star lucky charm. Glancing down, his thoughts returned to the complexity of problems he'd inherited on his return to Falerna. He would need all the good luck he could get if he and Liz were going to get through the next few days unscathed. *Anything, just keep Liz safe.*

Restlessness attacked him, worry gnawing at his insides. He hadn't slept well the past week, and eating didn't feel right. *I just want this over and done with.*

He rose, needing to stretch his legs, and walked to the arrivals screen. The flight number had 'landed' flashing beside it. Liz would've been through customs in Rome, so it was only a matter of minutes before she reached the arrivals hall.

Turning his gaze towards the large viewing windows of the tarmac, he was surprised he'd missed day turning into night, now that the landing strip lights flickered in the darkness. A quick glance at his phone and he breathed a sigh of relief. The plane landed on time, just before five o'clock.

Connor slipped the charm into a secure pocket inside his long, woollen grey jacket, with the sleeve pinned up halfway so as not to get in the way, and made his way back to the arrivals lounge. He leant his weary frame against a wall, giving him the best view of the arriving passengers. When he pressed on the sensitive stub, though, it tingled, shooting a phantom pain down to his fingertips. *The pain might keep me alert.*

He took a few moments to think about Liz and how much he'd missed her. Not just the past few weeks since last seeing her, but right back to the day he urgently left Falerna when his life changed forever. He pictured her snug in the blue Versace coat he'd purchased. Its thigh-length stylish cut would bring out her incredible natural beauty. Its slim-fitting belt would accentuate her figure. He dreamt of wrapping his arm around her small waist, with the electric blue colour dazzling her golden skin, and squeezing her close to his side.

Sally had sent a brief message letting him know Liz had taken off from Cairns. Hopefully, her stopover in Hong Kong was without incident and she made her connecting flight in Rome. He couldn't bear the thought that she wasn't on this flight.

Crowds of waiting family and friends expanded with each passing minute, giving a feeling of excited congestion.

Most of the conversations were in Italian, and he tried to piece them together, but the volume and speed of their speech blurred, making it indecipherable. The aroma of strong, black coffee reached his nose from a nearby table of young friends outside an eatery. He could have used a strong coffee to keep him focused. His mind wouldn't relax, and the tension in his shoulders left a dull pain across his back.

Moving away from the wall, he rolled his shoulders, trying to ease the knots when the first passengers trickled through the gate.

He clenched and unclenched his hand, waiting patiently for any sign of an electric-blue coat.

After the first few stragglers, Connor ran his eyes over the large groups of passengers making their way through. He didn't want to miss her arrival as it would be hard for her to spot him in the swelling crowd. Precious minutes passed, and still no sign of Liz as passengers and families hugged and cried in a sea of humanity. The noise leached into his skin, the fragile state of his mind causing a pulse to beat at his temples. *Where is she?*

The passengers coming through the gate were thinning, and his heart pounded faster. What if Liz changed her mind? In Hong Kong or Rome? There were no messages on his phone, but Sally wouldn't know yet. *Damn, why change her mind now?*

A small child running around in tight circles near his family fell against Connor's legs. He squatted to help the child to his feet.

And when he stood, there she was, standing with an apologetic smile on her face and no electric-blue coat.

"Hello, Connor."

It took him a few seconds to get over the shock of how he'd missed her coming through the gate, but he'd been looking for a certain colour. "Liz, you made it. Thank goodness." He went to touch her then pulled back. His gaze travelled from her worn, leather jacket down to her jean-clad legs, then onto her scuffed trekking boots.

When he met her gaze, she shrugged, wearing a sheepish smile. Sally had confirmed she'd given her the suitcase of clothes, but she wasn't wearing any of them. *This is one woman who doesn't care about my money.*

It was a refreshing change and only strengthened his feelings for her. All he wanted to do was nuzzle his exhausted face in the crook of her neck and inhale the scent of citrus that had been haunting his dreams for months. But he forced himself to drag his eyes away, his frown setting in. He'd worry about her clothing later. It was dangerous to linger too long in the crowd, and their transport to Falerna awaited. Connor placed his arm around her shoulder and steered her towards the luggage carousel. "We'll go collect your luggage."

◦◦◦◦◦

Connor closed the car door and indicated to the driver they were ready to leave. He eyed the vehicle ahead and the one behind, driving in the convoy. He was certain Liz had no idea about the extra security, but he was advised by his security team to take no risks. The streets were heavy with traffic, and as the car halted at the stoplights, the strong wind buffeted it.

He clamped his jaw tight, wishing he could relax. He had the most important person in his life beside him, but it was early days to slacken his vigilance. Turning in his seat, he looked across at Liz. When the vehicle drove forward, the streetlights flashed across her. She turned to look out the window; a small smile played on her lips as she watched a mother laughing with young twin boys on the street.

"Thanks for coming."

She whipped around. Moments passed, and her mouth remained open as though she'd forgotten to close it. In a rookie move, he'd sat on the left-hand side of the car. He wanted desperately to reach across and take her hand, except his right hand was missing. Another reminder he wasn't the same man she'd met all those months ago.

Then, as pain slid along his right arm and tampered with his missing fingers in jest, he winced. He closed his eyes for a couple of seconds, hoping to gather enough control to fight it, his teeth grinding hard to lend some weight.

"You asked me and...and I said yes." Her gaze darted from his missing arm to his face as though she understood this sudden phantom pain and why it reared its ugly head when he least expected it.

As pain sliced through his body, he managed to say, "You could've changed your mind."

"I know," she whispered, her chest heaving.

He struggled to breathe normally when their eyes locked. In the confined car, and in his thick jacket, sweat pooled in his armpits. He dragged his gaze away and started to unbutton his coat. Sensing Liz was watching him struggle, his breath caught in his throat when she reached across and completed the job. Before she could draw away, he gently squeezed her hands in his. "Thanks," he said before letting go.

She removed her woollen cap and mittens and rubbed her palms up and down her jeans. Taking a big breath, she said, "Connor, I'm really sorry about what happened to your arm." Wringing her hands on her lap, she continued, "I wish ... I ... I just wish it didn't have to be this way, and I'm sorry you left Italy angry with me."

His throat threatened to constrict, the lump too large to swallow. She turned to look straight ahead. He was going to have to work harder to get them back on stable ground. "I *was* angry and hurt. I planned to tell you everything that day. I couldn't understand how you and Roberta came to the conclusions you did. As for my arm, well ... I'm coping."

Am I? What if the pain never goes away?

She turned to face him again, her fingers twisting together on her lap. "I also have to apologise for something else."

He had an inkling of what she was trying to say, and he didn't try to stop her. God help him, he needed to hear it.

Her eyes, glassy with moisture, were visible enough with the street lighting. "I'm so sorry for what I said in Toronto."

The silence lay heavy between them, and Connor coughed, words choking in his throat. "Oh, Liz, I know this sounds selfish, but I thank God every day you came when you did. Of course, you should've been with your grandmother, but I needed you, too. The hardest thing for me to accept is that nothing I do will ever change what happened. I'm really sorry you missed your grandmother's final hours, and I hope one day you can forgive my selfishness."

She rested her hand on the seat between them, smoothing her fingers over the soft leather. "I already have."

Thank God, and relief swamped him, obliterating any pain for a small moment in time.

"I sometimes think Nan planned to leave as quickly as she did. My grandfather's death lingered for nearly two years, and the financial strain was overwhelming. Nan's health deteriorated so fast it was like she had a mission to accomplish." She looked up and latched onto his gaze again. "I'm starting to accept it was her way of saying she didn't want me to struggle like we did with Grandad."

Connor nodded, thankful one small step forward had been achieved between them. "I have a lot to tell you, Liz. I was hoping tomorrow would be a good time. Digging up the jewels is planned for the day after."

She nodded, her hand still smoothing over the soft leather. Connor turned to look out the window and noticed they were on the narrow, winding road leading into Falerna. He'd said enough for now. A lot was riding on his preparations and private investigations that had started a couple of months ago.

Two more days to go. The mantra ran round and round his head. *Keep her safe. Please keep her safe.*

Liz clutched the edge of the seat when the vehicle swerved around a tight corner. They were not far from Falerna, and she hoped no vehicles approached from the opposite direction. *With any luck, they'd hit the car in front first.* Too wound up at the car's speed, she didn't care about her selfish thoughts. Lights from the vehicle behind lit the interior, revealing Connor's tiredness. She hadn't missed the dark smudges under his eyes at the airport and hadn't seen a single smile yet. *Give him a reason to smile, girl.*

All too soon, the car came to a crunching halt and Liz immediately recognised the street. She opened the door to step out, and the wind whipped through her clothing. She fished her mittens out of her leather jacket pockets and hastily shoved them on. Too absorbed with trying to keep warm, she only just noticed a car stopped ahead of where they parked and another a short distance behind them. She frowned. This was odd.

Connor carried her worn suitcase and was halfway up the concrete steps before Liz finally made to move to follow him out of the biting wind. She jogged up the stairs, and just as she made it to the top, the door flung open and Liz fell into the warmth of the house and into the arms of Fiorina.

"We'll have lunch tomorrow. Sleep in as long as you want." Connor waved goodbye and closed the door behind him.

Chapter 35

Liz threw a few essentials like her purse and water bottle into her backpack and zipped it closed. Searching for her grandfather's woollen beanie, she found it in her suitcase and shoved it on her head. Then she reached for the mittens she'd left on the dresser the previous night. Southern Italy was not used to such cold winters, and their indoor heating had a lot to be desired. The frigid air was already turning her lips blue. Rubbing her teeth against them, she tried in vain to get her blood circulating again. What was it going to be like outside?

Fiorina was talking to Connor in the kitchen; their lively Italian conversation filled her room. She smiled, quickly made her bed and recalled how language had been no barrier the previous night. Fiorina had prepared a feast fit for a king and expected Liz to eat all of it. On a full stomach, she slept soundly and woke feeling 'as fresh as a daisy' as her grandfather used to say.

Lifting her backpack, she made her way towards the kitchen, her teeth beginning to chatter. She crossed her arms to keep her chest warm and greeted Connor with a smile when she entered the warm kitchen.

"Ready for lunch?" he asked.

Her hand fell to her stomach. "I'm not sure there's any room left after last night." Connor didn't smile but pulled his woollen cap back on and held the door open for her. When her attempt at humour fell on deaf ears, her smile slipped and she waved goodbye to Fiorina.

So, things *had* changed between them. Maybe for good. This was going to be harder than she thought. Outside on the top step, the icy gusts cut through her flimsy knitted jumper. In a matter of seconds, she was shivering so hard that she had to jog down the steps to keep warm. She stamped her feet, fast losing contact with her toes that were already numb. Connor's lack of communication didn't seem important anymore.

She looked up in surprise when Connor swore.

"Christ, you're shivering and blue," he hissed between drawn lips. With a scowl, he added, "Tuck yourself under that awning"—he pointed to a shelter used as a fruit honesty stall—"and don't you dare move another step." Turning on his heel, he left her standing alone on the narrow street, her day beginning to feel as grey as the clouds above.

He hurriedly disappeared next door, the empty sleeve of his heavy coat pinned up on his right side, swinging in time with determined strides. As time passed, her shivering got worse, and for the first time, she longed for the suitcase of winter clothes she'd turned her back on. She rubbed her mitten-covered hands together, praying it wouldn't take Connor too long to return.

Within minutes, he was on his way back with a bundle tucked under his arm. When he stood beside her, he planted both feet firmly in place and held the thick, woollen coat out to her.

"Bloody Australians. Think they know every darn thing about cold weather when they don't know a goddamned thing."

He fished into his coat pocket and pulled out a matching scarf, the colour of golden sand, and proceeded to wrap it clumsily around her throat. None too gently, he said, "If I accidentally strangle you, I'm sorry."

Connor had a point, and she tried her hardest to stem the quirk pulling at the corner of her lips. Reaching across to his other pocket, he unearthed a gorgeous woollen cap, complete with earflaps. He handed it to her and didn't hesitate to snatch her grandfather's worn beanie from her head, shoving it in his pocket.

"Go on, say it," Liz taunted, appreciating the immediate effects of the extra-large coat, cap and shawl. She pressed her hands against the earflaps, drawing in as much warmth as possible. She closed her eyes and inhaled a lung full of air through her nose, and her senses soaked in his masculine scent. She remembered it from last summer, and his spare coat carried a hint of it.

"I know what I'd like to say," he growled as the spell broke and she opened her eyes. He pulled up his coat and retrieved a pair of leather gloves from his pants pockets.

Liz sighed, replacing her crocheted mittens, the gloves' woollen insides providing immediate warmth as soon as they touched her skin.

"A few choice words," he burst out, "like stubborn, annoying, irritating and idiotic. Do you want me to keep going?"

Liz tried to stand her ground, retaliating. "But I checked the internet for what the temperature usually is this time of year. It didn't seem that bad."

Fuming, he ground out his next words. "Did it tell you this is their worst winter in decades? Did you get that sort of information?"

Connor glared until she couldn't stand it anymore and looked down at her feet. "Thank you for being so thoughtful and sending me the warm clothes. Sally drooled over the blue coat."

In clipped tones, he retorted, "Sally's a smart girl ... but ... but it wouldn't have suited her."

She was being chastised, and the time for smiling and joking seemed over. A few tense moments passed before his voice softened and he offered, "It would've looked stunning on you."

The cold air caught in her throat when she looked up, his eyes warming her plenty. "Oh, Connor, I'm sorry, I really am. I ... I just didn't want to be shackled with any more financial guilt. I barely paid a cent when I was here last time, including my medical costs."

Connor shook his head, his brows drawn together and his expression looking bleaker by the minute. "You know what?" He stalled as though trying to work his head around the next words. "Some women I understand really well ... some ... I just don't."

Liz choked on a laugh, but it came out sounding like a cough at best. The whole situation was ludicrous. Where was the man that fuelled her dreams every night? What about the laughing, joking, smiling man that had fed her imagination for nearly six months? In its place was a stranger with worry worn deep on his face and a grim outlook to match.

"Warm enough now?" he asked.

She nodded, quickly clamping her mouth shut. Retrieving her backpack from the pavement, she hoisted it back on and hugged the coat closer to her chest. She was deliciously warm, and grateful for it, *and* determined to make some attempt to smile during lunch. Pointing her nose in the air, she said in a posh Aussie accent, "I quite like this coat. You may never get it back."

They walked close enough for their shoulders to touch. No coat was thick enough to hide the jolt that zapped between them with every step. No day was cold enough to hide how being close to Connor warmed her from the inside out.

Until she turned in time to see Connor growl, and her heart dropped to the street, where she had no choice but to kick it along in her sensible trekking boots.

⁂

Connor inwardly sighed. The growl came out unintentionally. Why couldn't he just tell her? Because his anxiety overrode everything. Even the chemistry whizzing between them—every time his shoulder stroked against hers—couldn't budge the worry that had wormed its way inside his head. As they dodged a car on the narrow street, all he could compute was today she was still safe. He couldn't seem to bypass the premonition that tomorrow, everything could change in a split second. With so many unknowns to deal with, too much could go wrong. Was the recovery of the jewels worth it? He kept asking himself this same question but always came back to the same answer. *I made a promise to my grandfather.*

They didn't talk on the way to the café, but Connor knew Liz would want to know where the jewels were. He didn't blame her, but for her safety, there was only so much he could tell her before they started digging.

Now that she was properly rugged up, he chose to sit outdoors so they would not be overheard. He almost let his lips curve upwards, recalling how cold and blue she looked. *Damn stubborn Australians, so ignorant about how to dress for the cold.*

He placed his hand on her back and steered her towards a table protected from the wind. The faded red and white striped awning flapped in the strong breeze as they walked underneath it. One corner threatened to take off and sail over the rough ocean he could glimpse over the rooftops. The potted shrubs, randomly positioned to give diners some privacy, refused to welcome any visitors that day. Their leaves were turned inwards, shrinking away from the cold and wind.

The only two other diners outside were his security men. Plain clothed and dressed to look like ordinary tourists, they ignored him as they were trained to do. By the next day, there should be a dozen of them.

Liz's safety was paramount, they were told. The safety of the heirloom jewels could be taken care of after that. He clamped his jaw tight, recalling his instructions that his safety was to come last.

When they were seated, he asked, "What would you like to drink?"

Liz picked up the menu, concentrating on its contents. "Anything hot. Tea or hot chocolate, but—"

"Not espresso coffee, if I recall."

She attempted a smile as he called to mind previous conversations.

He remained grim, too nervous to relax.

With his back stiff, he knew she sensed tension pouring from him. *Does she think I no longer care for her?* But he didn't know how to hide it from her, couldn't tell her all the things that could go wrong. She had already suffered one serious attack.

When her smile disappeared, it seemed she'd given up trying to be too jovial, and he couldn't blame her. Despite her stubbornness and harsh words in Toronto, Connor sensed she was trying to make amends. Once upon a time, not so long ago, they'd shared something special. He desperately wanted it back, but not until he was certain the jewels were out and she was safe.

She looked intently at the Italian menu. "There was something Roberta ordered when we were last here that looked delish ... that's it ... frittata. You should try it. It's made with eggplant."

Shrugging, he said, "Okay." Within minutes, the short, homely owner of the café arrived and took their order. Too late, Connor realised he would have difficulty eating it one handed.

The silence stretched between them as they waited for their hot drinks and meal to arrive. Connor coughed into his elbow, then said, "Liz ... there are things I'd like to tell you about tomorrow."

She placed her elbows on the small round table and fiddled with the salt and pepper shakers before looking up. "Can I say something first?"

Nodding, his gaze lingered over her beautiful face, his missing hand itching to cup her cheek and draw her closer so he could kiss her. With his mind adrift for a few seconds, her voice startled him back to attention.

"I'm not sure how useful I'm going to be at digging." She dipped her head towards his missing arm and continued, "If we're relying on my digging, I wasn't too helpful last time. Roberta did most of it, and the ground had been softened with rain." She sat back and dropped her gaze. "The ground will be frozen in the morning."

Connor tried to fight it. Wanted to believe all his bullshit that 'no strings attached' could work, but his hand moved of its own accord. Placing it over hers, he didn't miss how her breath caught in her throat. She didn't retreat. Another small win. "I have a small petrol-powered mechanical digger organised tomorrow. You shouldn't need to do any digging at all."

Her lips formed a silent 'o' before she asked, "So how do you know where the jewels are? We got it wrong last time, didn't we?"

He squeezed her hand and nodded before withdrawing it, missing the comfort it brought for those few brief moments. "I learnt of their whereabouts on the day I left Falerna. Just before Phil phoned to tell me about my mother, an old man approached and called me Benito."

Her eyes opened wide. "Really?"

"He told me I reminded him of his childhood friend. Recalled how a week after their parents were murdered, he witnessed the brothers burying the jewels during the night. He never saw them again."

Connor's gaze lingered past Liz, and he saw Saverio's wrinkled and craggy face as he remembered it. Connor recounted their conversation and the genuine feelings Saverio expressed in ensuring the real descendant of the brothers recovered the jewels. "He was certain nobody had been back for them—and then he told me where to find them."

"Will you show me later?"

"I can't. Today being Friday, there are children in and around the building where the fontana is. Tomorrow, there should be no one."

Their food and hot drinks arrived, and Connor refrained from saying more until the owner was back inside. He stirred sugar into his coffee before taking a couple of sips. He enjoyed the hot liquid as it moved past his throat, wishing he were somewhere warm with his arm wrapped around Liz.

"Here, let me." She dragged his plate closer and cut his frittata into bite-size pieces. His heart lurched at the sight. It was as though she read his mind and, try as he might, for a few precious moments, he couldn't dredge up any pain coming from his missing arm.

He hastily blinked a couple of times, so overcome with what was probably a small consideration for her but a huge stumbling block for him.

"What do we do with the jewels if we actually find them?" she asked, unaware of the war raging in his brain.

He picked up his fork as she pushed his plate back to his side. "Thanks," he said and held her gaze, hoping his appreciation showed. Returning to her question, he considered how to answer it. He ate a forkful of the frittata, enjoying the savoury taste of the eggplant, and took another piece before answering. "After your visit to Toronto, I contacted my relatives in Rome. They were stunned, to say the least, and Antonio, the cousin we saw at the palace, sent me an envelope full of information about the family. In amongst it was a page on the missing jewels that were supposedly stolen when the murders took place. They have hand-drawn pictures of the jewels belonging to Giovanna, and copies of those drawings were in there, too. I haven't said anything to them about the jewels, but if we locate them, I plan to send them to the Frevannini Palace for authentication first. They have safety vaults where they can keep them safe until we decide what to do with them."

Liz kept her eyes downcast and concentrated on eating her food. She mumbled something Connor struggled to catch. "What was that?"

She drew her face level with his and said, "They don't belong to me. They should remain with the true descendants of the Frevannini family. I don't even know why I'm here." Her gaze fell, and she toyed with the frittata on her plate.

Connor's jaw dropped at her words. His fork fell against his plate when he reached across for her hand again. "Liz, look at me."

A tear dripped lazily down her cheek. He tugged at her hand until she finally looked up. "Liz, they belong to you, too."

She used her napkin to gingerly wipe it away and continued to eat.

God, we make a sad pair. Doubts had begun to crowd his head. *Why bring Liz here at all? Why didn't I get the jewels out and tell her about them later?* But the experts told him to make it look real. With Liz in tow, it would look like they returned to complete the job they'd started last summer. It was the only way to clean the mess that one stolen letter at the airport had created.

He sighed, his thumb continuing to stroke her hand. "Liz, I'm nervous about tomorrow. I'm sorry I can't relax yet."

She nodded, picked up her hot chocolate and took a sip.

"Fiorina has invited me to dinner tonight. Do you mind?" Connor asked. "I've been keen to ask her about the house and if she remembers anything of my grandfather and your Uncle Ben. It's still hard to believe this was where the brothers lived."

"Of course, I don't mind. I can't wait to hear what she has to say." She smiled at last. "And now I won't be expected to eat everything."

Relief flooded him. He would deliver her back to the house after lunch and finalise matters for the next day before dinner. He would be hungry by then and more than happy to eat both his and her share of the food.

Chapter 36

T he fringes of the coming dawn peeked from behind the dark and unwelcoming clouds, the wind continuing to blow a gale around them. Connor held her hand as they walked from their street, past the café and beyond. Through the leather gloves, she could feel his agitation. He'd squeeze her hand for a few seconds and then rub her fingers as though in apology.

Geez, what a bleary day. Not only is it their coldest winter in ages, but it's probably their windiest, too. They hadn't spoken except for a polite greeting when he arrived to escort her. The more distant Connor grew, the more confused she became. He hadn't stayed long after dinner the previous night, and she'd half hoped they would spend some time alone to reconnect.

Walking up a back street with a small incline, he darted glances in her direction. Then he would peer over his shoulder and look to his left and right. As unsettling as it was, she couldn't help but be disappointed with how this was turning out. Whenever she had pictured the recovery of the jewels, the sun was shining and it was a happy occasion. Right back when she first read Uncle Ben's letter, she'd pictured herself beside a mound of dirt, shovel in hand and a glittering array of jewels spread before her. The day couldn't be more different from her fantasies.

Thanks to Connor's clothing, she was warm, but they couldn't warm the chill that took hold of her, wedged deep in her bones. He wasn't the person she'd met last summer. The sooner they got this ordeal over and done with, the better. He never smiled, never joked, didn't want to hold her in his only arm and, God forbid, didn't feel inclined to kiss her like they once had. She had been determined to try and reconcile and had conveyed her forgiveness, but faced with this solid wall between them, it felt like nothing she did could penetrate it.

The jewels meant nothing to her anymore. Oh, yes, she wanted to find them. Get past the mystery of whether they were still there or not. She owed that much to Uncle Ben. But with the passing of her grandmother, so too was the urgent need to find them. All that was left was a reminder her grandmother was never going to greet her good morning again, and this always left a raw spot inside her chest.

She clenched her free hand tight by her side. To have money that did not, in principle, belong to her would only focus on how unhappy and miserable the whole adventure was leaving her. Keeping the jewels and wearing them didn't warrant consideration. *Where would I wear them?* As she told Connor the previous day, she had no right to claim their ownership.

She halted in her tracks when Connor stopped suddenly. Looking up, she recognised a building used as a school or childcare and tried to reconcile it with the drawing on the letter.

"We're here." He withdrew his hand and opened the steel gate, the squeaky hinges disturbing the early morning quiet. They hadn't encountered a single other person on the walk over, and why would they? She shivered as the frigid air bit at the exposed skin on her face.

Confused, she asked, "Where is the fontana dei povere?"

Connor tugged on her sleeve. "Come, I'll show you."

They walked up to the whitewashed building covered with a myriad of bright, colourful characters painted on its front, but the windy, grey morning dulled their brightness. She licked her dry lips and followed Connor to the side of the building where she spotted the remnants of an old water fountain long past its use-by date.

Yes, this is it. My God, Uncle Ben drew the details perfectly.

Connor stiffened when a vehicle stopped outside the gate. With worry etched deep on his brow, he said, "This must be the arrival of the digger."

They turned around together and watched as a man began unloading equipment. He looked up and waved with a smile. They made their way back to the gate, and the man started chatting to Connor in Italian. When he stumbled into broken English, Liz concentrated on making sense of his words.

⁘

Connor greeted the man as though they were strangers; meanwhile, he was one of his most trusted security men going by the name of Filippo. Connor continued to glance to his left and right numerous times and saw nothing. *Good.* The twenty security agents and Italian law enforcers should be in place but not visible. The plan was to dig until the thief turned up. With him would be an undercover security agent who had befriended the thief weeks ago when planning for this day had started.

"Finally, the jewels."

He looked at Liz with her lopsided smile. She was making an effort to be cheerful despite his moodiness, and he wanted to drop everything and wrap himself around her. Tendrils of her hair poked out from behind the earflaps of his woollen cap, and her nose had a touch of pink to it. He couldn't reciprocate the same feelings of excitement—yet, but he gave himself a moment to hold onto anything she was willing to give. Swallowing, he turned his attention back to the digger and mumbled, "Let's see if we can get this thing going."

When he chanced a glance at Liz, she was frowning. With the digger wheeled close to the fontana, Filippo was giving her instructions in halting English on how they would use it. He showed her how to hold the handle of the digger in place while he and Filippo would position the blades.

"I came here after the school closed yesterday and marked out where I thought we should start digging. What do you think?" Connor asked Liz.

She hesitated for a fraction, her hands on the handle of the digger before she looked at the position where they were set up. Then she looked at the building, her gaze flicking between the building and the spot he'd chosen. She looked to be mentally measuring the distance. No doubt she'd memorised her uncle's diagrams from his letter. No different to what he'd done with the instructions he'd received from his grandfather.

With a grimace, she said, "I say go ahead and start."

This hurt. He looked across at her, willing her to understand. But he'd given her nothing. No encouragement, no love and definitely no hope anything would come out of this for them. Anxiety, worry and a coming doom were all he'd conveyed, and he couldn't see a way past it until this entire matter was over.

Filippo fiddled with the levers on the digger, giving them a momentary reprieve. Liz, he noticed, looked away towards the ocean. He followed her gaze. Even from this distance, the shadows from the clouds left dark patches along the ocean's surface, reflecting his mood perfectly.

Ignoring the tug inside his chest, he reminded himself of the 'no strings attached' promise he'd made to her. There wasn't a single day—since leaving Falerna all those months ago—she hadn't featured in his thoughts, yet he'd given her the choice to leave after this was all over. If she took it, he'd never recover, but that was his problem.

As the frigid wind brushed cold kisses over his face, he wished for one last warm kiss from Liz. Anything to hide the premonition that retrieving the jewels would somehow hurt her. From her very first day in Rome when the thief stole her letter, a streak of bad luck had trailed her. No wonder fear lay thick against his chest.

If everything went to plan, it didn't change the facts. He wasn't the same man. He certainly wasn't the complete man he'd once been. He shook his head. Better to leave the memories where they belonged. In the past.

Filippo yanked on the starter cord. The sudden noise must have startled Liz because she jolted. She turned back and took control of the handle as she'd been instructed to do. As Filippo adjusted the throttle, the motor spluttered and backfired for a few seconds before falling into a rhythmic chugging. The disquieting noise of the motor reverberated in the silent street. The first sod of soil turning and the removal of the top layer couldn't suppress a tiny shiver of excitement, despite everything that could go wrong. He stood mesmerised by the action of the digger, distracted from everything around him.

Liz's strangled screams brought him from his reverie.

The thief held a thick-bladed knife against Liz's throat, and Connor swayed when faintness threatened to overtake him. *How had he not heard the approaching footsteps?*

"La ragazza muore se non consegnare I gioielli." The thief threatened to kill Liz if they didn't hand over the jewels. Connor's heart stopped beating. He couldn't seem to draw breath, and his legs were frozen to the spot. All the preparation in the world had not prepared him for the danger Liz was now in. Did his trusted security men know what they were doing? Was this part of *their* plan to draw the thief into a position where there was no way out for him?

He stared at the thief, whose face was as scarred as the Mars landscape. Liz's eyes bulged out of her sockets. The thief stood behind her, one hand holding the knife to her neck and the other over her mouth, muffling her screams.

Connor flicked his gaze towards their security agent acting as the thief's accomplice, begging with his stare for him to do something.

"Fare come dice," the security agent yelled in his face. *Do as he says, for God's sake.* Connor knew he had to listen to this man. They had drilled it into him repeatedly, the different options they would take depending on what the thief did. *But it's Liz he's holding. One slip and he won't hesitate to kill her.*

Connor ground his teeth and sourced every ounce of patience he could find as his heart kickstarted back into action.

Looking over his shoulder, Filippo appeared nervous and fidgety as he pushed the throttle down to make the digger go faster. Connor risked looking at Liz and pleaded with his eyes for her to stay calm. She struggled in the thief's arm, and her voice sounded raspy over the sound of the digger.

The digger stopped, and the sudden quiet sent shivers along his spine.

"Farlo partire subito." The thief yelled to get it started immediately, as he dragged Liz back along the yard and pressed the knife closer against her skin. She was crying as she tried to fight off the blade. A nick to her skin left a trail of blood trickling down her neck. With his nostrils flaring, Connor did everything in his power not to move. Any sudden movement on his part would make it harder for the law enforcers to do their job. *Oh, Liz, please don't move, I beg you.*

His silent message had no way of reaching her from where the thief now held her hostage, and he tried to stop from clawing at his cheek in frustration. Filippo pull-started the digger and it chugged back to life, the noise coalescing with the sounds coming from Liz. Now she kicked and screamed, and Connor understood real terror. He fought to swallow and breathe, sweat quickly building up under his heavy coat. *What the hell are they waiting for? Do they want him to slit her throat?*

He wanted to scream at the twenty agents close by to do something. *God help you all if she dies.* Just as he thought this, numerous gunshots sounded; the thief and Liz collapsed to the ground. As he mobilised his legs, a primal scream left his lips. He dashed across the childcare lawn, closing the space between them.

Suddenly, people swarmed everywhere, but Connor's mind was filled with confusion and terror. The thief was not moving and was quickly pulled from atop Liz. The blood had oozed from his torso and soaked into Liz's coat.

Liz was crying uncontrollably and attempting to stand. To Connor, it was the sweetest sound he'd ever heard. He reached her just as she crumbled against his chest. Pushing him off balance, they both fell back onto the hard dirt. Connor wrapped his arm around her as tight as he could, probably at the risk of making it difficult for her to breathe.

When Filippo turned off the digger, an eerie quiet settled over the playground. The law enforcers and Connor's men completed their tasks quietly. A reminder, as they proceeded with respectful silence, that a man had lost his life.

Connor looked up to see the thief had been covered with a sheet. The Italian criminal unit were taking notes and photos. Why were his feelings towards the thief mixed? The thief had dogged them right from the first day he stole the letter from Liz in Rome. His determination to find the jewels did not falter because, when Connor waved a red flag months ago, he resurfaced very quickly.

Now, for the first time since leaving Falerna months ago, Connor drew Liz closer and rained kisses all over her face. "Shh ... it's okay, you're safe now." With his gloved fingers lying cushioned in the wool of her coat, he held her against him. He briefly closed his eyes as relief swamped his body. Tension and worry had persisted for weeks, and a sense of doom pervaded his everyday life. For now, the pungent smell of blood mingled with the scent of freshly turned soil while he held onto the only girl he'd ever loved.

The paramedic he had on standby tried to prise her away so he could check her over, but she gripped his coat lapels and refused to budge.

"It's okay, Liz, he wants to look you over. Shh ... everything is going to be alright."

She whimpered and settled her face under his neck, her grip on his coat stronger than a vice. Connor allowed himself a small smile but waved the paramedic closer and insisted he clean the cut on her throat. The paramedic helped Connor remove her bloodied coat and replace it with another before the paramedic tended to her wound.

Once she was safely in his arm again, he looked across at Filippo. One by one he was removing the rocks from the hole. Euphoria washed over him in waves. *After so many weeks of worry, I deserve this.*

"Look," Connor whispered near her ear, "they're removing the rocks. Soon it will be the jewels."

She made some indistinguishable sound but refused to move.

Chapter 37

S haking uncontrollably and with disbelief coursing through her veins, Liz prised her fingers from Connor's coat and eased away from the safety of his chest. *How did this happen again?* She used the back of her hand to wipe moisture away from her face and noticed a sticky streak of blood on her glove. A shriek escaped her lips, and in an instant, Connor wound his arm around her again.

With tremors in her voice, she asked, "Did ... did I get shot, too?"

Shaking his head, Connor grimaced. "No, darling. You are perfectly safe and okay."

Darling? Her thoughts jumbled and tears welled behind her eyelids. All she wanted was for Connor to hold her tight again. She collapsed against his broad chest, feeling light-headed. Her throat thickened. Images of the huge knife flashed across her vision, causing tears to slide past their barrier and down her cheeks.

Connor rocked her back and forth. She briefly closed her eyes and drew a deep breath. She needed to concentrate on how to do the simple things again, like breathing.

"I think Justin would like us to be near the hole. They've reached the jewels. Would you like to come with me? I'll hold onto you."

Justin?

His lips lingered near her mouth. "I've missed you so much, Liz," he whispered so only she could hear. "Come, we better not keep him waiting any longer."

Connor bore the full brunt of her weight against his side while Liz tottered on shaky legs. When they reached Filippo and the digger, Liz asked, "Who's Justin?"

Filippo was close enough to hear her question and, without hesitation, proffered his hand. "Hi Liz, it's my pleasure to meet you."

She looked up at Filippo. His accent, similar to Connor's, was in direct contrast to the halting English he had previously used. She looked towards Connor and frowned in confusion. "Is this Justin?"

Connor nodded, physically lifting Liz's hand towards Justin's. He took a good, firm grip and pumped it up and down, saying, "Yes, Ma'am, at your service."

Despite the near-death experience that would rattle her for years to come, it was beginning to unravel in her mind what Connor had executed to recover the jewels. She recalled the vehicles driving in convoy from the airport and now it all made sense.

As Justin released her hand, Connor said, "Justin is my right-hand man. I hope you get to see a lot of him." Turning to Justin, he asked, "Does it look like the jewels are down there?"

A wide grin broke out on his face. "I was just attending to that matter, boss." He asked for a two-handled shovel from one of the other men and used it to reach down into the hole. Liz held her breath in anticipation, her fingers impatiently knotting.

Minutes later, with a light sheen across his forehead from lifting the dirt out, Justin grinned. "I've got something."

The trapped air in her lungs rushed out. *Could it really be the jewels after all these years?*

She looked over her shoulder at the shrouded body and shivered, despite the borrowed coat she wore. *My god, is that the same thief who stole my letter all those months ago?* Connor would explain everything later, but for now, she wanted to enjoy the moment of discovery.

A gasp left her lips when she spotted the leather-bound bundle between the twin shovelheads. Justin prised it free and handed it to Connor, who looked at the dirty and tatty bundle in awe.

"Doesn't look like there's anything else down there, boss," Justin stated, lowering a light down the shaft.

Stepping away from Connor, Liz moved closer to the hole and reached for one of the smaller rocks. Connor followed; his brow furrowed when she looked back at him briefly.

She clutched it to her chest and turned around. "The last time these rocks were touched was by Uncle Ben and your grandfather. I want to keep one."

Connor relaxed a smidgen. Not enough for a smile, but for a split second, his expression wasn't so grim. To Justin, he said, "Could you collect the rocks and keep them safe? I have an idea."

Liz entrusted the rock to Justin. "No worries, boss. By the way, Phil has already been on the phone. The private charter is due in Lamezia Terme in two hours."

⁂

Connor nodded, placed the bundle in his pocket, then took hold of Liz's hand and led her away from the hole, the shrouded body, the army of swarming men and the gradual increase in spectators as the village slowly awakened. He led her towards a concrete seat under a tree where only the hardiest of leaves clung to it in this bitter winter.

Once she was seated beside him, he didn't hesitate another moment to brush his lips over hers. He pressed firmer, drinking in her sweetness, something he had desperately missed all these months. When she opened her mouth and accepted him, Connor dared to keep going.

When he finally released her, he drew back and rested his forehead against hers, filling his lungs with much-needed air. "I have so much to explain."

When she didn't say anything, he swallowed, latching onto her hazelnut eyes. Her mere closeness tightened his throat. "I'll understand if you don't want anything to do with me ever again, but I've been wretched since leaving you here all those months ago." He clamped down on his teeth, trying to fight off the build-up of emotions. Too much had happened since the summer in Falerna. So much pain and heartache.

Tears suddenly sprung up, and he rapidly blinked. Now was not the time to show weakness. He wanted to be the man he was last summer. He needed to banish the mess of a man she'd walked in on that day she arrived unannounced in Toronto. If he could never unsee it, how could she be expected to?

With all the pent-up frustration, worry and anxiety crowding his head of late, it didn't surprise him when a rogue tear trickled down his frozen cheek. Was it a sign of relief? They had the jewels, Liz was safe and he was safe. The only downer was the deceased body. While not totally unexpected, it was never part of the plan and left a streak of sorrow that nudged his conscience. Violence was not something he dealt with well.

But now to convince Liz she was in sound company. Not some bizarre world where people in the way were shot dead. While his competent security team would deal with the legalities of what happened today, it was his job to deal with Liz.

Liz reached up and took his face in her hands, her tears beginning to tumble when she looked into his moisture-filled eyes. "Oh, Connor, I've been so miserable too. I wouldn't have blamed someone like you for forgetting I existed once you left Falerna."

"Why not?" Connor asked, his voice husky with emotion.

"When I learnt who you were and didn't hear from you, I thought you had. I only found out about your accident when your mother phoned a few days before I came to Toronto."

Connor slumped closer as he fought his emotions. Pressing her closer, he allowed her tears to rain over him. "I love you, Liz. This thing between us happened so fast my head was left spinning. I've never experienced anything like it. You are the only person I have ever said this to, and I want you to be the last." Their noses rubbed, and their lips touched over and over.

Liz reached into her jeans pocket for a packet of tissues. She used one to wipe his cheeks and handed over another. He used it to blow his nose, sniffling in the cool morning air. She did the same, their gazes refusing to leave each other. Then she smiled. It radiated a warmth that spread through him, thawing out the frozen parts of his body he didn't think would ever feel warm again. It'd been a long time since he'd properly smiled, and he had to think about how to do it. It must have worked because she looked momentarily dazzled.

Before she could make any sort of response, he lowered his mouth and kissed her again. Everything inside his body came alive like a volcanic eruption exploding into a clear blue sky; the cloud of dark ashes and dangerous gases quickly evaporating to leave a euphoric feeling that had been missing in his life since leaving Falerna.

When he pulled back, she asked tentatively, "Do you think ... ah ... do you think we should check if we found the jewels?"

With his hand, he cupped her cheek, caressing her still-moist skin. She offered him a small smile. As her earlier ordeal flashed across his mind, he was surprised she could manage that. "Depends," he hedged.

"On what?" Her smile quickly disappeared, and now a frown marred her beautiful face.

"If there are no jewels in the leather pouch, will you still take a chance on me?"

This time she smiled for real and quietly chuckled. As if right on cue, a beam of sunlight struggled past the thick, dense clouds and spread its paltry ray over her face. "You had me after saving my money pouch for a second time. You saved me again today. What choice do I have?"

His breath jammed in his throat. "I'll always be here to save you, I promise," and with a possessiveness new to him, he reached for her mouth again while his heart thundered in his ears.

When he was satisfied his kiss had stolen her soul forever, he sucked on her bottom lip and her breathlessness brushed against his skin.

Drawing back just enough to speak, he whispered, "Would you like to open it?"

She shoved her used tissue into the pocket of her jeans and reached into his coat pocket for the bundle. Discarding the soiled outer leather layer, she untangled the next couple of leather layers. A drawstring pouch remained, larger than the size of her palm.

He held his breath when the leather lace broke. She gasped at the damage, but Connor reached in and kissed her forehead, reassuring her it didn't matter.

When the pouch fell open at her prodding, the glitter of the jewels sparkled up at them and shone in her eyes. Gold, silver, emerald and ruby glittered back. Liz's mouth opened in awe.

He closed his hand around the jewels and whispered, "We did it, Liz. My God, we finally reunited the brothers."

EPILOGUE

*E*ighteen months later

Liz giggled as they tumbled onto the bed. Connor's shirt was twisted around his arm, half on, half off. Liz was laughing so much she didn't have the strength to remove it. He looked so adorable, baring his teeth and threatening all sorts of things.

And she wanted every single threat he proposed. A newlywed couple of barely three months, this insane desire to always be naked and in bed with this man was frightening, if not so satisfying.

"We are going to be so late," Connor admonished, pulling back the sheet and letting it drop to the floor.

"We have a whole hour before the ceremony starts, Connor, and a four-minute walk to get there. We are not going to be late."

Connor didn't sound so sure. "We'll have to make this quick. Think you can handle it?"

"Yes, sir," Liz smiled, wrapping her arms around his neck and peppering his face with kisses. "But I still want all the works, Connor. Everything, as usual."

Connor groaned. "We don't have time," he said, latching onto her naked breast.

Liz gasped at his touch. It never failed to arouse. "Yes, we do; come on, show me what you're made of."

And he did. Like he always did. Sometimes it started slow and worked its natural way up. Other times, it started frenzied and ended that way. Just like it was going to happen this morning. Connor didn't hesitate to work his hand down to her pool of desire, touching all the right places. He knew her so well. She reciprocated, holding onto his hardened penis, stroking it how he liked it, her hands and mouth never leaving a square inch of his body to wonder. Their climax came fast and together, their time constraint adding an extra buzz. In the eighteen months since they'd unearthed the jewels, they'd never spent a day apart.

Liz rolled onto her back, panting and dazed; always amazed by how he managed to leave her shattered and wanting more.

"Now, we have to get ready. Fast!"

Connor was already out of bed and preparing to dress. They were back to where it all began. At Zia Maria's Casa in Falerna, but this time for the unveiling ceremony they worked so hard to achieve.

Liz rose, messily throwing the sheets and quilt on the bed. Today was not a day to worry about leaving it neat and tidy. They were in a hurry, and she still had her hair and make-up to rush through. *So worth it.* Her skin tingled, and all the memories of that day eighteen months ago came back to remind her of how lucky she was.

Within two hours of unearthing them, the jewels were put on a private charter from Lamezia Terme to Rome with Antonio, who came personally to collect them. As far as she was concerned, they were back where they belonged.

At Connor's insistence, she wore the emerald and diamond encrusted necklace on their wedding day. She had never been so nervous and terrified of losing it. As she fished out underwear from her suitcase, she smiled at the memory of Connor removing it from her neck after they'd retired to their honeymoon suite. How he'd kissed every spot that every diamond had rested upon. Memories of their wedding night still had the power to create a blush along her neck, and she reached up to rub at the sudden warmth, recalling how tender and beautiful a night it'd been. She'd been relieved, though, when the necklace was returned to the safety of its vault in Rome.

"Nearly ready?" Connor asked from his side of the tiny room.

Liz groaned. "Not even close, but I'm trying."

Connor laughed, reaching for this prosthetic arm.

Donning it, Liz couldn't help smiling. Connor tapped the screen on the prosthetic arm, giving it instructions, sending messages, whatever.

Honestly, it had every gadget known to mankind embedded in it. It was any wonder he even had to lift his arm for it to function.

"How is your missing arm this morning?"

Connor waltzed past her, kissing her cheek before heading for the bathroom. "I never feel a thing when you're touching me in all the right places."

Liz mock groaned. It was a serious question. The phantom pain attacked him randomly, and he'd described it perfectly once by telling her it was like holding a handful of hot coals and someone forcing his missing hand closed. She shook her head. If holding him and touching him in all the right places reduced the pain, then she would do it every single day.

"Do you have the shooting star?"

Liz froze for a second. She double-checked the side zipper of his travel bag and let out a whoosh of relief when she touched its smooth surface. Something so small and insignificant had become important to both of their lives. Connor had told her the story of how he found it and how it became his lucky charm when he needed it most. She would protect it for everything it was worth. Together, with the two letters written by the twin brothers, they were worth way more than the jewels would ever be.

Now for my hair and make-up. Liz dashed to the bathroom and nudged Connor away from the pokey mirror. "My turn, Conno."

Connor chuckled before gently kissing her cheek. "I owe you," he whispered.

"But I thought I owed you?"

"You do and I will be collecting soon, but *I* owe you for agreeing to be my wife. I still can't believe you said 'yes'."

Liz smiled, manoeuvring her make-up bag on the vanity. The well of love she received from this man astounded her. Every day he thanked her in a hundred different ways, always thankful she'd agreed to share her life in his crazy world. They hadn't settled on one place yet, and finishing her degree was tricky, but the end was in sight. Travelling between Canada and Australia made for hectic times, but she wouldn't have it any other way. The old mechanics shop and the home she was raised in, were getting a complete makeover, making it harder for Liz to part with either. This connection would always give her a reason to return to Malanda; to her family and her roots.

"I love you, Connor." She pecked his cheek, looking up and latching onto his amazing green gaze. "But I need to get ready now. Go!"

"Hey, what happened to Conno?" he asked, leaving the bathroom.

She smiled. Every time she called him by his nickname, it reminded her of spectacular sunsets dropping into the ocean, waterspouts and picnics, and always of one special village deeply ingrained in her heart.

⁕

Liz shuffled in her seat under the official marquee, the summer air dancing around her face, lifting wisps of hair. The light breeze caressed her cheeks, and she smiled at the private knowledge that only an hour ago, she and Connor were still in bed enjoying each other.

She lifted her arm, and the diamond on her left hand caught the morning sunlight, glinting fiercely. No different from her love for Connor. Fierce, strong and unbreakable.

Showered and dressed in record speed, Liz didn't need reminding why it was important they arrived on time at the same place where the jewels had been retrieved.

No longer a childcare facility, it was now a fully renovated library for the small village, with the Frevannini Palace committed to sponsoring it for years to come.

As a special guest, Liz waited in the front row. Official members organised the stage where speeches would be read and a monument to the memory of Benito and Nicolo unveiled. Connor stood on the raised platform and chatted with the mayor of Falerna and numerous Frevannini cousins. She took this opportunity to appreciate his strong, sculptured features and again, her pulse rippled through her veins as though he had just touched her naked skin. His trimmed dark hair was neatly combed away from his face, his muscled body tucked within the confines of his well-cut black suit. His white shirt was in stark contrast to the swirly purple and red tie he insisted on wearing. Love had transformed her life, and she knew it was doing the same for Connor. Fate had thrown them together with such intensity that each day left her breathlessly in awe of how her world had changed so rapidly.

She fished a tissue out of her bag just in case the ceremony got emotional. It took nothing for Connor to get teary over the smallest thing, and she liked to have them handy. Then she straightened her stylish knee-length dress in the palest of pinks and crossed her stockinged legs resting in nude heels. The likes of which she'd never owned before. While she'd embraced this wealthy life, she was determined to stay true to her upbringing.

She looked from left to right, locals and visitors beginning to fill the empty seats behind her. Sally and Roberta were wandering through the crowd, and she waved to get their attention. They chose to stay on the marina for the week leading up to this day's festivities and were not short of suitors with the Frevannini crowd travelling from Rome. Her lips curved, suspecting there was more happening between Roberta and Antonio than Roberta was letting on.

Roberta plonked herself beside her and groaned. "Is this going to take all day?" Liz looked up in time to notice Antonio wink at Roberta, and Liz laughed out loud.

Sally leant across Liz's lap to speak to Roberta, who sat on her other side, when Liz heard a soft beep from her wristband. More than a piece of jewellery, it was a smart watch with an app connected to Connor's prosthetic arm. Liz looked up to see Connor pointing to his wrist.

She looked down and read the message: **I love you.**

She couldn't contain her smile as it stretched across her face.

Roberta leant in to read it after hearing the beep and groaned. "Christ, you pair. Do you have to in such a public place?"

Sally laughed beside her and Liz joined in. Connor raised his eyebrows in confusion. She couldn't send back a message without her phone, but motioned, hoping the message, "I'll explain later," was clear.

With more guests arriving, Liz spotted Belinda, Phil and Lucia. Fiorina was in the crowd alongside Zia Maria herself. In fact, everyone from the village was invited. Later there would be food, festivities, a special mass to commemorate the day, music and dancing to carry on into the night.

Out of the corner of her eye, she saw an elderly man arriving, flanked by two young, robust teenagers. With the aid of his walking stick, each step looked like a herculean effort. It wasn't until Connor raced off the stage to give him some support that the penny finally dropped. The man's suit looked stiff and new, and her heart lurched at the sight. This was the surprise guest Connor told her about but wouldn't give any details. This was Saverio, who had been the most instrumental person in helping Connor and Liz reunite the twin boys and unearth the jewels. She had yet to meet him, but his lined, weather-beaten face was a canvas of a lifetime of living. His rheumy eyes could still smile and dance at his honoured position that day.

Liz sighed. Everything was coming together perfectly. Turning back to the stage, she waved to Justin and he winked back. Security was everywhere, and Connor never planned anything without his most trusted by his side.

A stillness descended over the crowd as the mayor of Falerna called for everyone's attention and opened the proceedings with a speech. All spoken in Italian, it meant Liz could enjoy the spectacle. A couple of other dignitaries spoke for a few minutes each, including Antonio, representing the Frevannini Family. Then it was Connor's turn.

He began his speech in English and paused at intervals to allow the translator to fill the audience with his translated words. He started on the night his grandfather died and explained how events between himself and Liz had conspired and how fate should dictate they arrive in Falerna at the same time. Finally, he shared how one man found the courage to approach Connor and reveal he had witnessed the boys burying the jewels all those years ago. He pointed to Saverio and thanked him for coming and his family for standing by his side.

His final words in English had her heart beating faster. "Falerna will always hold a special place in my heart because it was here I fell in love with my wife. What started as a journey over seventy-five years ago finally ended when two brothers were reunited. Not in person, but in love. I present my wife, whose family adopted Benito all those years ago."

Connor paused, the translator taking over. His gaze never wavered from her face. Leaving the stage, he stepped off and stretched his hand towards her. She rose, took it and followed him back. A collective sigh from the crowd wrapped around her as the translator delivered their love story.

She stood beside Conner, her hand securely clasped in his, and looked out into the crowd as he completed his speech. "Finding the lost Frevannini jewels meant a mystery could finally be solved. But no priceless jewels worth great fortunes could give me the one jewel that has become precious to me."

Tears stung her eyes when his hand squeezed hers.

When the translator caught up, he finished with, "I pray the two brothers are now resting in peace and can look down upon this memorial with lightness in their hearts."

With his speech finished, Connor turned and left a lingering kiss on her cheek. The crowd cheered and clapped. She was sure her cheeks weren't the only ones wet with moisture.

When he pulled back, he whispered close to her ear, "I love you," and she held onto the love shining at her as she went to unveil the monument, knowing it was her task to complete.

When the sheath of material slipped away, it revealed the biggest surprise of all. Incorporated into the memorial were the rocks Uncle Ben and Connor's grandfather had used to bury the jewels, minus the one sitting proudly in their home. Visitors would read about their importance, but only she and Connor would ever appreciate how fitting it was to use them.

She peered down to read the inscription. Most of the words were in Italian, but at the bottom were the words they had laboured over to get just right.

Born of this world in Falerna.
Separated and sent to far horizons.
Reunited again in spirit.

She swallowed. The words were still powerful enough to affect her no matter how many times she read them. Standing upright again, she knew Connor struggled too, his hand continuing to squeeze hers. Then they took a step back, allowing the crowd to mill around the monument and read its message.

As the excited noise of the crowd soaked through her, she placed her hand over her heart. Already it felt lighter. They had finally achieved what they set out to do, and she sent a prayer of thanks to Uncle Ben for sending her on this wonderful journey.

Uncle Ben's Letter

I write this letter in the hope that one day it will fall into the hands of the right person. My full name is Benito Enrico. If you are from Malanda, you will remember me as Uncle Ben. I ran my motor mechanic workshop in partnership with Thomas Emerson.

I was born a twin, and my brother was Nicolo Enrico. We were from a small village in southern Italy called Falerna to parents Frederico and Giovanna Enrico. My mother belonged to the Frevannini Dynasty of central Italy, and in many ways, we were a very wealthy family in what was considered a poor province.

Just before our eleventh birthday, our parents were brutally murdered. My brother and I escaped, and we fled the house in fear. We hid until nightfall until we remembered words of advice our father gave us a year earlier. He swore us to secrecy and showed us where he'd hidden our mother's precious jewels. The year was early 1944. Six months earlier, Mussolini had been removed, with Italy surrendering to the Allies. You didn't know who to trust.

When we returned to our home in the dark hours of that morning, our parent's death had not been discovered yet. The murderers ransacked our home but were unsuccessful in finding the jewels they were probably after, as we quickly recovered them.

We took what we could in warm clothes and food and, with heavy hearts, left for the last time. We hid in the mountains for a week before deciding the jewels were too dangerous to carry with us. We vowed to return one day together to recover what rightfully belonged to us and with great anguish, we debated on the best place to bury them.

There were a number of fontana dei povere in our small town, but we chose the oldest one that rarely worked and decided to bury it about five feet facing west. In the middle of a wet night towards the end of summer, we dug a narrow hole four feet down. The jewels were already in a leather pouch surrounded by further layers of leather. We placed it in the hole, piled rocks around and above it and then covered it with soil. I have drawn a diagram on the back of this page to the best of my memory.

Our plan was to leave Falerna and make our way to Rome, where my mother's family lived. Within a matter of days, we were captured by an isolated German military unit and separated. I never saw my brother again.

Upon my arrival in Australia and still fearful of my parent's murderers, I decided to change my surname to Menorico. Nicolo and I had spoken once about changing our surname. I never learnt the fate of my brother, and all attempts to find him have failed. I refused to return to Falerna without him as we made a pact to return together.

I was fortunate in my life to meet my long-life friend and business partner, Thomas Emerson. He taught me how to speak and write English in my teens, and I have always felt a part of his family. I never married but was able to enjoy the spoils of family life with his wife and children and later his grandchild.

Still, nothing could take away the pain I carried every day at the loss of my parents and my twin brother. I have never spoken to anyone of my past, and this letter is my first attempt to put it down on paper.

I need someone to go in search of my family's past. I owe it to them, and I regret not doing something many years earlier. If you find my brother and his family, tell him I never stopped searching.

I know for any of this to happen, God must play a role and create a miracle. Many years have already passed since we buried our mother's jewels. So many changes have been wrought on the face of this earth, that to think the old fountain is still there is an old man's dream.

Chances are, if this letter is in your hands, then I am no longer alive. If you take this journey, I will watch from above and send you an angel to guide you as best I can.

Take care, and with my blessings, I ask you make the journey someday.
Ben Menorico

AUTHOR NOTE

This story is entirely fictional, except for my personal connection with the small village of Falerna. It's where my ancestors were born, including my parents.

World War II tore a lot of families apart. My grandfather's decision to bring his family from a war-torn and depressed Europe to Australia after the war is something I will always be grateful for.

Australia, at the time, needed people. Lots of people. And they came in their droves. Hard workers, they certainly were, but they were also lovers of food, music, dancing and wine. It's no secret Europeans from all walks of life made a new home in Australia. My family included. Being raised in Australia with a European background is something I will always cherish.

I travelled to Falerna as a young adult and spent quality time with my other grandfather before he passed away. I don't doubt, in the years since I've been there, that even this small village has changed a lot.

I guess it's time I went back for another visit, to meander over Il Ponto and watch the old men playing cards, gossiping and smoking a pipe. Yes, I guess it is.

THANKS FOR READING

Thank you for reading, **The Shooting Star.** It is book one in a brand-new series, **Sway of The Stars**, so keep an eye out for when the next book is due out. I have all sorts of plans for Sally, Roberta and Lucia.

The original version of this story goes back to my very first finalist placing with the prestigious Romance Writers of Australia Emerald Award for unpublished authors. It was this success that got me thinking that maybe, just maybe, I might one day be an author.

I know what you're thinking. What grand ideas! Trust me, Rome wasn't built in a day! Six years later and a complete rewrite to modernize the story, it was finally time to publish.

Family is so important to me and this story takes you to a small, out-of-the way dot in the Calabrian region of Italy. So many families in Australia can claim their family originated from this small province. It gave up its youth and hardworking citizens so that a brand-new generation could flourish and prosper on the other side of the world. No longer were they just Italian. They were now Italian Australians, enjoying all their traditions with a completely new lifestyle — the best of both worlds. As we know, this wasn't exclusive to Australia.

I am forever grateful for the risks and heartache my grandparents went through to make such a life-changing decision to move to a country where they didn't even speak the language. Oh, the courage they showed.

Above all though, this story is an emotional and passionate one, with the promised happy ending I always give my readers.

As usual, a big shout out to my critique partner, Author Lisa Stanbridge. I owe a lot of my writing success to our great partnership and her unwavering support.

And a final thank you to my family, who continue to let me sit in my corner and thrive on my imagination.

ALSO BY FRANCES DALL'ALBA

The **Australian at Heart Series** tells the stories of four interconnected siblings.

<u>Little Blue Box – Book 1</u>

Regrets, lies, and earth-shattering secrets. When Ella learns the identity of her biological father, nothing will stand in her way. Not even his power. When things don't go to plan, can one little blue box put Ella and Zane back on the same path? This second chance contemporary romance is filled with suspense, emotion and a life-changing sizzling romance.

<u>The Stone In The Road – Book 2</u>

Emotional, passionate and heart-wrenching. This suspense-filled captivating romance will have you dancing in the rain and smiling through your tears. Set in tropical northern Australia, we don't always get to choose our path.

The Silk Scarf – Book 3

An unravelling silken scarf ... mysterious gold ... a breathtaking romance.
An emotional and unforgettable contemporary romance set in Australia.

Rustic Denim Love – Book 4

Forgotten secrets ... blazing fires ... burning love.
She's busy and diligent, doing the best she can to save her crumbling family.
He's funny and witty, with a solution for every problem.
This one may just beat him.

Link to read more and BUY.

**https://francesdallalba.wixsite.com/francesdallalba/australianathe
artseries**

Sway of The Stars Series will share the stories of a group of friends.

The Shooting Star – Book 1

Hidden treasures ... broken spirits ... tangled love. A modern-day treasure hunt where hidden treasures will tangle their love and break their spirits. Duty or love, or can they have both?

The Glittering Star –Book 2

Shimmering waters ... towering giants ... buried mysteries. She's the no filters chick. Funny, full of life and always ready for a good laugh. Until her mother drops a bombshell. He's the environmental warrior. Passionate, driven and determined to save the world. Burnt once before, he's moving on and doing things his way. So how did they end up hand cuffed together on day one?

The Giving Star – Book 3

Endless roads ... timeless discoveries ... unbreakable love. She's packed up her life ready for change, with one regret still hanging over her head. He's working his way back from hell, adamant he's never going there again. But one stumble, one discovery, and one hotbed of attraction ... and the entire game plan changes.

The Priceless Star – Book 4

Forgotten treasures ... a perilous ransom ... shattered hopes

She's chasing answers long buried since the war.

He's content with a steady working life. Until he's not...

Sent to Far North Queensland to research a wartime mystery, Lucia Levorico escapes her privileged life and finds unexpected passion with reserved local, Theo Mather, under an outback sky – until a sudden goodbye and a devastating worksite tragedy tear them apart. When a ruthless ransom plot targets Lucia's wealth, their only reprieve will come from sharing the unravelling of a wartime mystery and its priceless treasure. Unless they're willing to fight for what they have.

Link to read more and BUY.

https://francesdallalba.wixsite.com/francesdallalba/swayof the stars

Eight Seconds, is a standalone story inspired by Australia's first female open bullrider. She pushed past the barriers and succeeded in a male dominated sport, creating a new legend showcased in two Australian halls of fame.

Triumph, hardship, true grit ... and one crazy dream.
An inspirational story about one woman, with one dream, and one almighty driving passion.

Link to read more and BUY.
https://francesdallalba.wixsite.com/francesdalla lba/eightseconds

Jack& Eva, is a standalone contemporary romance set in tropical North Queensland. It showcases our unique and adorable Lumholtz tree kangaroo and the valuable work done by Dr Karen Coombes in her care and continued research of them.

Broody meets bubbly ... and a bunch of cuddly tree kangaroos.
When the tempest blows over, will Jack and Eva be able to find a way forward, or are they destined for a train wreck with a bunch of furry animals caught up in the middle?
Fall in love with our adorable tree kangaroo while reading an emotional and passionate contemporary romance set in Australia.
Link to read more and BUY.
https://francesdallalba.wixsite.com/francesdallalba/jackandeva

ABOUT THE AUTHOR

As a contemporary romance author, Frances loves nothing more than losing herself in a good romance. She's all about helping you forget the housework, or the bus to work you're going to miss, if you don't put the book down now!

She's devoted to giving her readers an emotional, passionate, possibly some ugly-cry, fairly steamy love story, that'll melt your heart and have you fighting for the happy ending right until the end.

Frances sets her books in North Queensland. She makes no excuses if some of her settings include amazing lakes and waterfalls, stunning views from tops of mountains, spectacular outback scenes, or crystal-clear creeks shadowed by tropical rainforest.

When she isn't writing, Frances is climbing mountains, searching for waterfalls and swimming across lakes. She loves to exercise, would prefer it if someone else cooked dinner every night, and never notices dust on the furniture.

She lives with her husband in tropical Far North Queensland, Australia, and uses her great baking skills to tempt her family to visit home often.

Say hello to Frances

Visit her website: https://francesdallalba.wixsite.com/francesdallalba and subscribe to her newsletter. It will keep you up-to-date with everything happening in her author world.

Follow Frances on Facebook, Instagram, Bookbub, TikTok, and Goodreads. To do so, click on this link: https://linktr.ee/francesdallalba

Still have a question?

Ask her at: https://francesdallalba.wixsite.com/francesdallalba/contact

Leave a Review

Did you enjoy this book? The best favour you can do for an author is to leave a **review**. If you'd like to leave a review, go to your place of on-line purchase of the book, or search for the book on **Goodreads** and leave a review. Thank you.